THE SONS OF MERLIN

Matthew Davenport
& Robert Reynolds

MYSTIQUE PRESS

Prologue

The wind rushed through his beard as the horse pumped furiously to stay ahead of the approaching riders. Keeping his head down and the bundle tight to his chest, Merlin, Wizard of Camelot, mumbled words of encouragement to the poor and tired beast.

It only had to get to the water's edge, then the old wizard would allow it to take its final rest.

Behind Merlin rode the largest group of knights he'd seen since his days in Camelot, before he'd faked his demise to live in peace among the people. Back then, he'd hoped to try to coax a different style of change among the common folk, a change from within. He'd lived in hiding among them for the last thirty years, acting as a subtle force for good.

His pursuers were proof that he'd left Camelot and the center stage that he'd created much too soon. These knights were not of the now-fractured round table, but instead were of a new country, formed to the north, that claimed to have its own wizard. It was said that they were attempting to create a better dream than even Merlin had imagined.

Merlin had no doubt about the validity of the wizard from the north. At any one time there were at least a handful of magical practitioners in the world, but in the last few years Merlin had sensed their light dimming and every ounce of scrying he had attempted only pointed him northward.

It would seem that these hunters of wizards had come for him now.

The ride wore on Merlin to a certain extent as well. The horse, her name was Beauty, was feeling the most of it, but Merlin's old bones hadn't ridden a horse in many years and weren't used to the jarring impact of a full gallop. Even more so than for his own weary bones, Merlin worried for the bundle that he now carried. He prayed for Beauty to make it to the water's edge.

The gods were not with him as an arrow struck the swift horse in her flank while Merlin was still only in mid-prayer. With a lurch and a gasp, Beauty surrendered to the shock and collapsed, her heart exhausted from the exertion and the wound.

Old and frail, Merlin launched from the now deceased horse with his bundle, but he wasn't completely helpless in his old age. With one hand around the bundle clutched to his chest and the other outstretched, Merlin summoned currents of air to catch him and lower him gently to the sod. Commanding the same wind once more, he used it to aid him on his march, knowing that he was not far now from the water's edge.

The mad old man leaped over branches and wove between trees as he did his best to stay ahead of the oncoming army. As arrows rocketed towards his back, he shifted the wind that carried him and deflected them safely to the earth. Another wave of his hand toppled the horse nearest to him. As this horse collapsed, he saw the water finally coming into view.

The greatest and most powerful wizard to have ever lived bellowed at the top of his lungs, "M'lady! Bring to me the weapon of the righteous, of fallen friends, and even more fallen foes. I offer my blood as trade." He took a breath and then continued his roar, "Guard it with your fury, train it with your grace, and show it your love." On this final shout, he let go of his bundle and let it arc over and towards the lake.

Just as the bundle was about to slap the surface of the water, a pale and almost translucent hand thrust out of the water and caught it.

Beneath the surface of the water were the cold and deep eyes of the Lady of the Lake. She stretched her other hand out and above the surface and unwrapped the bundle, discovering an infant beneath. The lake echoed with a deep resonance. "This is acceptable."

The baby was pulled under the water without a splash or ripple.

Merlin collapsed at the edge of the water gasping for breath as the knights all broke into the clearing and began circling him. As he gulped down the cold damp air, he showed them no notice.

The soldier in charge brought his horse before Merlin's back

Cremont gave his grandmother a sidelong glance. "Gregory said to tell you hello." He watched for his grandmother to blush, but she kept herself under control.

Annoyed for not catching his grandmother off-guard, Cremont gave up before he'd really began and moved on to the subject that actually had him concerned.

"How was your visit with Martin?" He asked.

Evelyn looked up from her potatoes. "Martin? Cord?" She shook her head. "I haven't seen Martin since he visited yesterday."

Dash and Cremont exchanged glances before Dash said, "He was rushing home from this direction. We thought he had come to see you."

Evelyn shook her head again and then stopped. "When was this?"

Dash aimed his thumb over his shoulder, indicating the trail. "We just ran into him on our way home."

Evelyn blanched. She'd only just been working the plants. She'd been touching the gift that her voice had told her about. The gift that she was supposed to keep to herself.

The gift that her grandsons didn't know she had.

"Did he say where he was headed?"

Cremont grabbed a potato and bit into it like it was an apple, causing Dash to grimace at his brother. Cremont answered, around the potato, "He said his father was expecting him."

Evelyn opened her mouth to change the subject when her special voice called out to her.

Danger.

and directed his voice towards their hunted quarry. "Merlin, Wizard of Camelot, do you have any final words before we execute our orders?"

Merlin nodded, keeping his back to them and continuing to look out over the lake. His eyes heavy with exhaustion he thought ahead to what he was ready to do and the weariness that hit him felt heavier than it ever had.

"I'm sorry for what I must now do."

Those were the last words that any mortal would ever hear Merlin say.

Spinning, his dust-heavy robe swept behind him as Merlin raised his hands at the thirty or more knights. Gulfs of flame erupted from his palms and cascaded over the right and left-most knights. Their horses' faces ignited, and the soldiers screamed in pain as their flesh seared within their heavy metal armors. The center and unaffected soldiers' horses kicked and leapt, causing their knights to fall. Only a handful of the men managed to stay on their mounts.

Raising both of his hands to the air, Merlin allowed the fire to fade as he closed his eyes and felt towards the lake. The Lady answered his call instantly, launching what he'd originally traded his precious bundle for directly from the lake and down into his outstretched palms.

The weight of the mighty sword Excalibur never registered with the old wizard. Arthur had claimed that the sword had sung to him in the heat of battle. He'd said that the sword danced with him from the beginning until the very end and only then had he realized that he'd actually been fighting instead of making sweet and passionate beauty.

It was not like that for Merlin. Suddenly, he fell back into another moment, and found himself standing in the same spot beside the lake with the only friend he'd ever known. He stood there alone with Arthur, former King of Camelot.

"You're not too old to teach me, are you, old fool?" His old friend prodded, raising his sword in a defensive stance.

Merlin smiled his first genuine smile in years and raised his sword. "I've missed you, young fool."

"Silence your tongue and defend yourself," Arthur barked through a face-spanning grin and then lunged at his old mentor.

The dead know no physical limitations, and Arthur bobbed

and swung and swept with the speed that his immortality had granted him. Only Excalibur and the wizard's years of experience kept him ahead of his former student. As he swung, Merlin put forth jabs and slashes that tore the air and felt none of the resistance they aimed for.

Arthur laughed as he twirled and spun, fighting as only he wished he could have fought in life, weaving and twirling around all sides of his master. Merlin spun and ducked slashing behind and forward, up and back, down and to the front. His attacks were expertly placed and still they missed the King.

This battle went on for minutes but felt to Merlin as if it were only an instant, as he was having so much fun being back in the training exercises with his true friend. Finally, the battle ended as Merlin swung the legendary sword at his apprentice's head. Instead of ducking or blocking with his own sword, Arthur raised his hand with remarkable speed and grabbed the blade. There was no reverberation into Merlin and Arthur was unscathed from the act.

Raising his eyes to Merlin's, Arthur stated. "I'll have to take this back with me."

Merlin nodded.

Arthur mimicked his mentor's nod and said with a heavy sadness, "I'll see you for the rematch?"

Merlin nodded again, and added, "Soon."

With that, and a slight breeze, Arthur and the miracle sword that was Excalibur, vanished allowing for the real world to return.

Around him, Merlin took in the sight he had expected to see. The beach beside the lake was littered with the blood and dismembered pieces of the fallen knights who had raised their weapons to kill the famed wizard. Kneeling for only a moment and allowing himself to feel the weight of every saddening death he had caused while in his dream state with the sword, he closed the eyes of the nearest soldier.

Standing and taking it all in for a heavy moment, Merlin finally turned back towards the Lake.

"Open your doors, my love. I'm done with this useless world and the pain it causes. Give me back my days of glory and service at your feet. Give me unto my friends who have already fled this mortal coil."

As he said those heavy words, heard only by the trees, the

wind, and, most importantly, the lake, he walked into her and once he was fully submerged, he left the world behind.

It was only hours later when the tranquil lake setting was disturbed for a second time on that fateful day.

Breaking from the woods, another large contingent of knights from the Northlands trotted their steeds onto the beach, coming to rest around the still present corpses of their fellow soldiers. In their lead and wearing armor that was as black as the night and only barely large enough to encompass its owner's immense frame, came Lord Bonnevist, ruler of the Northlands. Bringing his equally large horse to rest, Bonnevist took in the sight before him.

Along with his dark armor and large frame, Lord Bonnevist was completely bald, with tanned skin and a heavy brow. His smooth face told nothing of his age and showed none of the wear that one would see in the faces of the region. Aside from his size and armor, there was little to imply the power that he held at his fingertips, yet one look into his stone-grey eyes and none would doubt that this man had dominion over them.

Not a single soldier was to utter a word as their leader surveyed the carnage that lay at their horses' feet.

Bonnevist wrinkled his nose as the scent of roasted flesh wafted before his face. The giant of a man swung down from his horse and waved for the three nearest soldiers to do likewise.

Once they had dismounted, Bonnevist waved his hand, indicating the nearest corpse. Without hesitation, two of the knights scooped their deceased companion up and faced him towards Lord Bonnevist, while the third knight righted the corpse's head. The dead knight was only a boy.

Bonnevist snapped his fingers and the young man's dead eyes snapped open. They were grey, vacant eyes: the eyes of the dead.

"Report," barked Lord Bonnevist. The magic in his words carried and reverberated through each of his men's very souls. "What happened here?"

The corpse worked its mouth slowly, grinding together as if attempting to remember something that it had been allowed to forget. It worked at this for several seconds before a wheezing sound finally emitted from it.

Raspy and distant, the voice stretched across the lands of the dead and only just barely could be heard as they left the boy's mouth.

"The wizard commanded the fire first, and the sword of legend second."

Lord Bonnevist looked towards the lake. Merlin had come here for aid and had received it. As per his relationship with the mythical Lady of the Lake, she had given him the sword, Excalibur, and he had danced upon the field of battle for a final time.

He snapped his head back towards the corpse. "Where did Merlin go?" Bonnevist demanded.

The corpse worked the stubborn jaw again and rasped, "The wizard left the world to rest in immortality at the feet of the one he serves."

Lord Bonnevist could see it now. Merlin finished slaughtering his men and then receded into the bosom of his lady. *The coward chose death*, he thought.

Bonnevist smiled, "Then I am the last of the wizards." All was proceeding to plan, and then a thought occurred to him.

He squinted his heavy brow at the corpse. "The legendary sword you speak of, it only comes at a cost. The first summoning of the sword cost Merlin a promise. He promised the Lady of the Lake to return this land from corruption. The second summoning could only have been met with just as high a commitment. She already had Merlin's life, so tell me soldier, what did the wizard promise the Lady of the Lake."

The dead boy's spirit found his eyes at last and rolled them to face his leader in life. "My lord," he cracked, "the second summoning was met with the promise of his bloodline."

Lord Bonnevist frowned. Merlin had surrendered and left this world, but not without promising the continuation of his power. Reports of the mad pursuit of the old wizard had said he'd been protecting a bundle. Could this bundle have been a child? An infant?

Very well. Let Merlin plan his plans and set in place his contingencies. A baby would not be a problem for many years. Bonnevist would have time to prepare.

Waving his hand at the corpse, it blew apart, showering the three who had supported it with the blood and gore of their fallen companion.

Ignoring the mess he had made, Bonnevist walked to the water's edge and peered into the cool, flat surface. Reaching out with his senses, he pulled and tugged at what little he could find in an attempt to scry for any information regarding the child. He found nothing. Distantly he thought that he could hear the cry of an upset infant.

Perhaps it was only in his head, but that same cry sounded too much as if it were mocking laughter from the old dead wizard.

Still kneeling, Lord Bonnevist pulled off his gauntlet and touched the surface of the lake ever so gently. Then he whispered, very quietly, but loud enough for the goddess and her wizard to hear. "Send your babies. I care not for what power they might possess. Watch as I tear down all that you built."

He stood quickly, replacing his gauntlet as he did, and marched back to the three knights who were still attempting to remove corpses from their armor. Picking the one most covered in gore, Lord Bonnevist grabbed him by the shoulders.

"What's your name?" He asked in a booming voice.

The young knight hesitated, fear flashing momentarily across his eyes before he found his voice. "Thordon, sir." He straightened as much as Bonnevist's tight grip would allow. "Richard Thordon."

Bonnevist nodded, "Richard. That is a good, strong name. That is a name fit for a king, would you agree, Richard?" Bonnevist didn't wait for the knight to respond, and Thordon doubted he could have answered if the leader of the Northlands had. "I now declare you King Thordon of Camelot, undisputed heir to Arthur himself!"

Richard was in complete shock and greatly confused, thinking this some odd joke by the Lord. "We have no presence in Camelot, sir, and... I am only the son of a farming family with much land and no kin to Arthur."

Bonnevist turned and stalked back towards his horse. "Then we will have to rectify that." He swung back up onto his horse. "We will take Camelot and tell your people of your newly discovered lineage." He took off back towards the forest and into the direction of Camelot. "Mount up!" he shouted. "We have a land to conquer!"

Falling to the muddy earth, only miles from the slaughter that was being discovered by Lord Bonnevist of the Northlands, Annette Farthing clutched at her flat belly. The laundry that she'd been carrying from the riverbank toppled with her, launching into the mud and ruining her entire morning's work.

Annette had forgotten about the laundry's existence, as the

pain from her belly was far worse than anything that she'd experienced previously in her twenty-three years. Radiating through
her body, the new fire begged for her with one excruciatingly loud
demand for water.

Annette had to get to the river if she wanted the pain to stop.
She knew nothing in the world as well as she knew this.

What happened in the following moments Annette would
never be able to recall. She would be incapable of recounting
how she gripped at the mud, pulling and kicking to drag herself
towards the water's edge that she'd only left moments ago. She
dragged herself over mud and stone over a hundred yards and
the only moment that she would ever remember of that never end-
ing journey through endless fathoms of pain would be when she
finally splashed into and beneath the rushing water of the river.

That was the moment that the pain flowing from her center
truly sang and jumped to every corner of her body, filling her chest
and limbs.

Every muscle in Annette Farthing's body tensed further than
it had ever been intended to tense. Then, as suddenly as it had
erupted, her pain subsided until it was only unbearable in her
belly and shifting lower.

As the pain in her flat stomach reached her pelvis, she noted
blood mixing with the river water and Annette's screams mutated
from pain to panic. As the river carried the blood away and past
her, the water started to pulse with a light as bright as the sun. It
emitted from between her legs and beneath the surface and shone
out and up from the river. Following the light, Annette watched in
horror as a woman's pale and almost translucent face slowly rose
from the water, directly above the radiating pain.

"What?" Annette managed to gasp as the pain finally subsided.

The Lady of the Lake's shoulders crested the water's surface
and were followed soon by the rest of her arms. In them rested the
calm and round face of a dripping wet baby.

Another second passed and the naked goddess stood on the
surface of the water and before the submerged Annette Farthing,
her arms outstretched as she handed the child to her new mother.

"Bound by the power of the twice born, I give unto thee the
mortal of immortal blood." For the first time, the Lady of the Lake
cast her eyes upon the adoptive mother. "Protect her, as her lineage
will be hunted. Teach her, as she will need to be prepared. Love

her, as she is your child, if not by blood, and your love will be the tool she truly needs to defend her line from those who would seek to eliminate it."

Annette raised her sore and tired arms and, without understanding why, accepted the baby girl. She clutched the infant to her own breast and, as she held the baby in her arms, the Lady of the Lake scooped Annette up and held mother and child in her arms. As she held them aloft, the Lady extended almost no energy as she leached the moisture from Annette's clothes and hair, leaving the new mother completely dry, as though she'd never touched the river.

The Lady of the Lake walked over the surface of the water and as close to the shore as her domain would allow. Reaching forward, the goddess gently rested Annette and her baby upon the soft earth.

Smiling translucent lips that radiated love and hope, the Lady of the Lake queried, "What will you call her?"

Annette tore her eyes from the infant for the first time since accepting her into her arms and took in the watery deep eyes of the goddess. "Evelyn," she answered without hesitation. She'd known this child from the moments she had laid eyes on her. "Evelyn Farthing."

Fear suddenly leapt to Annette's eyes. "What will I tell her?"

The Lady of the Lake stretched forward with one transparent hand and cupped Annette's face, absorbing the tears from her cheek. "You will tell her only the truth: that she is loved. You'll tell her that you are her mother, and you will tell her nothing of this day. Do not lie to her, only refuse her this instance. If you must, explain that it is to protect her, but no one must ever know by what grace Evelyn has come to you." The Lady of the Lake withdrew her hand and stepped back and further into the lake. "It will be difficult, as she is different from all that she will meet, and she will know this. Continue to be there and support her. Teach her that being different isn't something to be ashamed of but is something to nourish and allow to grow."

The Lady began to sink back into the river and before she was completely submerged she said with hope in her voice. "She will live a wonderful life, and her children will bring us the hope that will carry us through the darkness."

Chapter 1

Fifty-seven years later.

Cremont Farthing ducked under the fence with his satchel, splashing the mud as his feet slipped. Behind the 17-year-old boy came cries of alarm.

"Someone, stop that boy!" came the calls from behind him.

He ignored the calls and twisted through the back streets of Camelot, his satchel held tightly to his chest. His whole life had been lived on these streets, between these buildings, and among these people, and Cremont knew every corner and stone out of place. His grandmother Evelyn had told him that it was because he'd been born with the blood of Camelot running through his veins, but Cremont didn't think that it felt like that.

It felt like Camelot had been born with the blood of Cremont running through its veins.

There was only one thing that Cremont knew better than Camelot and that was his twin brother, Dash.

Turning another corner without slowing, Cremont tossed the satchel he'd been guarding so closely directly into the lap of one of the many downtrodden souls who lived unseen in the gutters of Camelot.

Except it wasn't a downtrodden soul any more than Cremont was. Dash Farthing was wearing rags and waiting for his brother to turn the corner of that specific alley behind the stables, ready for whatever his brother needed. The fraternal twin had blended right into his surroundings, and moments after Cremont had sprinted by, two palace guards took the same path, directly past Dash.

Cremont burst out of the alley and into the crowded Camelot marketplace. The sun beat down and Cremont flinched as it assailed his eyes, adjusted as they had been to the darker alleys. The boy skidded to a halt amidst the crowd and walked over to a barter selling potatoes.

Cremont gave the man a coin and began filling a bag, careful to pick the best that his meager payment would allow. Before the shopkeep could say that Cremont had picked enough, the twin tied the bag off and turned back toward the crowd.

His slow turn back to the crowd allowed him the chance to see his pursuers checking everyone that might have come close to his description. Cremont had been fast and knew that the guards didn't have much of a description to go by. Other than his plain brown shirt and simple britches, they'd maybe have his hair to go by, which was shoulder length and brown. Both qualities were far from unique in this crowd.

Pleased with himself, Cremont turned to walk past the potato stand and out of the marketplace and met a fist with his nose.

The boy fell back and onto the ground, grabbing at his nose as it started to bleed.

Before he could look up at his attacker, Cremont was pulled to his feet roughly by a gloved hand. Following the arm to its owner, Cremont recognized the Head of the Guard, Samuel Grand.

"Boy, where's the bag?" He demanded.

Samuel Grand stood a head taller than most men but was eye to eye with Cremont and his equally tall brother. His rough face had seen many battles at the side of King Thordon, and the scars spoke much to his ruthlessness.

"I don't know what you're talking about," Cremont said through the trickle of blood that ran over his mouth.

Samuel shook Cremont. "You think that the death of the King will stop us from arresting thieves, boy?"

A shopkeep stepped forward, and Cremont was suddenly hopeful.

Gregory Rogan was a friend of Cremont and Dash's grandmother. "The boy has done nothing wrong, Samuel. He's been helping me tend the shop this morning." Gregory wore an apron over his rotund belly, into which he slid his hands.

"Rogan, no one asked for your lip." Samuel spat. "A witness specifically saw this Cremont grab a bag from the wagon entering the city. He's stolen. Do you argue this claim?"

"I do." Gregory said plainly.

Samuel threw Cremont back to the ground and turned to Gregory. "What proof do you have?"

"Aside from my word that the boy has been with me this morning? Where is the bag he supposedly took?" Gregory didn't back down from Samuel's glare.

Samuel took his eyes away from Gregory and looked down at Cremont. A cursory glance told him that Cremont didn't have the satchel, so he instead turned his eyes to the stall and then Gregory. He directed his words to Cremont. "Where is your brother?"

His nose had stopped bleeding, and Cremont wiped his face on his sleeve. "He's with my grandmother. She needed help pulling in crops."

"Crops?" Samuel barked. "What crops? The ground has been too dry."

Cremont stood slowly, carefully. "My family has been blessed with better luck than most. Everyone knows." He brushed himself off but didn't take his eyes from Samuel who, in turn, hadn't taken his eyes from Gregory's. "Grandmother said it has something to do with our dirt."

"See?" Gregory added. "They have less reason than anyone to steal. Stop wasting your time with him and start looking for the real criminal."

Samuel's gaze hardened on Gregory. "Watch your tongue, shopkeep, or I'll cut it out." He turned to Cremont. "You came close today. Very close. Tomorrow is another day." He stormed off, slamming his shoulder into Cremont and knocking him back to the ground as he left.

Gregory helped Cremont up and checked his nose, yanking the teen's head about as he examined him roughly. Under his breath he asked, "What the hell have you done, Cremont?"

"It was a bag of feed," Cremont answered.

Gregory yanked Cremont's chin. "The Guard would have killed you if they'd had any proof."

Cremont yanked his chin back but kept his voice low. "The Cord's horse is starving. Not everyone can be as lucky as Grandmother."

Gregory poked Cremont in the chest. "You might be doing well for your friend Martin today, but don't lose your head over a horse, boy." Gregory turned back toward his shop and spoke over his shoulder. "Where's Dash?"

Cremont smiled. "He hid in the alley."

Gregory turned, a smile matching Cremont's spread over his face. "That boy could have hid in the crowd. He has a talent."

Cremont's smile vanished. "What did Samuel mean by the King being dead?"

Gregory's smile also fell away. "Exactly what he said. The King succumbed to his age today. His son might take over, but not until we've heard from Lord Bonnevist from the north."

"Thordon's son?" Cremont looked surprised. "He lost an entire legion in the woods north of here for weeks. He wouldn't make a wise choice."

Gregory hushed him. "Watch your tongue. You still wish to lose your head?" Gregory's eyes softened. "It doesn't really matter who will lead Camelot, does it? It was never the blood of Arthur ruling Camelot, only the wizard."

"Bonnevist," Cremont said quietly.

Gregory nodded. "As long Alec Thordon is willing to accept the council of Lord Bonnevist, it doesn't matter who rules Camelot. Our days will not change." There was a somber note to Gregory's tone, and Cremont could see the shopkeep's age then. He was a little older than Cremont's grandmother and still remembered the times before Lord Bonnevist came from the north. He still remembered the times before the resurfacing of Arthur's bloodline.

Cremont only knew Dash had been standing behind him in the crowd because he'd learned to look for his brother's subtle steps, but Gregory had no idea, and jumped nearly out of his skin as Dash stepped up to him and pronounced a loud "Hello, Gregory."

Gregory took a moment to compose himself while the boys laughed. Finally, Gregory voiced, "What are you doing here, Dash? Cremont just vouched for you, saying that you were with your grandmother. If the Guard sees you…"

Dash smiled. "Then they'll see that Grandmother needed a new shovel, and I came into town to check the prices and report back to her."

Gregory shook his head and returned to tending his wares. "There's no sense in either of you boys. You dance with fire and risk being burned. How that dear Evelyn can put up with your antics I'll never understand."

Cremont looked around and saw that the market was filling up more than he'd expected. He looked at his brother and, without words, understood that Dash had already seen to hiding the satchel somewhere else. Together they thanked Gregory who only grumbled at them to get out of his sight and headed out of town and back toward their farm.

The day progressed and the sun crawled across the open sky. The lands surrounding the city had been without a good rain for weeks, and no one knew this quite as well as Martin Cord and his father as they ladled cups of water onto their withering crops. Martin had carried the bucket of water behind his father for the fifth time that day, and together they each scooped cups of the precious liquid onto the plants, careful to not miss with a single drop. All too quickly, the man and his son were scraping the bottom of the wooden bucket with their ladles. Emptying what was most likely the hundredth bucket, Jacob, Martin's father, looked across the field at the work they'd done and the direction of the stream. Ache filled both of their eyes. Martin had already crossed from the stream about twenty acres away.

The process was futile. They'd emptied the barrels long before they'd started the trek to the stream and Jacob couldn't keep pushing his son this way. They needed rain.

Jacob sighed and looked at his son.

Martin would never quit. He was as dedicated to his family and the farm as his father was. The water, every ladle of it, was necessary for their survival. The boy knew it.

Boy, Jacob laughed inwardly. *He's more man than I was at his age.*

"That is all we can do for today. Tonight, when it is cooler, we can begin bringing buckets up to our barrels in preparation for tomorrow." The look on Martin's father's face was that of defeat, and it brought Martin's spirit to the brink of collapse. Jacob recognized what Martin was seeing and forced pride into his eyes. "You worked well today. No matter what comes of it, don't ever doubt how hard you worked."

It was only just past midday, the hottest point, and Martin knew his father wasn't planning on working again until near dusk. *Don't burn water when we ain't got water to burn,* his father had been known to say.

"Cremont and Dash are probably home by now. Would it be alright if I visited with them until dusk?" Martin asked.

Jacob already knew what he was going to say but went through the motions of plotting what needed doing and how much time they had to do it. It took him at least a minute of pure silence before he nodded. "Go, have fun, but don't be late." He smiled at his son. "I can't do this without you."

Martin smiled and thanked his father. He took the bucket back to the barn before running in the direction of Dash and Cremont's farm.

Martin didn't use the path to get to their farm, although over the years his own feet had started to dig an unofficial road between the two farms and through the woods.

As he broke from the brush and walked through the thick dying grass, he could hear Evelyn Farthing, the twins' grand-mother, singing to herself. Cresting the hill before their farm, he saw the older woman among her own, surprisingly green crops. The small plot that the Farthings tended, small by Martin's stan-dards, wasn't all as green as the center crops. The outer edges of her field were browning and starting to whither, but the bright green of their surviving crops put instant jealousy in Martin's heart.

As deep in song as she was and her eyes tightly closed, she didn't see the young friend of her grandsons as he approached.

Entranced by her song, Martin decided against interrupting it by announcing his presence, and only stood and listened. The song rose and fell but there seemed to be no actual words to it. She kept her voice flowing with the breeze and it was almost as if her crops danced to her song. The older woman raised her hands as if directing imaginary listeners in the proper method of dance.

This carried on for minutes and Martin felt as if the music of Evelyn's song would carry him away. It flowed through him and soaked into his skin. Martin felt like the music was kneading his sore and worn muscles and energy flowed through him, washing away hours of his ache. He swam in this ocean of relaxation for what felt like minutes before a subtle thought entered his mind.

This wasn't just music.

Martin opened his eyes and saw that the crops were reacting as he was to the music of Evelyn's song. The few crops that were browning and closest to the elderly woman were swaying with the music. As they danced to Evelyn's beautiful voice they also grew greener and took on a much healthier look, much as Martin was certain he had. As Martin cast his gaze across the rest of their small acreage, he saw that all the plants were now in sway with the grandmother and realization dawned on him.

This was magic.

Illegal, immoral, and all-corrupting.

That's what the King had said when he'd put the laws into effect demanding that magic be stopped. Cremont and Dash's grandmother was practicing magic and the only punishment for that crime in Camelot was beheading.

Martin was awash with emotions. First, he was struck with fear for his friends' family. Someone could see this. Someone other than himself. Then Martin was filled with jealous rage. How could she keep this to herself when he and his family were on the verge of losing their entire farm?

Somewhere in this mix of emotions, Martin was also feeling a sense of awe. This wasn't only forbidden, but it was unheard of. He had never seen magic used before, and it was exciting.

His admiration shifted back towards the negative; to fear. Before he knew what he was doing, Martin had turned his back on the Farthing farm and was running. His feet were hitting the ground hard, and he'd made it to the road before Evelyn could finish her song and lay eyes upon her only witness. Not knowing where to run, he avoided his usual trail home to his farm and instead took the path toward Camelot. Martin didn't know what he was going to do, and the trail would give him time to straighten his thoughts before he arrived back at home.

Martin didn't know whether to tell his parents, tell a city guard, or to tell no one. It was all so much bigger than anything Martin had ever encountered before. His friends could be killed. He could be killed. His family could starve. There were so many paths before him, and Martin was overwhelmed with this new experience.

Sprinting down the roads with so much panic on his mind, Martin didn't even notice as he barreled into his two friends heading home by way of the same trail.

"Martin, what's the rush?" Dash asked his friend.

Martin only looked at both. "I-I-I…" He stammered, still at a complete loss as to his goals. "I-I was running home. I had much to tell my father." Pride swelled within Martin for himself as he realized that he'd just stumbled upon the best course of action. "Yes, I need to go home. Father is expecting me."

Cremont and Dash helped their friend to his feet. "We should meet up later," Cremont said. "Maybe we could go to the stream and fish? With the waters so low, it should be easy picking."

Dash nodded and then remembered the satchel. "Martin! We managed to get some feed for Geraldine!" He pushed the satchel into his friend's arms and Martin took it, confusion filling his eyes.

Suddenly, the confusion vanished as he realized that his friends had just saved his horse and guilt took the confusion's place, filling his every bone as he realized that these friends were willing to do anything for him.

"Yes," he answered. "I mean, thank you. You don't know what this means to me."

"Don't worry about it. Maybe later you can swing on by for dinner if not fishing?"

Martin hesitated before agreeing. His greed mixed with the reemergence of his confusion. Dinner would be from their garden, Martin had no doubt. These friends would steal feed for his family's horse, but not give them an ounce of magic to save their farm? The idea turned the confusion to anger.

Martin bid his friends a quick goodbye, thanking them again for the grain before running back down the path and toward his home. This was too much for him to decide alone, so he would tell his mother and father and they would decide as a family what needed to be done.

Adrianna Cord slammed her hands down on the tabletop. "Calm down!"

Jacob looked at his wife while Martin kept his eyes to the floor. "Calm down? Adrianna, do you know what this means?"

"We do not have all of the facts." She looked at Martin. Sensing this shift in attention, Martin looked to his mother. "And while I trust our son, we cannot be certain of what it was he saw."

Martin shook his head. "I know what I saw." He shivered involuntarily. "I know what I felt. Evelyn Farthing was chanting and waving her hands about. The plants were moving with her, and they were green." Martin lost control of himself then and slammed his own hand down on the table. "That's the most damning truth. No one has green crops. How does she?"

Adrianna ignored her son's outburst and leaned forward, slowly lowering herself to the chair beside the table.

"The Farthings have been friends to our family for a long time. This kind of accusation could destroy them. We should not begrudge someone else's good fortune." Adrianna had no strength in her argument.

Jacob leaned forward in his own chair and brought his eyes to meet Adrianna's across the table. "I wish no ill will on our friends. I only want to ask that they share in their fortune."

"We can't ask that of them," Adrianna pressed.

"They could save our farm!" Jacob's voice was raising but not with anger, only excitement.

"But at what cost?" His wife asked. "Magic is outlawed for a reason. If we ask the Farthings to help us, how long could that go on before others begin to notice our farm?" Her eyes widened. "What if they accuse us of using magic?" Adrianna shook her head adamantly. "No. We can't ask them for their help. We must choose to ignore them if we are to save our own farm."

Martin spoke up then. "We wouldn't use them much. Only ask that they get us through the summer. Once we have enough to last us the winter we can thank them and go our separate ways."

Adrianna gave her son a look of annoyance. "Until the next dry season." She sighed. "If we do this, there will be no coming back. We will have lost our friends."

"But saved our farm and family." Jacob added.

Martin thought of his friends for a moment and then asked. "What do we do if they say no?"

Jacob grimaced, "The reward for magic users will get us through the winter and beyond." He nodded to his wife. "I will give them the choice. Either us or the gallows. They will understand and choose us."

Evelyn had brought in a box of potatoes from the garden and placed them on the table. Their house was small, and smaller still since the death of the twins' grandfather. Evelyn had thought that her heart would never heal from that tragedy but, as had been the case when their mother died, her love for Cremont and Dash had brought her back from the dark places of her heart.

Now, almost five years since her husband's death, Evelyn could only barely feel his ghost trying to turn her head. The boys would be home soon, and she knew that the house wouldn't be lonely for long.

It was no sooner than she had thought about Cremont and Dash, that she heard them walking up the path. They were young, and therefore loud, and she could hear them entire minutes before she actually saw them.

Evelyn walked to the window and shouted, "I left a basket of radishes in the garden. One of you grab them, please?" She noted that Dash broke from the road and ran toward the garden while Cremont continued toward the house.

She frowned at that. Evelyn knew the boys had left with a satchel, and it took no special insight to know what had happened to it. She'd been cutting vegetables a day earlier when she'd heard their young friend, Martin, talk about the starving horse. She admired her grandsons' large hearts, but they couldn't keep up with these bad habits. It would get their hands cut off and she had said as much only last week. She contemplated disciplining the boys but stopped. A voice that she knew all too well, but also knew not to be her own, sent out a warning.

Not today.

She nodded. Evelyn had never known the source of the voice, but it had been right too many times for her to believe it a product of a madness.

"Not today, then," the grandmother echoed.

Cremont came in first and gave his grandmother a quick kiss. Evelyn could see how he tried to hide his eyes from hers as he did this. The boy was young and thought himself more clever than anyone. He had much to learn. She allowed him his fantasy and followed the voice's advice.

Dash came in with the small basket of radishes and set it on the table.

Radishes set in their place the boys came up to their grandmother. Dash followed suit and greeted her with a hug.

Evelyn asked, "Anything exciting happening in town today, boys?"

"King Thordon is dead!" Dash exclaimed in a hushed voice.

"So I had heard," Evelyn responded without surprise. She had heard, but the boys needn't know that she heard from her secret voice. The boys' confusion was evident for only a second before they dismissed it. They had become used to this omniscient attitude their grandmother took on and assumed that she did it only to make them wary of their own actions.

Cremont gave his grandmother a sidelong glance. "Gregory said to tell you hello." He watched for his grandmother to blush, but she kept herself under control.

Annoyed for not catching his grandmother off-guard, Cremont

gave up before he'd really began and moved on to the subject that actually had him concerned.

"How was your visit with Martin?" He asked.

Evelyn looked up from her potatoes. "Martin? Cord?" She shook her head. "I haven't seen Martin since he visited yesterday."

Dash and Cremont exchanged glances before Dash said, "He was rushing home from this direction. We thought he had come to see you."

Evelyn shook her head again and then stopped. "When was this?"

Dash aimed his thumb over his shoulder, indicating the trail. "We just ran into him on our way home."

Evelyn blanched. She'd only just been working the plants. She'd been touching the gift that her voice had told her about. The gift that she was supposed to keep to herself.

The gift that her grandsons didn't know she had.

"Did he say where he was headed?"

Cremont grabbed a potato and bit into it like it was an apple, causing Dash to grimace at his brother. Cremont answered, around the potato, "He said his father was expecting him."

Evelyn opened her mouth to change the subject when her special voice called out to her.

Danger.

Chapter 2

Evelyn grabbed a sack from a drawer and immediately began filling it with any food that was within reach. Potatoes, radishes, and only a small amount of bread went into the sacks as her confused grandsons watched.

"Gran, what are you doing?" Cremont asked.

Before Evelyn could answer, Dash added, "What's wrong?"

Evelyn didn't know how to answer her boys. She couldn't tell them that the voices in her head had warned her that their friend might have seen her use her highly illegal magical ability. The same magical ability that her grandsons had no idea that she even had.

She would have to tell them.

Never before had she been so afraid to be honest with her grandsons.

"Cremont, Dash. I think that I may have put us all in terrible danger."

They both gave her an incredulous look. How could their grandmother, the sweetest old woman in all of Camelot, and possibly farther, have brought any danger to anyone, let alone them?

Before they could get any sort of explanation from their grandmother, a shout came to them from outside and down the path.

"Evelyn Farthing! I'd like a word with you."

Cremont's look changed from that of confusion to that of a teenage boy attempting to out-think his way out of trouble. His eyes went from his grandmother to his brother and the look became contagious.

The Farthing boys didn't know what the problem was, but they weren't going to wait for a solution to present itself.

Dash said nothing as he grabbed his cloak and then scooped up the food sack that Evelyn had been filling.

Cremont ignored his brother and went to the window to peek out. "That's Jacob Cord, Martin's father." He glanced back at his grandmother as Dash ducked out the back door. "What's going on, Gran?"

Evelyn Farthing shook her head, trying desperately to shake away the entire situation. "It's too late," she said and moved to stand closer to Cremont. "Jacob Cord has come to accuse me, and probably you boys, of using magic."

"Magic?" Cremont's eyes went wide, allowing Evelyn to see the disbelief in them.

"Yes, and he won't be wrong. I've kept it to myself, but I've known...tricks. Small things, and I've used them for keeping our farm alive when the droughts came."

"How does Jacob know?" Cremont wasn't sure what to believe but felt that he couldn't doubt his grandmother at all. Concerns about the legality of her abilities didn't even enter his mind, as he grappled with whether it was even true.

Evelyn was about to answer when Cremont stopped her. "Martin saw you," he realized. Evelyn nodded.

Another call echoed across their field, much closer this time, and Jacob Cord could now be seen from the window.

"I'm sorry," Evelyn told her grandson through eyes that were starting to fill with tears.

"Sorry for keeping us fed?" Cremont smiled. "You vile woman. You're the Devil himself."

Evelyn laughed with her grandson. "I should go meet him."

Cremont's smile vanished and a flash of the morning's previous adventure came to him. "I'm going with you."

Evelyn knew she couldn't stop Cremont, so instead she only nodded. Together, they walked out the door to greet their friend and neighbor.

Jacob Cord had stopped his march toward the Farthing home right next to their small field of crops. All of them were green, and there was no doubt in Jacob's mind at the truth behind his son's claims. This was magic.

His hands in his pockets and his mind still in shock, Jacob didn't hear Cremont or Evelyn as they approached until they were standing right next to him.

Finally taking notice of their approach, Jacob thrust his hand out to indicate the crops. "What is this?"

"Years of friendship about to be washed away over a moment of weakness," Evelyn said through hard eyes.

"It's witchcraft!" He exclaimed.

Cremont spoke up then. "We know what it is, why are you here?"

Jacob tore his eyes from Evelyn and gave Cremont a menacing look. "Save our farm." It wasn't a question, and though his eyes were still on Cremont, his words were for Evelyn Farthing.

"I can't," Evelyn said, her hard look softening to sympathy. "It doesn't work that way."

Jacob's look of menace turned to one of outright rage and he shifted his focus from Cremont to Evelyn. "Don't play around with me, Evelyn." He jabbed his finger back toward the crops. "Make it work, or I can't be held responsible for keeping to my loyal duties as a citizen of Camelot."

The look on Evelyn's face couldn't have been more sympathetic to Jacob Cord's need. Still, she persisted. "It takes from my own energy, my life. I can't make it work for your farm because I've already used it on ours." Evelyn sighed. "Your farm is much too big. The effort would kill me."

Jacob stepped forward, toward Evelyn, shouting, "You lie!"

Jacob only made it one step before he found himself on his back and looking up at the sky.

Cremont stood over him, his face red and his fist clenched. "You have your answer. Now leave, Cord."

Jacob stood and was about to flatten the young Farthing boy until he saw the look in Evelyn's eyes.

Evelyn's *glowing* eyes.

Jacob Cord let out a roar and stormed off back the way he had come.

Once Jacob Cord was out of their sight, Evelyn sagged. "What do we do now?"

Cremont didn't take his eyes from where he'd last seen Jacob. "We wait for Dash."

Dash stayed hidden among the trees, just off the path and about forty yards behind Jacob Cord's left shoulder. His cloak, though Evelyn hadn't known this when he'd asked her to make it, was the perfect mix of browns and greens for hiding in the denser growth along the path. Unlike his brother, Dash had no want for nefarious dealings, no matter how noble, but he was quite fond of not being seen.

Dash loved to see how much he could get done without being seen.

He was getting much done now.

From the crops, Dash had watched quietly as Martin's father had accused his grandmother of using magic. While it had surprised him, he hadn't been nearly as surprised as his brother. Dash assumed that Evelyn had to be doing something miraculous to keep the farm producing enough food for them.

Dash had brought the sack of food with him just in case Cremont or Evelyn wouldn't have time to grab it themselves. Of course, everything that might happen to them was still vague and uncertain. The Farthing family's future relied entirely on where Jacob Cord decided was his next destination.

With the sack of food tied to Dash's belt, he continued to creep slowly in the older man's wake. If he chose to return to his home then the Farthings would have time to take some sort of deeper look at their options. If Jacob instead chose to go to Camelot and get the guards, then their options were down to only one: run.

This wasn't the first time that a magic user had been discovered hiding among the people of Camelot during Dash's lifetime. Almost four years ago, Holy Priest Neville Strommer had been discovered, by a member of his clergy, to be using magic in lighting the holy candles. It was a simple spell, they had said. One that he must have used a hundred thousand times before he had been forced into hiding. It had only been natural for the hiding wizard to light the candles with magic, and when he'd been seen, it had been just as natural for the holy man who witnessed the act to turn Strommer in to the nearest guard that he could find.

Lord Bonnevist had joined Camelot, and King Thordon, on that day in coming down from his hidden home in the north to assist with the execution. It was so much worse than a simple execution, though. Lord Bonnevist wanted an interrogation and King Thordon wanted a demonstration. In the end, drawn-out and bloody as it was, Strommer gave no names and Lord Bonnevist agreed that this meant that there were no names to give.

"Magic isn't illegal out of spite or jealousy," King Thordon had bellowed over the still gurgling corpse of the former priest. "Magic is illegal because it goes against the very nature of Camelot. It goes against our souls as free and innocent people." He raised his hands to indicate everyone in Camelot. "Merlin ruled Camelot with an iron fist. He manipulated my great-grandfather and together they waged many wars, a bloody crusade, and shed more blood than ever in the history of our people." He lowered his arms and Thordon's face took on a somber look. "Magic, and those who command it, corrupt and leads only to death." King Thordon pointed to where Lord Bonnevist stood. The Lord returned his acknowledgment with a nod. "For this reason, we are forever grateful for the wise council of Lord Bonnevist and his vigilant hunting and removal of magicians and wizards from our beautiful home."

King Thordon had left Neville Strommer's corpse to rot in the sun that day and for the rest of the week. If you had been fortunate enough to miss the execution, you would most certainly have seen the result in one of your needed trips to the city.

It was said that Lord Bonnevist's focused goal of removing magic users caused many to hunt him in return. While he was a favorite patron of Camelot's, it was rumored that he'd acquired several enemies. Dash and Cremont had spent many hours debating on the location of the Lord's hidden home to the north.

At the divide in the path, Jacob Cord hesitated, stopping for almost a minute before making his decision. The thinner grass-covered path to the left led to the Cord farm, while the beaten and dirt-covered path to the right led to the walls of Camelot.

Dash began to sweat in his cloak, but not entirely from the heat of the drought.

Finally, after what felt to Dash like an eternity, Jacob Cord chose his path.

He chose left. He chose home.

Dash almost sighed out loud with relief. They weren't out of the woods yet, but the Farthings would at least not have to make a run for it now.

Dash reached into the sack at his waist and pulled out a radish, popping it into his mouth before pulling the tie on the sack tight again. When he raised his head back to the path, his blood went cold.

Jacob Cord had come back to the division in the path. Without breaking his stride, he turned down the path to Camelot, his mind changed. Dash was frozen with disbelief.

The boy shook his head, snapping out of his shock. Turning away from Jacob Cord, Dash didn't try to be quiet as he hit the road and sprinted back to the farm.

He arrived back at the house in minutes and burst through the door.

Inside sat Cremont and Evelyn at the table. Dash threw back the hood of his cloak and spoke between his gasps for breath.

"Jacob is heading into Camelot now," Dash gasped. "The guard will move fast." Gasp. "We have maybe an hour."

Evelyn stood, the sadness the boys had seen in her eyes earlier was now long gone as she spoke, replaced instead with solid determination.

"Dash, grab your bow and dagger," their grandmother walked over to the wall and grabbed Cremont's rarely used walking stick. "Cremont," she tossed the staff to her grandson, and he snatched it from the air, "grab your hunting knife as well."

Evelyn took the sack from Dash and set about adding more food to it while the boys did as they were told. When they returned, Dash had slung his bow over his shoulder with a quiver of arrows at his belt, while Cremont had donned his own cloak. His hunting knife peeked out from where the cloak was tied.

Evelyn gave the sack of food back to Dash who then returned it to its place on his belt.

"There isn't much time," she said. "East of here is the creek. You both know it. I want you both to go there and then follow it upstream. Keep following it until you get to the lake."

"We aren't going without you," Cremont declared.

Dash looked with confusion between Cremont and Evelyn. "You're not coming?"

"Like hell she isn't," Cremont said, his face reddening.

Evelyn's face turned stone-still. "I am the only one with the ability to slow them down. I can't go with you. I must stay here to stop them. When I know they've been slowed and can't find you, then I will meet you at the lake."

Both boys exclaimed "No!" at the same time.

"This cannot be debated," Evelyn said through gritted teeth. "The magic has told me that if any of us are to survive than this is how it is supposed to be."

"Damn the magic!" Cremont said, but his eyes showed that he was reluctantly accepting that he couldn't convince his grandmother otherwise.

"The magic speaks to me... as it soon will to you. It tells me that the gift skips a generation. Your poor mother never showed any special use of it, but I know that you two have it. Lord Bonnevist won't be happy with killing me, he'll want to make sure that my line is dead, too."

Dash's eyes were filled with tears that he tried to hold back while Cremont's eyes were filled only with rage.

"How," Dash started to ask before his sadness caught in his throat. "How are we ever supposed to escape this?"

It wasn't Evelyn who answered, but Cremont. "We won't. They will come for us, and they will hunt us for every day of our lives. They will do it until we finally decide to turn around and fight."

"But," Evelyn added, "that day is not today." She pointed east. "You must make it to the lake."

"Why the lake?" Cremont asked.

"It will be safe," is all that Evelyn could tell them. It was all that she knew.

"What do we do when we get there?" Dash asked.

To answer, Evelyn's eyes lost focus and she repeated the question. After a moment, their grandmother's eyes regained focus and she replied, "When you get there, you must wait by the shore. Do that and you will be safe."

Cremont's face showed none of his anger. "The lake is out in the open. If we wait by the shore we will be seen by any who chase use."

Evelyn shook her head before stepping forward and hugging Cremont tightly.

"I know, but you must trust in the magic; mine, and soon yours. If you wait by the water's edge you will be safe. I promise you."

Dash said again what Cremont and himself had both been struggling with. "We can't leave you here. The guard and Bonnevist will be here; you will die."

Evelyn took Dash in her arms, engulfing him into the same hug that still held Cremont. Looking into Dash's eyes, she gave him a wink. "You have never seen what I can do. Don't count your old gran out yet."

Evelyn Farthing stiffened then. She gave them both a quick kiss and said, "They are on the property. Out the back. I love you both so very much."

The boys started to move, but Evelyn stopped them. "Follow Dash's lead to the lake. Whatever he tells you to do, do it without hesitation. Once the lake is in sight follow Cremont's instructions.

Whatever he commands, you must follow!" This wasn't their grandmother speaking, but the magic speaking through her. In shock and surprise, both boys had no doubts to the truth of the words. "Do this and you will live."

The twins ducked out the back door as quietly as they could. They were uncertain if they would ever see their grandmother again.

Chapter 3

Ducking out the back door, Cremont and Dash only made it a few steps before Dash held up his hand, halting their progress. Cremont skidded to stop and raised his eyebrow at his brother.

"Why are we stopping?" He asked.

Dash put his finger to his lips and then brought his hood over his head.

Pointing the way they'd been about to head, Dash said, "They're coming from all around us. We can't take that path to the stream; they are already on it."

Cremont's look turned to one of anger. "What do we do now?"

Dash looked panicked for a moment and then brought his mind back under control. Closing his eyes, Dash listened for the clumsy Camelot Guard as they moved about the Farthing property.

"We move quietly and quickly. This way." Dash whispered before taking off in another direction, only slightly different from the path they were previously set to take.

Together, the boys kept low to the ground, continuing toward the forest. Dash would periodically hold up his hand, stopping their movements and tilting his head to the side, listening. Twice he adjusted their course, working them through the tall, dry grass toward the tree line.

To Cremont's credit, he did not argue his brother's directions. Not only did he know his brother's strengths, and that his own strengths were not those of the shadows, but he also could hear his grandmother's words still echoing in his mind. He would follow Dash's direction as best he could until they reached the lake. Cremont did not envy his brother's command, and he did not look forward to the moment in which the decisions would become his own.

Once they made it to the forest line, Dash pointed at the ground and then knelt. Understanding the signal, Cremont followed suit.

"Look," Dash's whisper was barely more than a breath. He pointed into the tall grass and then moved his finger to near the house and then again to the tree line.

It took Cremont a moment to see, but once he saw the first, the rest stood out easily. Each location was a member of the Camelot Guard, stalking slowly toward the house. Cremont was immediately furious and began to rise.

Dash grabbed his arm, hard and with enough force to bring Cremont's senses back to himself.

"She already knows," Dash added, and Cremont, though filled with rage, knew the truth of his brother's words. "We need to keep moving." Dash added.

"No," Cremont's eyes were hard. "I must see this."

Dash was eager to see how the events played out as well, and his grandmother was down there, but he didn't think that standing here and watching was in any way safe.

"Fine," Dash said, "but we do it my way." He stood and started along the tree line, keeping low. Cremont followed close behind his brother.

They came to a low group of fallen trees. Last year the drought hadn't come; instead, it had been the opposite situation. The rains had come down in an intense thunder and lightning storm that had taken down some of their trees. The boys had been slowly harvesting them for firewood and hadn't come to this collection of the fallen yet. Crawling between the branches, and careful not to make any noise, the boys climbed between the fallen dead trees and took positions.

Cremont was happier for this new location. From the other position they could only see a few of the Camelot Guard and the back of the house, but from this new position Cremont could see the front of the house, the plot used for the crops, and the Camelot Guards hidden along the front of the property.

They could also see the three members of the Guard escorting Jacob Cord to the front of their home. The head of the Camelot Guard, Samuel Grand, led the charge while Jacob walked behind him, a somber look on his face. The sight of Jacob was enough to raise the anger in both of the Farthing boys, but the sight of Samuel Grand almost made Cremont leap from their hiding place.

Dash saw this and touched his brother's arm. This small

gesture calmed Cremont, but only barely.

Samuel walked the path that passed the crops and led directly to the door of the Farthing home. His look radiated with smugness as he stopped just short of the house by about ten yards.

Samuel Grand drew his sword and bellowed, "Evelyn Farthing! The Camelot Guard demands that you answer to charges!"

There was a moment of silence that echoed across the farm before the door finally opened and Evelyn Farthing came out very slowly. She walked at that same pace toward Samuel as he stood still with his sword held out. The grandmother's face was unreadable by everyone present, even the boys at the forest line.

Samuel took this moment to explain the Guard's and Jacob's presence. "A witness has come forward to accuse you of using magic. As you know this is a highly illegal act of—"

He was interrupted by screams that came from all around them. Evelyn's face hadn't changed, and she hadn't stopped walking.

From their spot on the hill, the boys were the only people present who could see what had caused the screams. The tall grass around the farm had come alive and grabbed at the hidden members of the Guard. Many were grabbed and pressed to the ground by their limbs while the others' screams were cut off short by the grass wrapping tightly around their throats.

Evelyn continued her course toward the three members of the Guard and Jacob Cord as the screams of their companions made them look all about. Evelyn used the distraction to raise her hand at them. The ground beneath the two guards on each side of Cord split open with an eerie silence and consumed both, leaving Cord and Samuel unharmed.

Cremont took grim satisfaction in seeing that, for the first time since he'd met Samuel Grand so many years ago, the big man was paralyzed with fear.

Evelyn stopped her approach only inches away from Samuel. Jacob was standing just as terrified and directly behind the head of the Guard. Gently, and with a look of sympathy that only a grandmother knew how to show, she reached up and caressed Samuel's cheek.

He let out a gasp of pain that the boys couldn't hear but could definitely see in his face. From their vantage point, it took the boys a minute to notice that Samuel had stopped moving, his chest no longer rising and falling with his terrified breaths. Another moment of study and Cremont and Dash could see that Samuel Grand had been turned into wood.

Evelyn returned her hand to her side, the sadness evident on her face, even from where the boys hid. She stepped slowly around the newly created statue of the guard and approached Jacob Cord.

Evelyn came as close to Jacob as she had to Samuel but made no further movements.

"I asked you not to do this." Cremont and Dash were both surprised to find that they could hear their grandmother as clearly as if they had been standing where Jacob Cord was. It was the magic. She knew they were here, and she wanted them to know what she was saying.

"You had to assume that I would do everything and anything, just as you would, to protect my family." Evelyn waved her hand back and toward Samuel's now wooden corpse. "His death, their deaths, are all the result of my self-defense against your attack. We were friends, Jacob." She lowered her head. "It didn't have to be this way."

Raising her eyes back to meet Jacob's, Evelyn no longer had a look of sympathy. Instead, the grandmother carried the look of finality. She was prepared to destroy this attacker of her nest.

Evelyn Farthing raised her hand, just as she had only moments previously, and stretched it toward the quivering man's face.

A swift jerk of her body stopped her hand's approach, letting it fall to her side. Evelyn looked down at her chest, and Jacob's eyes followed.

Nestled between her breasts, and forcing its way through her dress, was the point of an arrow.

Cremont and Dash were shocked silent and immediately began searching for where the arrow had come from. Their eyes fell upon a member of the Guard near the corner of the house. He must have managed to cut his way free of the tall grass and stood there with his bow still aimed at Evelyn.

"No!" Cremont shouted, and everyone's heads turned to face the fallen trees that they now stood in.

Dash grabbed his brother, and together they grappled as Cremont tried to run to his already dead grandmother's aid.

It suddenly occurred to Dash that Cremont needed to act on his anger. This realization came to him because he had the same urge. They needed to do something, anything. He wanted to kill the man standing with his bow, prepared for another shot if their grandmother decided to stand back up. Rationality was screaming in the back of his mind, though, and it had the voice of his grandmother.

"Cremont, listen! Listen! We can't stay here, and we can't take them." He risked taking one hand away from his brother to point. "Look! The grass isn't holding them anymore. We need to run!"

Cremont's wild-eyed look began to find focus and it fell on the nearest guard as he was standing up and brushing the grass from his legs. He was looking right back at Cremont.

Through gritted teeth, Cremont said, "Fine." He stopped struggling, but he didn't move. Dash decided that Cremont wouldn't move until Dash did. He would still follow their grandmother's instructions.

Dash climbed from the fallen trees and ran into the woods. Momentarily, worry slipped into his mind that Cremont might not have followed, but soon he could hear sounds of his brother coming up behind him. That brought another concern to Dash's mind, and he slowed.

"We need to move slower. We're too loud," He told Cremont.

Cremont let out a grunt of frustration and then slowed to match his brother's pace. The sounds they'd been making quieted considerably and Dash kept them moving through the more dirt and grass areas. He kept their path to the areas least affected by the drought.

At this pace, it took them only slightly longer than they planned to get to the stream. It flowed to the south. Turning north, the boys continued their march along its edge.

Now that they'd become quieter, Dash and Cremont could both hear the approach of the Camelot Guard as they crunched through the woods. Their armor and weapons were making rattling noises and giving away their positions. At their speed, Dash knew that they wouldn't be able to outrun their pursuers. Dash slowed to a stop and grabbed his brother's arm.

"They're split up," Dash explained. "Some are close behind us, but the others must have taken more time to get free." Dash pulled his knife from his waist and turned south, the way they had come.

Dash put his finger to his lips and Cremont complied by not asking why they had stopped or what Dash was doing.

Grabbing his knife by the blade, Dash stretched his arm back and over his shoulder, preparing to throw, but waited. Dash tilted his head to the side and listened for the Guard. When he thought them to be close enough, he launched the knife as far as he could to the south and away from the direction they were headed.

The knife disappeared from sight, but they soon heard it hit something and then bounce on the dry grass and broken branches in the woods. A sudden snap of twigs told Dash that the pursuers had heard and changed course, but he could also tell that he'd let them get too close.

Turning to Cremont, Dash pointed at the tall grass by the stream and then ducked down into it, sliding his bow free and rolling onto his back.

Cremont hesitated for only a moment before joining his brother.

Lying incredibly still, Dash moved only to free up an arrow from the quiver tied to his waist under the cloak. Slowly, he knocked an arrow to the bow and drew the string back, keeping the bow flat to his body.

Idly, Cremont noticed that the grass by the stream was almost as dry as everywhere else. The drought had turned the stream into little more than a trickle. Even he, less subtly-minded than his brother, could hear the crunch of the grass as the nearby members of the Guard came closer.

There were two of them, so far, and one of them had definitely followed the direction of the knife. Whether incredibly stupid or incredibly clever, the second had chosen against following that path, instead continuing in the direction that boys had decided to hide. Cremont could feel his brother's tension rise. Dash hadn't killed anyone before, but from what Cremont could tell, he was prepared to. Cremont worried for his brother. He'd taken it upon himself to follow his grandmother's wishes, and to do so looked as though he'd have to lose pieces of himself. Cremont's anger at the day's events was starting to change to fear. He and his brother had been pushed onto a journey that in just an hour's time had already began turning them into completely different people.

The guard had come close, only feet away, and both boys had stopped breathing. Dash knew that the guard was going to reach them, but he didn't want to do what he knew would have to be done.

His steps came closer and suddenly he stopped. Dash moved

only his eyes and noticed that now the guard stood with his nearest foot only inches away from his outstretched arm and bow. The guard was looking toward the stream and hadn't noticed the boys in the tall grass just inches from him.

It didn't last. As he brought his eyes around to search for a sign, they fell on Dash and Cremont's shapes in the grass. He drew his sword and opened his mouth to call out.

Dash didn't remember bringing the bow up and he had no idea as to when he'd let go of the string, but he saw the arrow leave his bow and place itself firmly into the middle of the Guard's throat.

Cremont gasped. Dash assumed that he was breathing but he couldn't hear it over the sound of his own heartbeat. It felt similar to the excitement he'd felt when he had felled his first deer, but it was different. His heart beat loudly, and he couldn't feel any of his muscles, but the satisfaction wasn't there at all. Instead of the butterflies filling his stomach, he could feel lead in his heart.

It wasn't until Cremont grabbed his arm that Dash came back to himself. They had to move; this wasn't over yet.

Leaping to their feet, they knew that they weren't far from the lake and so surrendered their stealth for speed. They had covered about a hundred yards before more of the Camelot Guard spotted them; arrows began to hit the ground ahead of and behind them. Not hundreds of arrows, not even ten, but enough to keep the boys moving.

Cremont's staff still in his hands, he stopped when the arrows began to get closer and turned to face the charge. Dash caught up to him then and grabbed him. "We can't win a fight here, and you're easier to hit if you stand still."

Cremont growled in frustration and turned to follow as his brother took off past him. More arrows continued to assault the ground.

It was another two hundred yards of weaving between trees and barely avoiding arrows before they burst from the brush and into a clearing. Ahead of them they could see the lake, its surface mockingly calm during this day of turmoil.

Dash and Cremont looked at each other, not sure what to do now that they'd reached the lake. Silently reaching an agreement, they ran to the water's edge, hoping for answers to present themselves.

Once they'd reached the edge of the lake, Cremont shouted, "What do we do now?"

Dash shook his head. "Gran said that I was to listen to you once we were at the lake."

Cremont knew that and had dreaded it this entire journey. He had no idea what he was supposed to do. With water on one side of him and the Camelot Guard on the other, he had no real answer for anything.

Three members of the Camelot Guard broke from the tree line. Two of them had their swords raised while the third was setting another arrow into his bow.

Suddenly, Cremont was filled with calm. He couldn't understand it, but this felt better to him. He wasn't like his brother, and he needed to confront his problems without clever subterfuge. He needed to hit something. It might get him killed, but that didn't bother him. He was more in his element at that moment than he had been in the woods.

Cremont didn't take his eyes off the approaching guards as he turned and said to Dash, "Prepare your bow and be ready to protect me." Dash didn't hesitate and knocked an arrow. Cremont continued. "Save your arrows. Only take your shots if you think I'm in danger." He took his eyes from the guards and looked at his brother. "Dash, I know what I'm asking. I'm sorry about back there, in the grass."

Dash returned his brother's look. "We're surviving, and they killed Gran. Do what you have to do, and I will do what I have to do."

Cremont nodded and then turned back to the oncoming guards.

He squeezed the wood of his staff tighter and then ran at middle of the three.

The archer raised his bow, but before he could finish his draw, Dash's arrow took him in the chest. The archer fell to the ground where he stood. The center guard brought his sword down to cleave Cremont in two, but Cremont's staff was ready and batted the sword aside.

Cremont didn't slow his charge at all. Having batted the sword away, the boy crashed into the guard and knocked him back onto the ground. They landed together with a thud, and the wind was forced from Cremont's lungs from the impact.

Before Cremont could bring his arms up to attack the guard, a meaty hand grabbed Cremont around the back of his neck and tore him from the fallen man. He flew backward, managing only barely to keep his grip on his staff. While in the air, Cremont noticed that two more of the Guard were coming out of the forest. He landed hard on the dry beach of the lake.

Before Cremont can get back to his feet, the Guard who had tossed him was already to him and bringing his sword down toward his head. Cremont had no time to bring the staff up and expected to die then, but he had forgotten that his brother was only a few yards behind him with his bow.

The guard fell, an arrow in his chest, and Cremont came to his feet quickly, trading his staff for the sword of the fallen guard.

The two approaching members of the Guard joined the first that Cremont had attacked and stood watching the boys.

Cremont brought the sword up and couldn't help but feel as though the weapon were completely foreign to him. He'd never held a sword before and while it felt well-balanced, it also felt incredibly clumsy in his hands.

Inside, Cremont was a torrent of terror, but he decided against showing it.

The members of the Camelot Guard that stood before him thought that he was speaking to them when he loudly said, "Are you ready?"

The first guard that he'd tackled snickered at him. "Leave this boy alive. His Lordship will want to interrogate him personally."

An arrow went through that guard's eye, and he fell to his knees and then to the ground.

The guard to the right yelled, "Edmond, get the archer!"

Edmond brought up his own bow which, until now, he'd kept at his side. As he drew the string, Cremont overhanded the sword at him. The sword went wide, but so did Edmond's arrow. In the extra second it took for Edmond to recover, Dash's last arrow took him in the chest.

The last guard stood there, not ready to move on the two boys, even unarmed. His hesitancy disappeared when he heard another guard approaching from behind him.

This most recent guard had his own bow already drawn and trained on Cremont. All their tricks spent, the boys only stood there, watching and waiting for the guard to release the string.

The nearest member of the guard pointed his sword at them. "Lord Bonnevist wants you both alive. Get on your knees."

Together, the archer and the guard approached the boys slowly. Cremont immediately started backing up and toward Dash. When they came together, he looked to his brother.

"Any ideas?"

Dash shook his head.

Cremont placed his hand on his brother's arm and together they continued to back up. They heard a splash, and the cool water was around their ankles. Dash and Cremont only took another two steps before it was up to their knees, and the guards were shouting for them to stop.

Not knowing what else to do with the bow trained on them, Dash and Cremont both stopped their retreat.

A loud boom of thunder erupted from all around them, and everyone grabbed their ears, the archer lowering his bow to do so.

As the thunder continued, the boys and the guards watched as the cool water of the lake climbed the legs of both the Farthing twins.

Dash was screaming, confused and terrified, and finally his mind was at the edge of what it could handle for the day. Cremont had been pushed just as far as his brother had, but he couldn't bring himself to scream, instead shuddering in the shock of the event as the water climbed up and over both of their shoulders and then encompassed their heads.

The Camelot Guard watched as the water then froze into solid ice surrounding both the boys. Both of the guards were almost as afraid as the Farthing boys had been.

Another burst of thunder caused both guards to fall to their knees. Together they watched in complete shock as the frozen twins began to crack and shudder.

Thunder erupted a third time and the boys shattered into thousands of pieces and fell into the water.

Nothing was left of them.

Chapter 4

Camelot had grown a darker place in the last sixty years, and the only place that it wasn't evident was in the Hall of the Round Table.

Arthur's original knights had long passed, and it had fallen to the subsequent kings to appoint the new knights. Of King Thordon's original twelve knights, only four were still allowed to sit around the famed table.

Their head, Sir Parker Willingham, sat in the seat directly to the right of King Thordon's now empty chair. His was a position of power; if the King was unavailable or, as was the case, deceased, he was the one to make decisions until the heir to the throne was found or chosen.

Sir Willingham held no reservations about his post, or the King's for that matter. The real decisions of Camelot were all made by the absent wizard, Lord Bonnevist. Until he arrived, though, Parker Willingham was as powerful as the King had been.

"An entire family of the Magic-Born. How did we miss them?" Sir Keith Harrigan was asking. This was the third time that he'd asked, and he wasn't pleased with the answer that he continued to receive.

Sir Brandon Barrier put his face into his hands. "They aren't of a bloodline that raised suspicion, and we could only have known through witnesses, such as Jacob Cord."

The last knight in attendance, Sir Darrel Hudnall, slammed his hands down onto the legendary table. "We damned well should have known, bloodline or not!" He stood, kicking his chair back. It was no easy feat as the chairs were just as old, legendary, and heavy as the table they rested at. "Of all the children in this city, the Farthing twins have been trouble since before they could walk. They caused so much heartache that their own mother couldn't bear it. Then, raised by that damned witch?" He sighed loudly. "We are all lucky that they didn't bring all of Camelot down with them."

"Agreed." A deep and dark voice radiated from Sir Willingham's left.

Seemingly from nowhere, a large shadow had taken residence in the former King's chair. Lord Bonnevist, his immense frame dwarfing the old chair, wore a black cloak, emphasizing his gray eyes and his completely hairless visage.

"I must ask, that if we knew them to be such a terror, how they have never before been taken care of?" His eyes were staring at his folded hands as they rested on the table.

"Lord...Lord Bonnevist!" Sir Willingham choked out. The knight didn't dare mention that he hadn't seen the ageless wizard arrive, because he never saw him arrive. "We...until...they are just children, being rowdy, as children are. We had no reason to assume that they were of the Magic-Born."

"No, no, no." Lord Bonnevist stood. Sir Hudnall returned to his seat immediately. "You all are approaching this threat to our kingdom incorrectly." He rested his hands lightly on the table, leaning onto them. "Everyone is suspect. If they have ever lived in the walls of Camelot, then they are suspect. If they are visiting Camelot, then they are suspect." His voice climbed in volume. "If they are damned rowdy children who can be described with terms such as 'We are all lucky that they didn't bring all of Camelot down with them,' then they are *suspect!*"

The knights, chosen for their courage and strength, looked as terrified as rabbits before a wolf, and in many ways the comparison was accurate.

After a long moment of silence, all the knights began apologizing, speaking over each other. Lord Bonnevist waved his hand, and everyone became silent.

"What is the situation?"

Sir Willingham's voice cracked as he hurried to explain. "Evelyn Farthing was approached by the Camelot Guard and her accuser, a neighbor named Jacob Cord. Somehow she was able to kill more than half of the guards that left to apprehend her, including the head of the Guard, Samuel Grand, before they could kill her." His face was turning red with embarrassment. "She has two grandchildren who escaped into the woods. They were pursued and managed to kill several more of the Guard before they...they disappeared."

Lord Bonnevist raised his eyebrow. "Describe 'disappeared.'"

Sir Willingham was worried that his neck was on the block, and he had no idea as to where this fear was coming from. "They fought our men at the nearby lake. As they became overwhelmed, they retreated toward the lake. Once they were in the lake, the guards claim that they vanished. Evidently... swallowed by the lake."

Lord Bonnevist was suddenly filled with energy. None of the knights had ever seen him like this, and it did little to quell their terror.

"The lake?" he demanded. "Are you sure that they disappeared into the lake?"

Sir Willingham hesitated just too long for everyone's comfort and Sir Hudnall jumped to answer. "Yes, my Lord. The two members of the Guard were very sure of what they saw, the lake consumed them. They believed it to be something of their magic."

Lord Bonnevist smiled, and it was a vile thing. "No. It was not of their magic, but this is a very good thing."

Sir Willingham found his voice. "Lord? How is this a good thing?"

Lord Bonnevist ignored the question and instead directed his attentions toward finding more answers. "My quarters are prepared?"

Sir Willingham nodded. "We had expected you."

Lord Bonnevist returned the nod. "I need the witness..."

"Jacob Cord," Sir Harrigan supplied.

"I need Jacob Cord taken to my quarters. Supply him with food and make certain that he is comfortable. If he has a single thing to complain about then I will have all of your wives killed." The knights nodded quickly. "As for the Camelot Guard, have the two who saw what happened to the Farthing boys carry their grandmother's corpse to the cells." He pointed at each of the knights in turn. "The members of the Guard, the corpse, and myself are not to be disturbed. Is that understood?"

All four of the knights answered in unison, "Yes, my Lord."

In a movement that was only dramatic in its complete lack of drama, Lord Bonnevist left the Hall of the Round Table.

The knights left in his wake were each suddenly struck with a strong feeling of confusion.

The cells were where Lord Bonnevist preferred to hold his interrogations. What would he want a corpse taken there for?

Alex Ronstead and Harold Thomas held the corpse, clumsily, at each end. Alex stood at the Farthing woman's feet, with one leg under each arm, while Harold had his arms uncomfortably around her chest.

The cells were in the basement of the castle of Camelot. They weren't used for their designed purpose and hadn't been since the days of Arthur and his wizard. The town proper had its own holding cells and stockades for those who dared attempted to break the law, but King Thordon had been an advocate of extreme punishments, and criminal behavior had managed to decline.

Or the crooks just got better at not getting caught.

Alex and Harold had both been very hesitant to move upon receiving Lord Bonnevist's instructions to carry the Farthing woman's body to the cells. They'd seen what she'd done, and they didn't want her springing back to life and finishing them both. Then there was what had happened to her grandchildren. This family was cursed, and just touching her made them feel violated.

It was easy to tell what cell they were supposed to bring the corpse into. None of the other cells had ever been used by Lord Bonnevist. He preferred his usual: a small cell in the back, furthest from the stairs.

He had a lit candle on each wall and as the members of the Camelot Guard came in, he was mixing a mud-like concoction in a bowl with his thumb.

In the middle of the cell was a long table that just barely fit between the bars and the far wall.

"Put the body on the table." Lord Bonnevist didn't look up from his mud as the men brought the body in and laid it gingerly on the table.

Alex and Harold had been told that they would be required to recount the disappearance of the Farthing boys for the Lord and didn't make to leave. Instead, they remained near the cell door at the head of Evelyn Farthing's body.

Lord Bonnevist pulled his black-stained hand from the bowl and pointed at Alex. "Don't say a word."

Without lowering his hand, Lord Bonnevist swung it to the

right and halted it when it aimed at Harold. "Tell me what *you* saw."

Harold didn't understand why, but he was filled with dread as he began speaking. "After the," he nodded to the corpse, "witch killed Samuel Grand, myself and Alex here managed to break away from the spell that she cast. We managed to stay close to the boys as they made their way, but they obviously knew the forest better than we did and remained ahead of us."

Harold stopped for breath and it was at that moment that Lord Bonnevist set down his bowl of mud and tore open the top of Evelyn Farthing's dress, exposing her pale breasts and the small hole between them that the arrow had produced.

Shaking away the awkward distraction, Harold put his eyes to the nearest candle and continued his story. "Alex had drawn his bow and was shooting at the boys whenever he saw them."

Lord Bonnevist retrieved the bowl of black mud and dipped his fingers into it. While Harold of the Camelot Guard continued his story, Lord Bonnevist began drawing odd symbols across her chest, covering every inch of her naked top with a muddy image.

"When we arrived at the lake, there were several of us, not just Alex and myself, and the boys had already managed to dispatch several of our fellow members of the Guard."

Harold stopped again, but this time it was because Lord Bonnevist had turned his mud-covered fingers toward their foreheads. As the Lord raised his hand to Harold's forehead, he halted mid-reach and said, "I did not ask you to stop."

Harold nodded and returned to his report while Lord Bonnevist spent detailed time on his forehead.

"As Alex and I approached, the boys became disarmed and began backing toward the lake. It was odd, my Lord." Lord Bonnevist turned his artistic attentions to Alex while Harold continued. "As they stepped into the lake, the water seemed to crawl up their bodies until they were covered by it. It was our hope they'd drown, but that wasn't what happened."

"What happened?" Lord Bonnevist asked as he finished the symbol on Alex's forehead.

"Well, they froze, my Lord. And after they froze, they shattered. Nothing was left of them as the ice fell into the water." The mud was surprisingly cold against Harold's forehead. "Not knowing what else to do, we instead returned directly to Camelot to give our report."

"Are you working magic?" Alex asked as the mud drizzled slowly onto his nose.

Harold's eyes closed in shame. He'd been told to be quiet. Silently, Harold prayed for Lord Bonnevist to not notice Alex's lapse.

"At what moment, precisely," Lord Bonnevist was asking Alex, "did you decided to become a traitor?"

Alex flinched and gulped. "A traitor? I'm no traitor, sir!"

"You willingly disobeyed a direct order from the King's advisor." Lord Bonnevist shrugged. "That's treason."

With a quick movement, Lord Bonnevist shoved his finger deep into the mud mark on Alex's forehead. "To answer your question," the Lord said through gritted teeth, "I wasn't working magic; I was preparing to work magic. This," he pressed his finger harder, "is magic. *Bite your tongue.*"

Harold watched as a shiver ran through Alex's body and terror filled Alex's eyes. With no hesitation and his lips still closed over his mouth, Alex worked his jaw.

The slicing of his tongue could only have been more gruesome to watch if Alex's mouth had been open. His eyes watered in pain and his face was red with pain. While his lips remained closed, blood began to seep out and over his chin, dripping down the front of his tunic.

Not minding the blood, Lord Bonnevist reached up and touched Alex's chin. "Now swallow it."

A large gulp only made the tears turn from a drizzle to a torrent down Alex's face.

"Unfortunately," Lord Bonnevist continued as if nothing had happened. "Magic is a necessary evil. It is rumored that Merlin himself worked a curse into the stones of Camelot that a wizard must always be at the call of the King. It was done to keep the wisdom and council of one wise enough to use the magic forever at Camelot's aid." He sighed and started wiping the blood from his hand onto his robes. "The wizard is the beating heart of Camelot, and no matter how horrendous the act, someone must play the part." He flourished and bowed for his captive audience. "I used to be like the witch on the table, full of pride for my power, but I soon saw that I had nothing to be proud of. In such a big pond, what is another fish? Besides," he almost sounded wistful, "what's a fish when compared to a shark?"

He stepped back to Evelyn Farthing's body and began straightening her hair, almost as if he were concerned for her. "Merlin was the most powerful being ever born. His power was unmatched, and I have always been a firm believer in being the best." Alex's tunic was soaked in the blood draining from his lips and his face was as pale as the moon. "I learned during one particular torture that once a wizard's mind was cracked just enough, that it was possible to pull their energy, their magic, out of them and hold it in myself." Lord Bonnevist slapped Evelyn's dead face. "But they can't be dead." He stepped very close to Harold, their eyes only inches apart. "So, I came to Camelot over 50 years ago to meet and drain the vile wizard Merlin. Instead, he chose to kill himself and leave me without my prize. Now, I'm Camelot's wizard, and I choose to protect it by tearing the magic from every user I come across." He smiled then and it was an ugly thing. "Camelot is blessed in that way. It has a spirit, and the spirit has been sick since the death of Merlin. In an effort to heal itself, it has been subtly calling the Magic-Born here." He returned to Evelyn's body. "To me."

Placing his hands together he held them over Evelyn's bare chest. He pitched his head back and began humming a steady tone and wiggling his fingers, only inches above the corpse.

Slowly returning his head to stare forward, Lord Bonnevist let out a bark and then threw his right hand toward Harold's chest.

Harold felt something hit him in the back like a mighty punch and he rocked forward. He was surprised that it hadn't knocked him over until he realized that he was in pain. Looking down at his chest, Harold was surprised to see that a glowing arrow, seemingly formed from the light itself, was protruding from his breastbone. He tried to speak, but he could only move his lips, his voice lost in the torrent of light that pierced his chest.

"She must not be dead if I'm to take her energy. I give you her death, guard. Wear it well." Harold collapsed to the ground as the light evaporated, leaving a hole in exactly the same shape and place as the one on Evelyn Farthing.

Lord Bonnevist hadn't forgotten about Alex either and in a flash of movement he was standing next to the guard. Swiftly, Lord Bonnevist grabbed the back of Alex's neck and slammed it toward the table. The mark on his forehead cracked against the mark on Evelyn Farthing's forehead and he fell, just as deceased as his fellow guard.

"And I give her your life," Lord Bonnevist finished.

The life and death of the members of the Guard flowed into and out of Evelyn and she jolted awake as the hole in her chest vanished and the pallor to her skin shifted to a pink.

Evelyn Farthing's eyes darted around in a panicked search for understanding. Terror filled her eyes until they landed on Lord Bonnevist.

"Lord Bonnevist." Her entire demeanor calmed, and she paid no notice to her exposed breast. "Then I've already been dead." Lord Bonnevist didn't answer her, but Evelyn knew that she was correct. "The boys?"

Lord Bonnevist still said nothing, and that brought a smile to Evelyn's face. "Good."

Cremont and Dash's grandmother began laughing then, elated that her boys had escaped. Lord Bonnevist raised his hand quickly, preparing to backhand the revived woman.

He stopped himself though, as all his anger and frustration evaporated into fear and confusion. Both were feelings rarely known by Lord Bonnevist since he was young.

That laugh no longer belonged to Evelyn Farthing. It had turned deeper, huskier, and older. It was the laugh of an old man.

"What is this?" Lord Bonnevist demanded.

The laugh only became heartier, and Evelyn's eyes began to tear as her body rocked with the laughter.

He reared his hand back again, "Damn you! What is this?"

Before Lord Bonnevist could swing his hand down, Evelyn raised her own hand, palm out toward the dark magician. An unseen force slammed into his chest and lifted Lord Bonnevist from the floor and toward the wall. His back hit the wall hard, rattling his teeth, and the force continued to hold him tightly and painfully against the stone wall of the cell.

The dark laughter continued for another moment or so before stopping abruptly. Through gritted teeth and a masculine voice, the body of Evelyn Farthing spat, "Lord Bonnevist!"

Lord Bonnevist shivered when he heard the voice. He recognized it. That voice belonged to a dead man. "Merlin!" Bonnevist hissed. "This is impossible...unless..." Realization dawned on Bonnevist's face.

"I see," Merlin interrupted, "that you've met my granddaughter."

Lord Bonnevist smiled through tight lips before slowly

lowering to the ground. "I long ago surpassed the power at your command, Merlin." His feet touched the ground and Evelyn Farthing's hand fell to her side. "Your silly tricks are only that: tricks. If you thought that you could kill me, you would have done it by now."

Merlin nodded Evelyn's head. "Yes, in your purge of the Wizards, you managed to leech much power. It would be impressive if it wasn't so despicable." Merlin's smile returned to the borrowed face. "I think your time is about done now."

Lord Bonnevist ignored the comment. He had no idea as to how long he would have with the dead wizard, and he had questions.

"Tell me how to get Excalibur from the Lady. Tell me this and I'll end my...purge, as you call it, starting with your great-grandsons."

Merlin shook Evelyn's head, lowering it slightly to show that he pitied Bonnevist's lack of knowledge. "You're a curse to the title of wizard, and not just because of your murderous cannibalism. You forsake the title by trading wisdom for greed."

"Your sermon is moving, really." Bonnevist stepped closer to Merlin. "Teach me what it is I need to know." He was shouting now. "Save the lives of your damned offspring!"

Power was crackling along the edge of Evelyn Farthings body. "Why? To what purpose? Your word is nothing to the Magic-Born, and less to the mortals." Merlin shook with rage. "I am not blind to your motives." The crackle of energy increased with Merlin's rage. "The mantle of the sword would grant you even more power than devouring your fellow magicians would. And then what would you do? What would be your next conquest? I have no doubts that any promises you gave to allow the Magic-Born to thrive would soon be forgotten."

Lord Bonnevist's rage calmed to disinterest, and he turned away from Evelyn Farthing's haunted body. "I don't need you. I won't kill your boys; I'll torture them, or worse, convince them that I'm right in my quest. Who needs the great wizard Merlin, when I can have his two heirs show me the path to the sword?"

The laughter started again, and it was causing Lord Bonnevist to become very annoyed. "Go ahead and chase my boys." It was Evelyn Farthing who was speaking again. "They will know you for what you are, and they will end you."

"This conversation is over." Lord Bonnevist waved his hand in dismissal to Evelyn and her grandfather. Magic carried with the wave and Evelyn's neck snapped, returning her to the land of the dead.

Jacob Cord was somewhere between nervous and terrified. He had been taken to the grandest room he'd ever seen. While he sat on the edge of a bed, servants had continuously brought in different meats, cheeses, and fruit, encouraging him to eat any and all that he wanted.

He shoved as much as he could into his pockets but made no actual move to eat any of the food.

Jacob's heart was devastated by the turn of events. "Why couldn't she have just helped me?"

"Because magic corrupts," Lord Bonnevist had appeared out of nowhere, a look of compassion on his face. "The Farthings had lost their very souls to its dark touch."

Lord Bonnevist crossed the room and sat down gently next to Jacob. Jacob had never been this close to the King's advisor and was silent with shock.

"Evelyn Farthing and her grandchildren are descended from a long line of vile sorcerers who have been known to poison the crops and homes of their neighbors." He patted Jacob's arm gently. "You're lucky that you discovered them in time. If she'd have touched your crops, the corruptive influence of her magic would have spread from farm to farm and could have destroyed all of Camelot."

Jacob's eyes were wide with disbelief before shifting to relief. He'd saved Camelot. He was suddenly grateful that Evelyn hadn't accepted his offer to save his farm.

Except, if Evelyn had wanted to poison his farm, then why didn't she simply accept his offer?

Before he could find his voice enough to ask his question, Lord Bonnevist changed the subject.

"Unfortunately, I also have been touched by magic, a long time ago, and am cursed with certain abilities. To better lessen the risk to my immortal soul, I've devoted myself to protecting Camelot from the magic of others."

Jacob finally found his voice. "You're a wizard?"

Lord Bonnevist cringed, as if the word had caused him physical pain. "Yes, I guess that would be what I am. I am telling you this, my secret, so that I can ask you for your help."

"My help?" Jacob echoed.

Bonnevist nodded. "I cannot stop Evelyn's grandsons from spreading her evil without the intimate knowledge that you have of them. You've known the Farthing twins their whole lives, and that knowledge would be useful to me. I can use my curse to get that knowledge from you, but it could hurt you." Lord Bonnevist seemed torn by the concept.

Jacob Cord couldn't resist, he needed to help, to make things right for whatever part he might have played in the death of the Camelot Guardsmen who had gone with him to the Farthing farm. "Anything I can do to help. Please, use my memories."

"The pain will be intense," Bonnevist argued.

"Will I live?" Jacob asked.

"Yes, but—"

"Then I will do it. Anything I can do to continue to serve Camelot, I will do." Jacob found that he was no longer nervous. He just wanted to help.

"That is very generous of you, Jacob." Bonnevist reached out and placed his hands on top of Jacob's head. "Hold still, this is going to hurt."

Everything that was Jacob Cord flooded into Lord Bonnevist's mind. It wasn't only the memories of the Farthings, but also every moment on his own farm with Martin and his wife Adrianna. It all filled Lord Bonnevist, mixing with his memories, telling him all sorts of details about the Farthing family.

Jacob Cord writhed in pain, every muscle in his body taut almost to the point of tearing.

Lord Bonnevist tore his hands away from Jacob's head and they both fell away from each other. Slowly, they gathered themselves and returned to their places on the bed. Jacob was slower to return but managed to find his strength.

"Did that give you what you needed?" Jacob asked, his voice weak, his eyes barely open.

"Yes, it told me where to go next." Bonnevist smiled.

"It did?" Jacob was confused, he didn't know that he'd held the knowledge of where Cremont and Dash had disappeared to. "Where will you go?"

"To your farm."

"My farm?" Jacob grew concerned.

"Yes, I'm going to flay the memories of Cremont and Dash

Farthing from the twitching corpse of your son, Martin."

"What?" Jacob demanded. He attempted to jump to his feet, but his strength betrayed him, and he slid back to the bed.

"Jacob," Lord Bonnevist said, a look a mock pity in his eyes. "Don't you worry about him, or your pretty wife. I'll take good care of them." He placed a hand on Jacob's shoulder. "Stay here a moment and regain your strength." Concern filled Lord Bonnevist's eyes. "You look so very hungry, and there is so much food around. Why don't you *Eat?*"

Jacob suddenly forgot his confusion and his concerns for Martin and Adrianna. He was instead filled with an insane hunger. He began to reach for the nearest piece of cheese.

"No." Lord Bonnevist stopped him. "I'm sure you're hungry for...*something different.*"

Jacob looked to Lord Bonnevist and then slowly looked to his own hand. Somewhere in the back of his mind, Jacob Cord screamed that this was wrong, that what he was about to do was against nature itself.

Jacob bit into his hand and pulled, tearing away bone and fingers, the meat and veins stretching as he pulled his face away and began to chew with a vacant stare.

Lord Bonnevist smiled as an idea sprang to him

He reached past Jacob and grabbed a slab of ham from a platter and began chewing on it himself, watching Jacob consume himself. Through a mouthful of food, Bonnevist commanded, "Eat it all."

Chapter 5

His eyes felt as if they'd been covered with dust, and Dash decided that this meant that they should stay closed. His mind was still a fog as he continued to lie on his back, making no movement to get up. Wherever he was, Dash felt an overwhelming sense of comfort: the temperature was perfect, the ground was soft, and the light hitting his face felt inviting. He clenched his fingers into the ground and decided that he must be on a beach by the sandy texture.

As Dash became more alert, he opened his eyes and sat up. The first thought to confront him was the color blue. Everything had a hint of blue to it.

Dash had been right about his idea of the beach. He was sitting in sand, and the ground, as far as he could see, was sand everywhere. Dash sat up and took in the walls. He sat at the end of a hall, the walls of which were made of stone that had been stacked evenly. At his end of the hall was a dead end, leaving Dash with only one direction in which he could move. This thought quickly vanished as he watched the dust that he'd stirred while sitting up. The sand he had kicked up in his movements didn't just fall away from him. Instead, the sand drifted, slow and awkward, back to the ground. It was as if the sand was in no hurry to get where it was going.

The lighting for the hall, wherever he was, didn't come from above him, but instead radiated from the walls in faint blue shafts that shifted as if they were being produced by someone holding a glass or similar substance up to the light. As far as he could tell, there was no ceiling to the hall, instead the walls continued up and into darkness until they were well out of his sight. This combined with the dark shades of blue, gave Dash the strong perception of being at the bottom of a lake.

Placing his hands beneath himself, Dash stood slowly. When he was completely on his feet, Dash was hit by a wash of memory as he recalled the events prior to his waking.

Jacob Cord had invited the Guard of Camelot to come to their home and kill Dash's grandmother. An arrow had pierced her, stealing her life away and with it, Dash's heart. Dash had run, deep into the woods and along the creek to the lake.

The water had been alive!

It had climbed his ankles and further upwards, reaching for his mouth and face. He'd been terrified that he was going to drown, but instead he only fell asleep. At the time, his panic had almost consumed him, until he'd heard that voice.

Softer than any he'd ever heard before and possessing a strength that Dash assumed couldn't be matched by any soul in all of Camelot, the voice had begged him to stay calm, and told him that he would be safe. Dash wasn't certain if he should be listening to the voice, but something about it called to him. It was a woman's voice, and his first thought was that her voice sounded soft and kind, not unlike that of his mother's. Another soothing command and Dash realized that the voice wasn't his mother's at all but still felt as capable to be trusted as any voice that he had ever heard.

Dash felt that he knew the voice, even if he couldn't place it, and he allowed himself to be swallowed by the living water.

Dash took a few steps forward before realizing that this was much more than just a hall to some larger corridor. He could see around the bend and the halls continued and multiplied. Every bend had options, right or left, that made this entire walled area more than it seemed.

He was in a labyrinth.

Panic started to seep back into Dash's mind, and he felt as if he might succumb to the weight of the day's events when his brain was suddenly flooded with images, smells, and feelings.

There were no words, but Dash knew the voice behind the thoughts that invaded his mind. It was the woman from earlier and she was giving him knowledge. Specifically, she was explaining that this wasn't just any maze, and was actually a very simple labyrinth on a physical level. The challenges of this labyrinth were of a different kind that would test him and his reactions.

The path would be fairly obvious, but it would be laden with tests.

Something finally clicked in Dash's mind, and anger and confusion flooded throughout him. He suddenly realized that something was missing. "I have no time for tests." He was shouting into the air, at the walls, at wherever the voice was radiating from. "Where's my brother?"

The voice had returned to words and filled Dash's mind with a soft answer. "He is fine and faces other challenges. The Farthing boys are going to the same destination but are taking different paths."

Dash was annoyed, but he suppressed it. "Who are you?"

There was a hesitation before she answered, "I am a friend."

Cremont's head was slow to clear as he replied, "I think I've had my fill of friends, thank you."

There was the hint of a smile as the voice countered, "An ally, then." The humor vanished from the voice as she continued. "You will have much to learn if you plan to bring your grandmother's killer to justice."

Those words resonated with a piece of Cremont's soul— a large piece. Cremont wasn't naive enough to think that the death of his grandmother was because of some archer hidden in the grass next to their home. He'd had a commander, and that commander had been following his duty to bring law breakers to justice. The problem, and the killer of his grandmother, was the law itself. No one, as far as Cremont knew, who had ever been accused of being a Magic-Born had ever committed any actual crimes.

That realization blew apart the walls in Cremont's mind, and he suddenly found himself wondering why those laws were in existence. Had the killing of the Magic-Born been the deterrent for the crimes, or was the law broken and the Magic-Born were normal people.

Evelyn Farthing had never committed any crimes against anyone. She'd broken the law by simply existing and that wasn't right. The laws were flawed and those in charge of the laws needed to be brought to justice.

Except that was King Thordon, and the King was dead.

The voice must have been listening to his thoughts, because she answered them. "Yes, you definitely have much to learn if you still think that King Thordon held any sort of power."

This confused Cremont, but he let it drop. Stepping forward,

Cremont decided to get this maze over with.

He turned the nearest corner of stone wall and then stopped, waiting for the voice to give him some sort of warning. When none came, Cremont shrugged, assuming that whatever awaited him must be further down the path.

With nothing ahead of him but air, Cremont increased his speed, and ran down the straight hall. He made it only halfway down the hall before he realized that the air directly ahead of him was beginning to shimmer, as if the floor of that section was radiating intense heat.

Slowing only a little, Cremont didn't have time to react. For the second time that day, a large fist came from seemingly nowhere. It erupted from the shimmering air and punched him in the nose.

Cremont's feet continued forward while his face stayed stationary. His entire body rotated with his own momentum, turning him horizontal before he inevitably fell to the ground. It was only sand that he landed on, but the distance of the fall was enough to make a jarring impact that rocked through his back.

Cremont's head was the last of his body parts to hit the sand, but it didn't make any difference, because the back of his head wasn't in as much pain as the face was at that moment. Tears and pain blurred Cremont's vision, but he could see through his pain and confusion that the shimmering air had ejected more than just a hand.

Rubbing his eyes and scooting back as quickly as he could, Cremont looked up, and the shock of what he saw before him replaced all the pain that had filled his body.

"You were the death of me, boy," Samuel Grand, the former head of the Camelot Guard, said. "Now it's my turn."

Dash had surrendered to the voice in his head. He wasn't making any real progress in arguing with it and he needed to move if he was ever going to find his brother.

Dash was jogging down a short corridor, not far from where he'd originally started his journey through this sand-riddled labyrinth, when he came to a bend in the path. He took it, turning right, and then stopped.

The hall before him was impressive. He stood at one end of it and couldn't see the other end at all. The distant end of the hall faded away into blackness, much in the same way that the ceiling did. For a moment, dizziness almost overwhelmed Dash, and he had to grab the wall to hold himself steady.

If his feet weren't firmly attached to the ground, he'd have forgotten which way was up.

Finding his balance again, Dash straightened and started forward slowly.

He made it only three feet down this new hall when a stone pulled itself free from the wall to his right and came whistling toward his head. The stone was ridiculously fast, and Dash had barely noticed it before it had slapped into the side of his skull.

Dash didn't remember falling, but he was suddenly on the ground and his head was throbbing with pain. Reaching up to his temple, Dash lightly touched the place where the pain seemed to be radiating from. He let out a yelp and pulled his fingers away from the already swelling lump forming on the side of his head. Looking at his hand, Dash saw that it was covered with blood.

Dash turned his eyes from his hand and to the wall, giving it a look of incredulity. As he watched, the stone that had clubbed him was retreating back into its place in the wall.

Dash looked at the sand on the ground and noticed that when he had fallen, it hadn't been straight down, but instead he had fallen back the way he'd come from. Reaching forward, Dash tentatively watched the wall as his hand crossed a threshold that he couldn't see.

He had almost missed seeing the incoming stone, this time coming from the left while he watched the right. Dash's eyes caught the stone in the edge of his vision, and he pulled his hand back quickly. The stone that had dislodged itself from the wall sailed through where his hand had been, the breeze from it touching his skin coolly.

Having missed its target, the stone retreated just as quickly before wiggling to settle itself back into its home in the wall.

Dash's mind was finally beginning to clear, and his thoughts came quicker. He looked up and down the walls of the hall, keeping care to stay behind the imaginary line of attack. He needed to see the puzzle for what it was, and he had no doubts that it was a puzzle or test. There was a way to solve it; he only needed to think of it.

Finally, a simple answer came to Dash. He'd just return the way he came and find another path.

Turning around, Dash only managed one step back the way he had come before he realized that backtracking wasn't the answer to this puzzle either. The path that had led him around the corner and into this hall was gone and in its place was another stone wall. It stood there as if it always had, and the only proof that Dash had come from that direction were the footprints in the sand.

Fueled with an uncharacteristic surge of rage and confusion, Dash ran forward and punched the wall, slamming his fists against it repeatedly and hoping that it would give, fade away, or fall over.

Moments later, his anger spent, Dash pressed his back to the new wall and slowly slid down until his body touched the sand.

This was going to be harder than he had hoped.

Scrambling to his feet, Cremont backed away from the recently deceased guard. Blood was trickling from his nose, but that wasn't anything new, so Cremont chose to ignore it.

Cremont opened his mouth to ask if Samuel was dead but stopped himself. As his mind converted the panic to sharp clarity, he noted that Samuel Grand hadn't stepped out of the shimmering air; he had been the shimmering air. Now, the guard stood before Cremont with his hands curled into fists and Cremont could see clearly through Samuel. Samuel Grand was dead, and he blamed Cremont Farthing for it.

Cremont continued to back away until he felt he had enough space between himself and the apparition to turn and make a run for it. As he spun around and took the first step of what was likely to be the fastest sprint of his life, Cremont crashed into a wall.

The wall stood perfectly still and unaffected by his slamming into it. Cremont ran his hands up and down it quickly, confused by the sudden appearance of the evil wall. He hit it twice and begged loudly for it to disappear before terror forced him to turn around and watch as the deceased Samuel Grand turned and stalked toward him.

Turning back around when he did saved Cremont's life. Samuel had closed the distance on Cremont when the boy's back had been turned and was swinging at Cremont as he turned around. Cremont only barely managed to see the fist in time, sliding his head to the side as the ghostly knuckles crashed through the air and into the wall where his head had been.

Dust and chips of stone came away from the wall, and Cremont had no time to watch them slowly drift to the ground when another fist was coming from Samuel.

Cremont was just barely staying ahead of Samuel, pulling his body aside and sliding against the wall as the guard broke away chunks of the wall in an effort to destroy Cremont. Cremont, having decided that standing with his back to the wall, literally, wasn't the safest of places to be, finally found an opening and ducked through it.

He thought himself free of the guard's grasp, when Samuel's cold dead hand grabbed onto Cremont's cloak and pulled him from his feet as if he was made of the same air and mist that as the ghost.

Cremont flew through the air, apparently thrown by Samuel, before glancing off of one of the hall's walls.

Bouncing off of the wall and into the dust, a dizzy thought crept into Cremont's mind. He realized that he didn't blame Samuel Grand for whatever he was trying to do there. Cremont's concussed mind fell on the fact that every pain that the guard had ever had to put up with had been his fault. He'd made it his job to make Samuel Grand hate being the head of the Camelot Guard, and it had been Cremont's family that had directly led to Samuel's death. He didn't feel bad for the guard. Samuel Grand had brought the might of Bonnevist's laws down on his Gran, but Cremont did not blame the guard for his anger.

Understanding didn't mean surrender, though, and Cremont leapt to his feet and ran at the guard before the guard could run at him. Once he was within range, he jumped at Samuel Grand, putting all his momentum toward the guard's waist, hoping to bring him down.

To Cremont's surprise, he passed directly through Samuel Grand and slammed into the ground. Cremont rolled onto his back and kicked upward at the Guard as the dead man closed in on him. Exactly like his leap, his kicks failed, passing through Samuel. With a heavy swing, Samuel brought his fist down toward Cremont. Cremont rolled out of the way just in time and came to his feet as quickly as he could.

Samuel shrugged, seemingly enjoying himself, and spoke. "I could have had your hide strung up along the walls of Camelot a hundred times over for all of the pain that you've given me and the

Guard." He swung, clipping Cremont in the shoulder and sending him spinning toward the wall again. "I didn't, though." Samuel shrugged. "Instead, I considered it a service to you and your family that instead of having you executed for your many crimes against Camelot, I'd just thump you in the face or set the dogs on you. I wanted to scare you into being a better man." Samuel swung twice more at Cremont. Cremont ducked them both, crouching low, but couldn't avoid Samuel's ghost boot as it came up and took him in the ribs. He bounced high before hitting the sand. "Your grandmother was a great woman and a pillar of Camelot, and that meant that you had the potential to be a good man, too. I wanted to give you a chance." Samuel kicked at Cremont again, but Cremont managed to roll away just in time. "I had hopes that one day you'd be Camelot Guard." He picked Cremont up by the back of the head and punched him in the chest. The boy sprawled backward and crashed into the wall, taking deep breaths while he tried to bring his lungs back under his control. "What is my reward for keeping your carcass from bleeding out on a pike? Your grandmother is found out to be a Magic-Born! Outlaws, the lot of you. Hereditary, too, by the looks of it. All of my hope died for you died only hours before your grandmother killed me."

Pain and blood coursed over Cremont's face, and he was suddenly filled with rage at the accusation. The rage felt wrong, misdirected, and he took precious moments of his life to find the real source of his anger. It didn't take him long.

"It wasn't Gran's fault that you died," he said, blood trickling down his split brow. "Jacob Cord accused her out of greed. You died because an idiot wanted a shortcut in his life and chose to use you as his enforcer." This halted Samuel's march toward Cremont, so the boy continued. "But that isn't right either. You didn't die because my Gran was a witch, and you didn't die because of some greedy farmer. Think about it, Samuel: How many of the Magic-Born have died because of the laws of Camelot?" Cremont didn't expect the guard to answer and only silence followed. "Now, how many of them were using their powers to corrupt Camelot, to destroy it?" He didn't give Samuel a chance to speak this time. "You died because someone made a law that murders people. Death only brings death. You said it yourself that my Gran was a pillar of Camelot. How could you see her as such a source of goodness and think that her being a witch made her evil? She was still a witch when she was that pillar." Cremont's voice got quieter. "All of the Magic-Born have been pillars, standing tall to help Camelot even when Camelot didn't want their help."

The ghost shrieked, "No! Evelyn Farthing killed me!"

Cremont bellowed just as loudly as the apparition, "In self-defense!"

Samuel lunged at Cremont, swinging wildly. Cremont managed to avoid most of the hit but got brushed in the ribs. The hit launched Cremont at the near wall and he bounced off before hitting the ground. He was gasping for breath.

"The law is clear!" Samuel was continuing. "My death and the death of my men was proof enough that you and your family are in violation of the law. There is no law requiring you to live in Camelot, but you chose to bring your damned magic blood to the only place where it is illegal to be of the Magic-Born." Samuel grabbed Cremont by the hair and pulled him to his feet. "You call Jacob Cord an idiot, but how wise was it to live in the only place where your kind are outlaws?"

Cremont couldn't help but agree. *What had Gran been thinking? Why hadn't she moved them?*

In one hand Dash held his cloak, now off his shoulders, tightly in his fist. In the other he did the same, keeping the cloth between the two arms pulled as tightly as he could manage. Twisting his body, just a little, he held the cloak vertically, with his left hand up by his head and his right down by his waist.

He stepped toward the imaginary line and slowly crossed his arms, holding the cloak over it. With tense apprehension, he waited for the cloth to be struck by a stone.

It came when he was about to give up and drop his arm. The stone launched itself from the right wall and directly toward the center of the outstretched cloth. To Dash's dismay, the stone tore through it as if it hadn't been there.

Dash had been hoping that he might be able to tie a corner of his cloak to his leg and hold the rest tight above his head. It would have afforded him protection on at least half of his body, but it was useless. The stone had torn through the taut fabric and wouldn't work for any sort of lengthy journey through the hall.

Frustrated, Dash threw the cloak on the ground and sprinted at the line. Crossing it, he kept running as hard as his legs could pump.

To Dash's surprise, not a single stone touched him for a large length of his run. He could feel the brush of wind as they swept behind him, but they were always behind him. He'd made it a little further than a hundred yards when the stones began to catch him. Two scraped his back, but he was halted by a large one smacking into his arm.

An idea flooded into his brain then, and Dash, hoping that he'd survive the next minute, spun on his heel and sprinted back the way he'd come.

More and more of the stones started scraping at his shirt and he could hear tears as the fabric ripped apart. The sound was an incentive to keep moving quickly, but all the incentive in the world couldn't make his legs work fast enough to keep the stones away from his back. He was very close to the imaginary line when a stone caught him again, this time in the leg. His shin screamed with pain that racked Dash's entire body and sent him sprawling to the ground in a tumble.

He knew when he had crossed the imaginary line without actually seeing it. The stones stopped flying at him. Bringing his roll to a stop, Dash pulled his shirt from his back and, ignoring the bloody streaks on the back, ripped a piece off to tie off his bleeding leg.

When he'd finished with binding his leg, Dash wrapped the shirt around his head and then gathered up his cloak.

Cremont's contemplation of how Camelot's laws destroyed his family was cut short as Samuel brought a fist down into his face. Either the guard had let go of Samuel's hair or he'd taken a large piece of it out and Cremont collapsed to the ground. His entire body ached, but he wasn't willing to give up. He tried leaping at Samuel again but passed right through the misty abdomen of the guard.

It confused Cremont that Samuel could be made of air but his hands were as hard as stone.

Cremont was dazedly thinking on how to properly attack the wind when he realized that Samuel was still talking.

"—about my family? Why do the witch's children continue to plague me, but my baby girl has to be without her father?" He kicked out at Cremont and Cremont was sure that he'd felt something in his chest break. He tried to roll away, but the pain was excruciating. "Why did I have to die for you?" Cremont forced himself to his feet and tripped and he moved to get away from the raging ghost. "I will right what you've made wrong, boy."

Samuel grabbed the fallen Farthing boy and picked him up, higher than his feet should have been able to reach. About ten feet in the air, Samuel slammed Cremont into the wall and held him there. "It is time that you die now."

Cremont took a deep breath, the action making his chest shriek with another wave of nauseating pain. "I'm sorry, Sam." He wheezed. "I'm sorry for the trouble that my family has brought to you and I'm sorry that my Gran was the one that killed you." He took another painful and rattling breath. "Mostly, though, I'm sorry that we took you away from your family." A tear ran down Cremont's face that had nothing to do with the beating that he'd experienced. "I've only just lost my Gran and my heart is torn apart. I can't imagine ever feeling whole again and I don't know how I'll survive without her in my life. I can't even imagine what you must feel like knowing that you are the cause of that same pain in your family. Your pain makes mine look weak, and I am so sorry that my family had any part in giving you that pain."

Samuel's anger was evident in his eyes, and it had only grown stronger. "You're sorry?" he asked through gritted teeth.

With his head wrapped tightly in his shirt, Dash finished off by tying the cloak around his waist. He felt that he'd been going about this all wrong when he'd been trying to stop the stones with the taut cloth. This new idea was, hopefully, an improvement.

His head was wrapped multiple times, giving it a girth of shirt to protect it. Around his legs he still wore his pants, and the cloak had been tied high enough as to not impede his running, but loose enough as to not get shredded when hit by a stone. His chest and back were bare, but only out of necessity. He didn't have enough cloth to protect his midsection but was also fairly sure that he wouldn't be as slowed by a rock to his side as he would a rock to his head or legs.

Still limping from the rock having struck his leg on his earlier attempt, Dash stepped close to where he knew the imaginary line to be.

He bent his knees slowly, preparing to spring forward like he would when he would race Cremont to the stream.

Dash took a deep breath, said a silent prayer for his grand-mother to watch over him, and then he crossed the line.

Dash pumped harder this time than he had during his last test. He had thought that on the last attempt he had given it his all, but he was finding a new reserve this time around. His limp was the furthest thing from his mind as he felt the breeze from stones hurtling across the hall and only barely missing him. His mind flashed to escaping the archers in the woods and he pressed him-self to run harder and not slow down.

To Dash's surprise, he could suddenly see the other end of the hall. It was within sight, and he hadn't been hit by a single stone yet.

He renewed his speed at the sight of the far end of the hall, but he could still feel the exertion taking its toll on his body.

A stone from the wall finally clipped him in the shin, near to where the previous stone had hit his leg. Dash let out a yelp of pain and began to stumble, but his survival instinct was greater than his pain and he pushed through it, running as hard as his tired legs could carry him. He was only yards away from the end of the hall when two stones hit him in the ribs. He didn't have the breath to yell, and he doubled over in pain.

Dash continued to pump his legs, but another stone crashed into his makeshift head protection. Dash's vision blurred and he was suddenly incapable of running in a straight line.

A final stone hit him in the left knee, and he went down so fast that he couldn't remember the journey from vertical to horizontal. He crashed into the sand head-first and his only thoughts were of how close he had come to getting through the hall.

Samuel dropped Cremont the entire ten feet and sunk to his knees beside the boy. "You're sorry?"

Cremont opened his tear-filled eyes and looked into the guard's.

"How does that make it any better?" Samuel demanded between sobs. "My daughter will never have her papa in her life again."

Cremont slowly reached forward, the movement sending sharp pains throughout his entire body, and laid his hand onto Samuel's shoulder. For a brief moment, Cremont was surprised that he could touch the Guard, and wondered if he should press the advantage. He dismissed the thought as quickly as it came. No fighting was going to solve this man's torture.

"It doesn't make it better, and it wasn't supposed to." Cremont answered. "I'm sorry, but not because you think I'm responsible for your death, or the deaths of your men. I'm sorry," Cremont frowned as his own ideas registered their meaning inside his head, "because it took your death for me to understand what was wrong. Magic might have been the means of your death, but only when it was threatened." He shook his head. "The problem is that Camelot has become a place where murder is acceptable. What happened to the Camelot of our grandparents?" He shrugged and it was a painful thing. "I'm sorry that Camelot is filled with so much hate that you had to die before I could see that it is mine and my brother's job to fix it."

Samuel Grand looked confused. "How are the Farthing boys going to fix anything?" Cremont ignored the question and decided to pose one of his own.

"What if..." Cremont said, unsure of himself. "What if...you had to die to save her future?"

Samuel raised an eyebrow. "What are you talking about, boy?"

"I don't know much of anything, but I've learned a little bit about magic today." He waved his hand around, indicating the place they were in. "This is all training for something bigger. Dash and I are about to learn...something...and whatever it is, even if it's just how to build a handcart, I'm going to use it to save Camelot from its hate." He took both hands and grasped the shoulders of the ghost. His aches were a distant memory as he became excited about what he was about to say. "I promise you, Sam, that your death was for a reason. The best kind of reason, and I promise you that your daughter will be safe, and she will know how much her father loved her."

Samuel frowned and his look expressed that he held doubts in the boy, but he believed enough to let his anger go.

With a nod to Cremont, Samuel Grand vanished.

Cremont hadn't realized how much he'd been relying on Samuel to hold him up. After the disappearance of the ghost, Cremont collapsed in a heap on the ground. Every ache and pain in his body sang to him loudly, screaming for attention and rest.

From his lying position, Cremont watched as the walls shimmered and moved, reshaping the labyrinth hall into a larger room.

Across the room from Cremont, and wrapped oddly in bundles of clothing, was Dash.

Summoning his strength, Cremont stood slowly and moved as hurriedly as his body would allow toward his brother. Reaching Dash, Cremont sat and rested his brother's head on his lap.

Dash began to stir then, and Cremont noticed the bruising on his brother's chest and ribs and the blood oozing out from underneath the shirt on Dash's head. Cremont was bleeding as well, but he was at least still conscious.

"I made it?" Dash mumbled.

"What are you wearing?" Cremont asked with a smile as relief flooded through him that his brother was alright.

Dash winced. "Protection."

Cremont nodded gently and prodded the bruised ribs of his brother to see just how bad the damage was. Dash winced but didn't yell out. Cremont assumed he'd have to do the same poking and prodding of his own body, and he wasn't looking forward to it.

"Protection?" Cremont asked as he helped Dash slowly to his feet. "Doesn't seem to have done much."

Dash nodded and smiled. "It did a lot more than you think." He carefully pulled the shirt off his head and a huge lump could already be seen forming over Dash's right eye. Both of his eyes had already blackened. "You don't look any better," Dash said when he saw the terrified look that Cremont was giving him.

Cremont was actually bleeding from several different places on his scalp, and while he still had his shirt on, Dash could tell from the way that he held himself that his ribs were as badly injured as his own, if not worse.

With Cremont's help, Dash untied the cloak from his waist, tossed the shirt into the sand and threw the cloak over his shoulders.

Finally situated, Dash looked at his brother. "Now what do we do?"

Cremont nodded past Dash, "Ask her." Dash spun around as Cremont asked, "You're the woman who was in my head?"

The visage that greeted them was the shape of a woman, but she was also in a cloak with the hood draw over her head. They couldn't see her face, but the curves of her body told them that she was a woman. The cloak itself looked to be made of the same stone that surrounded them.

A nod from the hooded woman confirmed Cremont's question before she pulled her hood back and shocked the boys again.

She was beautiful. Her skin was as pale as granite, but her face was angelic. She had penetrating blue eyes and hair as black as the night itself. Her lips were only a slightly pink hue of the rest of her pale skin and her smile came easy, setting the boys into a whirlwind of emotions. Her smile alone made them want to do anything she asked. They were at her command and would have it no other way.

Deep behind that smile was something else, and it came to her as readily as the smile that disarmed the boys. Behind her smile was a strength of character that radiated. Hers was a will that no one would dare question.

"I am the Lady of the Lake and a friend of Merlin."

Dash nodded as if this was all to be taken in stride. As if to prove her claim, Cremont kicked the sand, sending it drifting slowly to the ground, as if it were in water.

"This is your home?" Was all that Cremont could think to ask.

The self-proclaimed Lady of the Lake nodded again. It was a subtle and almost impossible to see gesture, but they could feel her nod more than they could see it. "That is a...very mortal way of putting it. It shall be your home as well, for a while." She came forward quickly and touched a hand to both boys' faces. "Your lives were in danger, and I had to bring you here if you are to ever learn the truth. The truths about yourselves and your family."

"Truth?" Dash pressed. "We know the truth already. We are of the Magic-Born."

The Lady of the Lake nodded slowly. "That is only a small part of the truth." She clasped her hands. "You are of the Magic-Born, but that is only a small name for a very big truth." Her smile somehow got wider.

"You are the sons of Merlin."

Chapter 6

Dash looked slowly from the Lady of the Lake to Cremont and then back to the Lady of the Lake. He was figuring that he'd received more damage from the hall with the throwing stones than he must have originally suspected.

Cremont's mind was a mirror of his own. "The sons of Merlin? What does that mean?" Cremont asked.

The Lady of the Lake had expected this question and smiled to both the boys. Her face radiated an intense joy, and it helped the boys calm down even further than they had already been in her presence.

"It means that you are the direct descendants of the greatest wizard, Merlin." She spread her hands outward, aiming the palms up as if asking for a hug. "You are the only living heirs to his power." The Lady of the Lake brought her hands in and then waved her left one around, indicating the realm that was her home. "Otherwise, you would not have been able to enter into this…home, as you call it."

Instead of understanding, confusion washed over Cremont's face. "If this is your home or realm, or whatever you'd like to call it, then why did Samuel attack me?"

The Lady of the Lake's face took on a sadder visage. "You were attacked by Samuel Grand because Samuel Grand was angry with you."

Cremont shook his head. "I am sure that many spirits have been mad at lots of people, but they don't just appear out of nowhere and attack people!"

The Lady of the Lake looked confused as she raised her eyebrow at Cremont and asked, "Don't they?"

Dash cut in then, placing a hand on his brother's arm and watching carefully for where his hand fell to avoid any of the myriad of bruises. "Cremont has a point. If this is your...place... then why did that wall attack me, are we not wanted?"

Cremont looked at his brother with new eyes. "A wall *attacked* you?"

Dash shook his head, "It was more like an entire hall, but that's not the point." He looked back at the Lady. "Why were we attacked?"

The Lady of the Lake's somber look faded to one that was more alien, less readable to the boys. "You've been allowed passage into my world so that we can teach you and test you. I allowed Samuel Grand to attack you so as to teach you the first lesson that you needed to learn, Cremont." She folded her arms, and the very human gesture only made her foreign expression look even more so. "I have seen the possibilities of what you are to become. You will need to rely more so on your compassion than ever before during the coming battle. And you," she let her gaze fall on Dash, "Dash, your test was one of brute strength and speed. In the coming battle your skills will be useful, but you will need to be stronger and faster than ever before. You will need to adapt as your enemy adapts." She passed her gaze back and forth between the boys. "You are not here to hide from the enemies of the Farthing family. You are here to learn how to use the power that is your birthright and reclaim Camelot."

The silence that resided between all of them was so intense that Cremont wondered to himself if it was caused by more magic.

Finally, Dash broke the silence with a laugh. "You want us to overthrow Camelot? We still live at home. We are children."

Cremont couldn't help but agree with his brother's assessment. They had just been living quietly on a farm under the care of their grandmother only hours ago. Yet, agreement wasn't acceptance, and Cremont was ready to fight. He was ready to keep his promise to Samuel.

"Arthur took the crown when he was younger than you by two years," the Lady of the Lake stated. "I am not asking that you do that much, only that you save Camelot from the influences of Lord Bonnevist."

Cremont raised an eyebrow. "Lord Bonnevist? He is only the King's advisor, he has no power without the King's approval."

This earned Cremont a laugh from the deity before him. "Obviously, we have much to teach you." She sighed. "Lord

Bonnevist has been the only power in Camelot for over half of a century."

"But King Thordon—" Dash started.

"He's no damned spawn of mine," declared a newcomer from behind them.

Spinning as quickly as their injuries would allow, Dash and Cremont prepared themselves for whatever this new attack might be.

A simple tunic and pants couldn't hide the intense muscles that the man carried. His blond hair was shoulder length and blended in with his well-cropped beard. His eyes were a fierce blue and could almost have competed with those of the Lady of the Lake.

Almost.

Aside from his very plain clothes, he wore a belt and scabbard, with his palm resting on the hilt that resided within the scabbard.

Dash, understanding the truth of what was before him, dropped to his knees in reverence.

Cremont hadn't understood the intensity of what was happening and only looked confusedly between the newcomer, Dash, and the Lady of the Lake.

Finally, he let his eyes fall on the back of his brother's head. "What are you doing?"

Dash didn't raise his head, but Cremont could tell that Dash's teeth were clenched as he hissed, "He is King Arthur!"

Cremont returned his look to the man before him. The man wasn't wearing anything regal and only carried a nice-looking sword. This new man also failed to look almost one hundred years old. His brother was obviously addled.

"But King Arthur is dead," Cremont insisted.

Dash hissed again, "So was Samuel!"

Cremont suddenly understood. This world of the Lady's had the power to make the dead physical. He looked at Arthur and stared, in complete shock. It took a moment of his brother's tugging on his leg before he gave a half smile and dropped to the same position as Dash.

Arthur rolled his eyes at both the boys. "Get up! I haven't been a king in a very long time." His look of disdain evaporated into a smile that engulfed his face. "I should be kneeling before you!" He exclaimed. "The sons of Merlin! I had almost lost hope until I heard that you existed. The bloodline runs true and there is nothing that we cannot accomplish!" The former king stepped forward as the boys climbed to their feet. "You both have the potential to do more for Camelot, more for the world, than I ever did!" He let his hands fall, his left landing on the hilt of his sword. "Now, let's get on with it."

Dash frowned. "Get on with what?"

The Lady of the Lake stepped forward. The movement made no ripples in her dress, and it looked more as if she had glided forward, which could be the case, as they couldn't see her feet in the hooded gown that she wore.

"I have asked for Arthur to train you." She indicated the sword. "He is to teach you in the art of using a blade."

Cremont smiled. There was no one better suited to teach the arts of swordplay than Arthur himself. The echo of the promise he'd made to Samuel did not dull his excitement either. Instead, he was even more enthusiastic about the prospect of taking the fight to Camelot.

Hesitant still toward the prospect of fighting anyone, let alone the entire kingdom of Camelot, Dash asked, "To what end? We have the blood of Merlin, why should we learn to fight? Can't we just shoot fire at our enemies, or give them a plague?" He stopped and shook his head, causing more pain to sear through his body. "More to the point, why us at all? The Lady of the Lake and the Legendary King Arthur stand here telling us, two children fresh from the farm, that we are to overthrow an entire kingdom? Why do you even need us and why should we do it?"

Much to everyone's surprise, it was Cremont who answered Dash's question. "The laws of Camelot are disguised as those of peaceful people, but how many of the Magic-Born have died without even stepping forward to defend themselves? What harm did Gran cause? None, but because she was born differently, because she had the blood of Merlin, Camelot sentenced her to death." His excitement had fallen into the background, now replaced by his sense of what was right. "We need to free Camelot from the hate and make the world safe for wizards again, and it needs to be us because only those of the Magic-Born have the power to do it."

Arthur was smiling. "That's part of it anyway." He looked to the Lady before continuing. "It does need to be wizards who go against Camelot. The power at Bonnevist's command is greater than most wizards, and possibly greater even than that which you carry in your blood, but mostly, you are needed in this cause because of what Bonnevist seeks."

Cremont frowned. "What is it that he's after?"

"Excalibur." The Lady of the Lake said it plainly, but the power of the magical sword's name resonated deeply within the boys. They knew of it as they knew of Arthur. They were legends of a time long ago.

Dash, still surprised by his brother's answer to his question, and then shocked by the declaration that Bonnevist was seeking the sword Excalibur, stood in silence. In the back of Dash's mind, he wondered again at what must have transpired between Samuel Grand and Cremont to make such a normally unreasonable boy into a crusader for the justice of the Magic-Born.

"Why does he want Excalibur?" Cremont asked.

Arthur looked to the Lady of the Lake again. This time she raised her hand to the former king, stopping him, before explaining herself. "The power of Excalibur helped Arthur to destroy his enemies with minimal effort. Lord Bonnevist is a wizard of grand power. In his hands the sword would be a rallying point for the forces of evil." She lightly folded her arms. "If Bonnevist and Camelot are corrupted now, imagine their state with Excalibur in his hands."

Dash pulled himself together before picking up where he'd originally been taking the conversation. "Alright, let's say that I agree and that Camelot needs saving. Even so, let us add the fact that I desperately want to bring revenge down upon those who destroyed my family. With both of those reasons, I still ask you, what are Cremont and I supposed to do about it?" He shrugged. "We cannot walk into Camelot and fight Lord Bonnevist to the death. He has the entire Round Table at his command, as well as soldiers and lesser knights. All of Camelot believes in him and his fear of the Magic-Born. Even if you teach us how to fight," he looked from Arthur to the Lady of the Lake, "or teach us how to be wizards, what can we do? We are still only two."

Arthur frowned at Dash. "Merlin was only *one*." He smiled as a thought came to him. "Right now, you're thinking as a man thinks. That's the first mistake, and this will be your first lesson in wizardry."

The Lady of the Lake let out a small giggle. "A lesson in magic from the dead mortal? This shall be entertaining."

Arthur frowned at her but continued. "You need to think like a wizard."

Cremont and Dash joined the Lady of the Lake in laughing. "Think like a wizard?" Cremont asked. "How exactly does a wizard think?"

Arthur ignored their mirth, and continued, "A man thinks in a straight line, while a wizard thinks in circles."

Dash stopped laughing. "What does that even mean?"

Arthur folded his arms. "At best, I was only ever a man, but Merlin tried to explain it to me once, and I think I grasped the concept fairly well." He frowned as he tried to remember. "Imagine that a bear stands between you and the path that you need to walk. You cannot go around the bear and it is very large, and very angry. How would you go about passing it?"

Dash answered first, "I would shoot it." Cremont nodded in agreement.

Arthur smiled and shook his head. "That is how a man thinks. A wizard would not have found a bear in his path."

Cremont raised his eyebrow. "What?"

Dash looked the Lady of the Lake and saw that she was still smiling.

Arthur explained. "A wizard has a connection with the world and can sense the flow of events to come. He would have taken notice of the bear long before the bear had noticed him and even longer still than a mere man would have taken to notice the bear. Once the wizard had discovered the bear, he could have done one of many things to encourage the bear out of his path before he approached it. He could have shifted the winds to bring the smell of a recent kill to the bear's nose, or he could have made a stone raise from the earth and make the bear's position uncomfortable." He smiled and spread his hands. "A man approaching a bear on a path removes the bear while a wizard approaching a bear on a path convinces the bear to remove itself."

Cremont frowned and his brow furrowed. "Thinking like a wizard means using magic to make people do what you want?"

Arthur shrugged. "Yes and no, but mostly no. This example illustrates how a wizard thinks. A wizard doesn't come at an opponent from the front. A wizard plans, manipulates, and makes subtle suggestions. If magic is needed to help in those manipulations, then that is the wizard's choice, but magic isn't necessary."

Arthur's eyes took on a far-away look. "There was one time which I remember, in which Merlin had brought two beautiful women to Camelot to clean our main dining hall. No one had seen or heard of these women before Merlin had brought them, and at his request, no one asked about them either. They were to clean the main dining hall, and only the dining hall, every day and all day." He held up his hand with three fingers splayed. "Three days after Merlin had brought these women to our castle, a Duke from the southlands came. I don't remember the place he came from, but he had come to claim war on Camelot and myself over some land near his border. After a very short discussion in the dining hall, he no longer wanted to wage war. Instead, his eyes fell upon one of the two women, and he started crying with joy." Arthur smiled. "As it had turned out, many years previously the Duke's daughters had been kidnapped by slavers. Merlin had somehow known this, found them, and put them to work in the dining hall so that I could be the Duke's savior and reunite his family."

Dash was wide-eyed. "And he stopped a war."

Arthur nodded. "Wizard-thinking."

The Lady of the Lake spoke up then. "That is what magic truly is. Preparation for the proper application of power. The wizard with the weakest power could defeat a legion of the most powerful wizards as long as he has prepared accordingly and knows the proper places to leverage his power." She nodded to the boys and her hair barely moved, as if it was also in the same water that was affecting the movement of the sand. "Leveraging an impossible situation before the situation ever becomes impossible. Your grandmother might have Merlin's bloodline, but she was untrained. With her limited knowledge of her power, she was able to defeat most of the Guard of Camelot before she fell." She paused for the sad looks of the boys to change to understanding. "We are going to train you to be wizards and warriors, and you will make things right."

The boys could only nod. They were on board and ready for this fight.

Dash also noticed, only slightly before Cremont did, that he was standing straighter and no longer clutching at his bare side. Looking down, all his bruises were gone. He tested his leg while Cremont tenderly touched his own nose and face. All their damage was gone.

Arthur and the Lady of the Lake were both smiling. "I have

healed you," the Lady said. "I encourage you not to get comfortable, though."

"Why?" Cremont asked.

The Lady's smile took on a more sinister look. "I have only healed you so that Arthur can break you."

Dash's eyes grew wide. "Break us?"

Arthur's smile was joined with understanding eyes. "The only lesson that is learned is the lesson of pain." He shrugged. "Merlin taught me that one as well."

Cremont managed a weak smile. "Great Grandfather was just full of useful information, wasn't he?"

Arthur winced at a memory before saying, "You have no idea."

King Arthur of Camelot twirled the legendary sword, Excalibur, between his hands with practiced ease. In each smooth arch of the sword, the blade displayed the years of use and experience that it shared in the dead King's service. When the blade was in the ghost's hand the two of them would move as one and it was impossible to tell if Arthur was controlling the sword or if Excalibur was controlling the man.

Cremont didn't wait. Lifting his sword, he lunged at the former King of Camelot. Arthur stepped aside and brought the legendary sword around, defending his waist from the oncoming sword. Cremont's sword had a wider blade, much like Excalibur, but a thick guard between the blade and the hilt. It had a longer handle, but it was light enough that Cremont could handle it, most of the time, in one hand. While the Lady of the Lake's armory had been very impressive, holding more weapons than the boys knew existed, this sword spoke to Cremont and felt natural in Cremont's hand.

Cremont slid past Arthur, allowing for Dash to dart in and fill the spot Cremont had started from. The move put the boys on each side of Arthur, but they both knew from experience that Arthur wasn't disadvantaged by the positioning. This was possibly the hundredth fight they'd shared with the King in the last week...or month...they weren't certain.

Existing in the realm of the Lady, the boys had no idea of what had passed for days or nights. The sun didn't shine in her realm and the scene never changed. From time to time, they could see through the underwater rock and into a world of fish and weeds, but nothing that gave away any hint at a passage of time.

Added to that was the concern that Dash had voiced only just before the most recent battle practice: they hadn't been hungry or thirsty at all. After one fight in they should have been begging for water, but they hadn't been. However much time had passed since they had entered this world, it wasn't affecting either of the twins. They hadn't even been concerned about sleep.

Dash had selected a thinner sword than Cremont's. It was lighter and meant to be held in only one hand. The blade wasn't as wide, but it looked sharper. While it was narrower, it was also about a foot shorter, allowing for faster movement. This weapon, much like Cremont's, had seemingly called out to him once Dash had come near it. It was as if these weapons had been forged from whatever material made up the boys' souls.

Dash swiped at the back of the King's head and missed by only a hand's width as Arthur ducked the blade, turned, and punched Dash in the chest. Continuing his spin, he came back up and blocked Cremont's returning blade. Arthur followed it with a sharp kick to Cremont's solar plexus. The boy dropped to his knees wheezing.

"Hold!" Arthur commanded and then strode to the corner of their arena. The room they fought in looked like every other room in the Lady of the Lake's realm. Its walls were of stone with refracted light pouring through them as if they weren't there. The floors were more of the watery sand that continued to float slowly back to the ground in the aftermath of their battle.

In the corner of the room, Arthur picked up Dash's bow and Cremont's staff and tossed them to the boys.

"We are done with our playing. When you are out in the real world, you won't be fighting on your own terms." He strode toward them as they picked up their weapons. "You'll be surprised, and you'll be burdened, or blessed, with the things you carry." Arthur swung Excalibur at Cremont's chest. Cremont leapt back but kept the staff where it was. The blade struck the staff and edged into the wood. "The Knights of the Round Table carried sword and shield when they fought by my side. You are blessed by not being Knights of the Round Table." Arthur spun at Dash, bringing the legendary blade toward Dash's waist.

Dash stepped toward it, dropped his own blade to catch Excalibur, and then swung his bow as if it were a club, taking the ghost of the deceased King across the head.

Arthur shook his head and smiled. "That means you're blessed to not need a shield. Everything in the world is your shield. From the glint of the sun off a blade to the rush of the wind in the trees. Everything is your shield, and you need to fight like it is."

He turned to Cremont but kept his sword down. Even so, Cremont flinched and brought up his blade. "I don't know much about the magical worlds, boys, but I can give you your first real lesson in magic." He grabbed the staff away from Cremont and held it out lengthwise.

Cremont shot a half-grin. "You already gave us our first lesson in magic: to think like a wizard."

Arthur frowned at Cremont. "Pay attention, boy! I gave you your first lesson in wizardry. This will be your first lesson in magic!"

Cremont's smile vanished instantly.

"Concentrate on the solidity of the wood, and how strong it can be," Arthur began. "Imagine the strength of stone in the wood and put your will behind it." A ripple of light left the ghost's hand and climbed the shaft of wood. "As long as you hold it, it should be able to aid you without becoming damaged. It will work with almost anything, but don't do it to yourselves. Being stiff as stone won't help you in a battle, it'll only hurt you."

Dash was wide-eyed with astonishment. "How did you do that, Arthur? Are you a wizard?"

Arthur barked a laugh. "Not hardly." He waved his hand, indicating his own being. "I am dead, and the soul is where everyone's magic resides. If I was alive still, I would have no access to the power of my soul."

He tossed the staff back to Cremont.

The staff hadn't yet finished its arc to the boy, when Arthur swiftly turned and attacked Dash. Dash jumped back and slid the bow over his shoulder. The bow settled with the string across Dash's chest and the wood along his back.

Taking a chance, Dash closed his eyes and concentrated while Cremont caught his staff in his left hand and brought his right hand up with his sword.

Arthur stopped and smiled at both. "Good."

Dash opened his eyes and ran at Arthur. Cremont mimed his brother's actions, running at the King. Arthur caught Dash's blade with his own and spun at Cremont. Bringing his sword with him, Arthur blocked Cremont's blade, batting it away, but missed Cremont's staff that slammed forward into Arthur's chest. The King stumbled back and toward Dash. Using the momentum, King Arthur brought the blade over his head in an arc and brought it down at Dash's head. Dash ducked, Excalibur's edge deflecting off the now-solid bow, and dove into Arthur's waist. He drove Arthur back until Arthur clubbed him on the back of the head with the legendary sword.

Dash hit the ground hard, and stars filled his vision, but he forced himself back up.

Arthur was still recovering from Dash's attack as Cremont came at him with the staff.

The wood came up at Arthur's back and Arthur spun, catching the staff on his blade and drove it away. He silently noted that Cremont had also hardened up his staff. The King was impressed with how the boys had so quickly picked up on their first use of magic. As Arthur dragged the staff away, he moved to bring the sword back to his defense but realized with a broad smile that he would not be quick enough. Cremont's sword swung through a tight arc and cleaved Arthur's head from his body.

Or it would have, if the former King had been of the land of the living. Instead, the blade passed through the space of his neck like a knife through smoke and left no mark on Arthur.

Arthur raised his hands, including the one still holding Excalibur, and beamed his smile at the boys.

"That's your first win. We are far from done, but that's a start."

In the break of the battle, a thought crossed Cremont's mind. "Why haven't we started learning magic yet?" Dash and Cremont had no idea how long they'd been in the Lady of the Lake's realm, but whether it had been hours or days didn't change the fact that they hadn't learned any magic other than this one spell just then taught to them by Arthur.

"One step at a time," Arthur said cautiously.

As if he hadn't said anything, the twins heard the Lady of the Lake's voice in their heads as she declared. "Now."

Chapter 7

The walls of blue-hued stone, the sand beneath their feet, and even King Arthur melted away. The world around the twins was made of fluid and splashed out of existence just barely before the wave of a new reality crashed in around them.

The shift in the world was intense and the boys fell to their knees. The explosive rush of water roared in their ears and then it, too, changed. For only a moment the sound vanished, and the twins were surrounded by complete silence. Just as quickly as it had left, the sound returned, but it was different. Instead of the rush of water, the torrent of wind blasted over them, tearing at their clothes as violently as it screamed in their ears.

As quickly as the sound deafened them, their hearing returned. The wind hadn't died down at all, but it was no longer affecting their hearing. Blinking away the tears the sharp wind was pulling from their eyes, the twins stood and turned away from the gusts.

They were as far from the bottom of the ocean as they possibly could be. They were miles higher than they ever had been, and they now stood on top of a tower that rested at the peak of a mountain. The tower was made of stonework similar to what they saw in the ocean realm. The top of the tower had no lip and was completely flat.

Terror gripped at Cremont and Dash as they realized how the wind was fighting to push them from the top of the tower and they had nothing to hold on to. They subconsciously stepped closer to each other as they took in the rest of the scene. Clouds and fog hid the rest of whatever mountain range they were in, but the brothers knew that these mountains were too tall to be anywhere near Camelot.

They both started as Arthur's laugh echoed across the mountain range from somewhere behind them. They spun and realized that they no longer had their weapons as they tried to bring them to bear on what they thought was another attack.

Instead of turning and confronting Arthur, the boys finished their spin and were greeted by the calm, and not attacking, Lady of the Lake.

She waited for the laughter to stop echoing and Dash couldn't help but feel as though Arthur sounded like he knew something they didn't.

"Magic is the power of life that you control with your willpower. The Magic-Born are the people in your world who are gifted with the unique strength of will that allows them to shape that power." The Lady of the Lake wasn't moving her mouth, but they could hear her voice as if she was whispering in their ears. "It is your job, as wizards, to conform the world to your will. Most of this you will be able to do, over time, from your mind, but some thoughts are made stronger by using words." She nodded to both. "Most importantly, your training will never be over, and it starts now." She began moving as she spoke. "Arthur showed you how to make your weapons stronger through willing it to be so. The principle of all magic is that simple." She looked to Cremont. "Make the wind stop."

The flow of the air around the boys was strong enough that they still feared they could be blown from the tower at any second.

Cremont reached down within himself and found that same strength that he'd found before, and instead of focusing it around his staff, he focused it at the wind. At first there was no difference. The wind tore at their clothing and threatened to remove them from the tower. Pushing every thought from his mind, Cremont focused his will into a single powerful command and pushed it from his body.

Dash saw it before he felt it. Cremont's hair fell back to his head in a mess and his clothes relaxed and stopped being so tight around his body. Then whatever energy Cremont was projecting slowly expanded and washed over Dash, and Dash could see as it continued out further and encompassed the Lady of the Lake. As her own hair and clothing relaxed, Dash looked back to Cremont and saw strain in his face.

Holding the wind at bay was taking its toll on Cremont, and he wasn't going to be able to keep it up for much longer. As if reading Dash's thoughts, the Lady of the Lake nodded and Cremont relaxed. The wind did not return.

The Lady of the Lake turned to Dash. "Now, bring the wind back."

Dash reached down into his soul and tugged at the place where he'd found the strength to harden his bow. It was a strength of his conviction, of his beliefs. He understood exactly what the Lady of the Lake meant by magic being related to his willpower.

Dash exercised his will against the wind, demanding that it move.

Cremont was still panting; sweat dripping from his forehead, when he realized that the sweat was cooling. The breeze had begun to pick up and swept over his face, cooling it and giving him back some of his energy. To Cremont's relief, he didn't feel as though the breeze was any kind of threat to his staying on the tower, and he didn't attribute that to any weakness on Dash's part so much as an understanding that the wind didn't need to be dangerous.

Dash was looking just as tired as Cremont had been when the Lady nodded and allowed him to relax. She let the wind die down.

"All magic works on that basic principle. When those of the Magic-Born focus their will, they can change the world."

The Lady of the Lake made no movement and said no words, so the boys had no warning as the wind exploded around Cremont and Dash. It picked up speed until it was double what it had been when they had first arrived on top of the tower.

Dash's feet went out from under him, and he only barely put his hands down fast enough to save himself from breaking his jaw. Cremont twisted to avoid the wind, but it only sent him spinning and rolling across the tower. The wind stopped but the twins kept their momentum and went over the edge of the tower, grasping at the smooth stone and hoping to stop their descent.

They were airborne for less than the blink of an eye before they hit solid ground. Confusion and terror gripped them. Dash was panting in fear while Cremont seemed to be holding his breath. Looking around, Cremont and Dash found themselves on the top of the tower at the feet of the Lady of the Lake, and the breeze was absent.

"Stop being children." The Lady of the Lake barked. "I'm teaching you magic that you will use in *battle*. Act like it." She crossed her arms, much as Gran would when she was cross. "You know how to access your power. Now do it! Touch your will and shape it."

An interesting look passed between the boys and the Lady of the Lake laughed. "Your egos are extraordinary. Do not hesitate to bring the full force of your attacks to bear on me. I promise you, if the mighty Merlin couldn't touch me, no other mortal can."

The boys took their time, standing slowly to their feet. Once they were upright, they reached down within themselves and touched the very will at the center of their beings.

Cremont aimed his hands at the ground, directing the control of his mind at the stone beneath his feet. Behind him, the stones scraped loudly as they grew out of their positions and into a small wall behind him. Cremont's wall only went as high as his knees and he smiled, proud of what he'd accomplished.

Dash took another approach. His eyes still closed, Dash turned so that he faced Cremont, and his left shoulder was aimed at the Lady of the Lake. He lifted his hand, his palm facing the same direction as himself, and his fingers pointing at the Lady. His hand had become a wedge. Inches before his hand, the air shimmered, only barely noticeably. His wedge of a hand had projected a wedge of solid air before him.

The Lady of the Lake saw that they were defending against the attack that had already happened, and she could have chosen to change her attack, simply to teach the boys a lesson, but it was only one lesson in, and she had plenty of time to destroy the boys' weaknesses.

Once again, the Lady made no movement or indication that she was attacking. One second the wind was absent and the next it was roaring at ridiculous speeds.

Cremont's feet were braced against his makeshift wall, and he leaned into the rush of the wind as it washed over him. The wind pushed at him, and he had to take some of his energy from the wall and put it into strengthening his legs against the onslaught.

Dash was surrounded by the wind, but it mostly ignored him, instead hitting his wedge of willpower and going around him.

The Lady of the Lake liked the progress they had made and doubled her efforts.

No matter how much energy Cremont poured into his legs, they were already buckling with the wind. He shifted his tactic and pressed his will into the wall even more, straining as it rose higher behind him. It climbed as high as his waist before he felt he was safe to hold his position. His legs and lower body were pressed against the magical barrier, and his hands rested on the top of it, trying to hold himself up against the wind.

Dash found that the harder the wind blew, the more that it didn't matter what he held in front of himself. The wind tore around his wedge of energy and buffeted him at all sides. Still holding onto his construct, he poured power instead into his cloak, encouraging the sleeves to grow longer. He aimed his free hand at the ground and that sleeve shot forward, planting itself into the stonework. Releasing his wedge of energy, Dash allowed his other arm to do the same. The wind hit him with its full force, catching his cloak and yanking him of the ground. His tethered sleeves were the only thing holding him steady, and the wind washed into his face. Dash's eyes were forced shut and tears streamed back over his face.

The Lady of the Lake knew that the boys wouldn't last much longer, so she allowed the wind to stop.

Cremont fell forward with the sudden stop of the wind, landing on his stomach, while Dash crashed into the ground. They allowed their spells to stop, and Dash's sleeves returned to their normal length while the stones in Cremont's wall returned to the tower.

"I am impressed," the Lady said as the boys brought themselves to their feet. "You are grasping the basic concepts faster than most."

Cremont looked at where his wall had been. "I wouldn't have been able to do that yesterday, but now it seems almost easy. Why? If this is something I just had to will into existence, why hasn't it happened before now?"

The Lady of the Lake waved her hands and the world shifted again. Instead of standing at the top of a tower on the peak of a mountain, they were instead inside of a volcano surrounded by molten earth. The stood on a raised platform of stone, still in the same positions that they had been in. Heat surrounded them and the boys couldn't decide if it was safer to leave their cloaks on or take them off.

"You are still in my world, and it is a world constructed entirely of magic. A man will not learn to swim standing in a field, but if you submerge him in an ocean he will float or he will drown." She nodded to both. "You have chosen to float."

Dash was confused. "So, will we be weaker in our world?"

The Lady tilted her head to the side in a look that would have read as confusion on a human face. "I am teaching you how to flex a muscle that you did not know existed. It is hard now, but your muscle will get stronger. If your training goes well, then you won't notice any change in your abilities once you leave this place. If you allow your muscle to go weak, then it will be harder for you to flex it." She straightened her head. "If you left now, you would be very...weak and incapable of using as much magic as you are now. Over time, it will be nothing for you to use magic like this normally. If you leave at that point you will notice no difference in your grasp of control."

Dash nodded, slowly understanding while Cremont looked as if he was more interested in the boiling magma.

Suddenly, the Lady of the Lake was gone.

As if he had been standing there all along, in the Lady of the Lake's place stood Lord Bonnevist. They had only seen the man once or twice in the past, and not recently, but they had no doubt of who it was. According to the Lady of the Lake, this man was directly responsible for the death of their grandmother. For the death of Evelyn Farthing.

Being in a place of magic, they knew in the back of their minds that this couldn't actually be the advisor to King Thordon, but that thought was pushed from their minds by an outside source, and they reacted as if it was certainly that vile man.

"*Kneel*, Merlin's blood!" Lord Bonnevist shouted. The words echoed over the sound of the boiling magma, but the boys heard it differently. The words seemed to come from inside their minds, as if they had thought the commands themselves.

It took them each a moment to realize that they were already obeying before they found the willpower to break the spell. Forcing their legs to obey only their own commands, Cremont and Dash stood and glared at the snickering bald man.

At once, the twins ran at Bonnevist, both wishing that they had their weapons at their sides.

In response, Bonnevist raised a hand and a ball of bright light erupted from his hand and barreled at them. Lightning crackled around the ball of energy, and Dash barely dove out of the way as it careened past him. Cremont wasn't so lucky, and, while the main projectile hurtled past, a bolt of lightning arced off it and struck him, throwing him toward the edge of the platform. He grabbed and grappled at the ground and barely managed to stop himself from going over the edge and into the magma.

Clarity came to Dash as he realized that they couldn't just run at a wizard. He looked at Cremont, rage filling his brother's eyes, and shouted, "Together. Block and shoot."

Cremont's rage dwindled a little as confusion filled his eyes. "Shoot what?"

Dash shrugged, "It's your power. Shoot whatever you want, just shoot him, together!"

Cremont shrugged, flinched as the burn on his shoulder ached in the action, and stood up. Dash had just climbed back to his feet when Bonnevist launched another blast at Cremont.

This time, the hurtle of energy stopped, inches from Cremont's face as it hit an invisible wall in front of the boy. The lightning still arced past the shield, but the ball itself had stopped.

Dash saw this as his chance and focused his own power into energy. As his mind struck out looking for something to use, it found the answer. The heat from the air gathered into a ball of his own devising. Fire leapt from Dash's hand and struck at Lord Bonnevist.

With a snarl, Bonnevist batted the flame aside as if it were nothing and launched another ball of his own energy at the boys.

This time the energy came at Dash, and Dash instinctively brought up his own shield. The ball of energy and all its lightning stopped at the shield, and Dash cast all the collected energy away.

Dash glanced at Cremont, and Cremont shrugged. Collecting his own willpower, Cremont pulled at other sources in the air that Dash hadn't and jabbed his hand forward.

From his hand leapt a bright lightning bolt that curved through the air and hit Bonnevist in the hand. Bonnevist had attempted to catch it but instead the power burst through his defenses and blackened his hand. The jolt of energy sent the older man spinning and onto his back.

Lord Bonnevist jumped to his feet without hesitation and sent two more blasts of energy at the boys.

"Behind me!" Dash shouted. The boys had learned their rolls already from King Arthur, and Dash put up a shield.

Bonnevist's next ball of energy leapt toward the twins, but Dash had already put up his shield. As the dark wizard's power crackled in the air before them, Cremont let out a blast of lightning from his own hand. It arced through Dash's shield and across to Bonnevist, who tried to deflect the energy but only barely succeeded.

Back and forth the boys and the advisor dueled, continuing their game of shoot and dodge with their energy. Dash was sweating more profusely with each bolt of energy that his shield took while Cremont looked more tired as he threw more of his power.

The dark wizard couldn't deflect and attack, not like the boys could, and it was also tiring him out. The boys' coordination was allowing them to throw more power at a quicker rate than the more experienced wizard, and that advantage gained them ground.

In an effort to change tactics, Bonnevist hurled magma from the nearby pools at Cremont and Dash. It splashed about them, but Dash's shield worked just as well against the new attack as it did the old.

Cremont had found his rhythm, and instead of getting noticeably more tired, he seemed energized as he continued to hurl his power at Lord Bonnevist. He began getting new ideas, and soon his assault changed form until he was shooting alternating attacks of energy balls, magma, and lightning.

They had backed Lord Bonnevist to the edge of the solid rock that they all battled on. The man was beginning to look his age and satisfaction was spreading across Cremont and Dash's faces. With a quick glance to Dash, Cremont said, "Together."

Dash knew what Cremont meant and dropped his shield. Then, without realizing that he was doing it, Dash reached to his waist, where his quiver normally rested, and grabbed at an arrow that wasn't there. Then, continuing the motion, he knocked the arrow that wasn't there to the bow that he wasn't holding and drew back the string.

Cremont stopped hurling his power with just his one hand and placed them both together, concentrating all his willpower through the center of his being and pressing it out and through his hands. With only a thought, he released that power from both of his hands.

At that same time, Dash released his fingers from the string that was not there, and a silver shaft of light shot across the distance between the wizard and the twins.

Dash's attack was met with Bonnevist's upraised hand, and the arrow of light pierced his palm before plunging into his breast. Cremont's attack was met with no resistance as the lightning hit

Lord Bonnevist directly in the face, causing his body to flip, end over end, before hitting the magma without a splash.

The boys collapsed. They had used almost all their energy during the fight, and the heat was smothering them and sucking the life from them. Even on their knees, Dash and Cremont weren't going to let their pain ruin their moment. They'd killed Lord Bonnevist: the man responsible for their Gran's murder.

Just as suddenly as that wave of elation swam over them, realization did as well. They hadn't killed anyone. The reality of the situation had been subdued in their conscious minds. They had only been fighting a ghost of the Lady of the Lake's. Their hearts sank.

Cold wind rushed over them, and the magma around them steamed from the touch of it and darkened. Cremont and Dash were suddenly surrounded by scalding hot steam and tried to scream. As they did, the steam got into their lungs, and they choked and fell over.

In terrible pain and confusion, both Cremont and Dash looked at the top of the volcano from their positions on their backs. Just as they did, they saw water pouring into the mountain.

Dash tried to bring up his power to protect them from the falling torrent of water, but it was very suddenly inaccessible. In a panic he looked to his brother, who was thrusting his hands into the air in a futile attempt to put up his own shield.

The water washed over them, hitting them like a felled tree. At first it was warm, but then it cooled almost instantly.

Seeing light above him, Cremont touched his brother's shoulder and pointed. Together, they swam weakly toward what they hoped was the surface.

They broke the surface together and the wind rushed over their faces as they took deep breaths. They expected their scalded throats to explode with pain but were both pleasantly surprised to find that they no longer hurt.

Wiping their eyes, they looked around themselves. There were no landmarks of any kind as far as either of them could see. Cremont and Dash floated in a seemingly never-ending ocean. Standing on the surface of the ocean, only feet from where they treaded water, stood the Lady of the Lake.

The Lady of the Lake's face was stern as she asked, "What did you do wrong?"

The boys turned their heads to look at each other and it was evident to both that the other was confused.

"We did nothing wrong," Cremont answered weakly.

"We killed Lord Bonnevist!" Dash shouted over the rush of the wind. "We worked together and were able to destroy him."

The Lady of the Lake almost looked sympathetic as she answered, "What you fought was a weak ghost of what Lord Bonnevist really is." She shook her head. "Bonnevist is dead. You killed him. Now return to Camelot and tell them of your victory."

Realization dawned on Cremont, and he turned to Dash who still bore confusion on his face. "Camelot doesn't know Bonnevist for what he is." He looked from his brother to the Lady of the Lake. "We can't just kill him. We have to show Camelot what he is and that the Magic-Born are not the problem."

The Lady of the Lake smiled, and Dash nodded in understanding. Cremont had found the truth of it. It did them no good to fight Lord Bonnevist anywhere if there wasn't some sort of demonstration of how vile he really was. They weren't just out for revenge; they were out to free Camelot from its misplaced hate.

"You have to be constantly planning and adjusting your attack, changing it to fit all of the new information that you'll be gaining on your path," the Lady of the Lake said. "Lord Bonnevist has been planning for your destruction and the acquisition of the sword of Excalibur for more than half of a century." Her face took on a look of sympathy again. "You do not have the luxury of underestimating him. He will use your love and your anger to control you."

She walked across the surface of the water and closer to the boys. As she stepped closer they were no longer floating in a vast sea, but were instead standing on their farm, directly in front of their house. The Lady of the Lake was no longer with them. In her place, walking toward Cremont and Dash, was Evelyn Farthing.

Joy flooded inside of both the twins, and they hesitated for just long enough for Evelyn to say, "I've missed you, my boys."

That was all that was needed, and all three of the Farthings ran at each other with smiles and tears covering their faces.

Evelyn only made it a few steps into her run when an arrow burst out of her chest and blood spit from her mouth. The shock of what had happened, again, stopped the boys in their tracks.

Dash ran forward as Evelyn began to collapse, wanting to catch her this time before she hit the ground. Cremont reacted with rage and summoned fire to his hands as he scanned the horizon for the location of the shooter. Dash couldn't move once he had Evelyn in his arms and began sobbing, begging the heavens for this to not be happening.

Dash looked into his grandmother's dead eyes just as they seemed to lighten up. She looked at her grandson and then smiled a broad and wicked smile that was not his grandmother's.

From the air, the corpse pulled a knife, summoning it with her will, and she plunged it into Dash's neck with three quick jabs. The young Farthing boy fell back from where he'd been holding his grandmother and gurgled for his voice through the torrent of blood.

Cremont turned at the sudden commotion behind him just in time to see Evelyn shift into the form of Bonnevist and throw the blood-covered knife at Cremont. The knife sank to the hilt into his chest, and Cremont's strength was suddenly gone from him. He collapsed to the ground.

His knees landed on sand and not the dirt and grass that was directly in front of his home. Cremont looked around and saw that the knife was gone from his chest, as was the wound, and that he now stood on the shore of the Lady of the Lake's lake.

The Lady of the Lake rose from the water, and Cremont turned and checked on his brother. Dash was still poking at his neck where there should have been holes and relief washed over him when he hit solid skin.

"I have been hard on you to teach you some very valuable lessons. For this I am sorry, but it was necessary." She still had her look of sympathy, but there was hardness behind it. "It will not get easier. I will come at you harder and faster each and every time. Every time that I do, it will be different, and you will be taken, beaten, and killed. Your hearts will break, and your souls will beg for me to end you, but I will not. You must pass through this fire if you are to be strong enough wizards to do what must be done." The Lady of the Lake folded her arms. "I will destroy you because Bonnevist will not hesitate to destroy you."

Dash shook his head. "But it won't be like this. We will have weapons as well. We'll have swords. We'll have Excalibur!"

Cremont nodded. "If we're training for battle with wizards, give us our weapons so that we can train properly. Give us Excalibur so that we may have an advantage over Lord Bonnevist."

The Lady of the Lake laughed. "In good time, you must learn to use your skills before you learn to combine them with combat training." She tilted her head to the side as another idea came to it. "Perhaps another lesson is in order, though. One that you should have learned long ago."

From the air, much as Evelyn had pulled the knife, the Lady of the Lake pulled a sword.

No, the boys realized that it wasn't just a sword, it was *the* sword. It was the same sword that Arthur had been using in their practice battles. It was Excalibur.

The Lady allowed it to float over to Dash who took the sword in his hands and swung it through some practice movements.

Dash looked at the Lady of the Lake. "I don't feel anything different." He handed the legendary sword over to his brother hilt first. "You try."

Cremont took the sword and went through several similar swings to what Dash had before looking at them both. "I feel nothing different. I thought that the sword would give me power."

"No, the sword *is* power." The Lady of the Lake answered. She shifted her shape to that of Lord Bonnevist, and then in his voice commanded, "Attack me."

Bonnevist pulled a sword from his scabbard and stood in a defensive position. Cremont wasted no time and, raising Excalibur, charged with an attackFrom the side, Dash watched as the swords met. Cremont parried blows with the dark wizard, and Dash thought that it looked as though his brother was doing surprisingly well.

Just as the thought crossed Dash's mind, Bonnevist grinned his evil smile and sped up his attack. Cremont was only barely keeping up with Bonnevist and had to leap out of the way several times from attacks that he just wasn't fast enough to block.

With a spin, Bonnevist slapped Excalibur to the side, pivoted and brought his sword down hard on the wrist holding Excalibur. Cremont screamed in intense pain and continued to do so as Bonnevist picked up the sword, peeled Cremont's fingers from the hilt, and gripped it tightly in his own hands.

Fire filled the space behind Lord Bonnevist's eyes, and Excalibur glowed with the light of the noon sun. Dash was panting with terror at the sight.

Shaking and barely keeping his wits about him, Cremont weakly asked, "How?"

Everything was back to normal in the blink of an eye. Cremont had his hand back, and they each stood on the shore again directly in front of the Lady of the Lake. Lord Bonnevist and Excalibur were nowhere to be seen.

"In the hands of the Merlin bloodline," answered the Lady of the Lake, "Excalibur is only a sword."

"What does that mean?" Dash begged. He was still shaking from the sight of the overpowered Lord Bonnevist.

The Lady of the Lake explained, "The sword isn't anything but a conduit, or a passage, for the power of Merlin. Excalibur was only as powerful as the bloodline of the great wizard, Merlin. Many people, throughout history, have attributed the power of the sword to myself, the Lady of the Lake, but this is far from the truth. I never gave the sword any power. I only repaid a favor to Merlin. He came to me and asked that I create a sword that was as powerful as the magic in his blood. A sword that a mortal could use to rise above the dregs and become a king. I warned him of the danger of having such a weapon in existence, and he promised that he would forever be the deciding factor of who would wield the sword. On that oath, I forged Excalibur, a tool for channeling the power of the bloodline of Merlin. The sword created, I had to also forge the other end of the connection, which I did so with a title: The Mantel of Excalibur. The Mantel could only be inherited and whoever the Mantel rested with would be the source of the power of the sword as well as the one who decided who should wield it. They would both be Merlin.

"By right of blood, you boys, born at the same time and to the heir of Merlin, have both inherited the Mantel. With your combined power filling the sword, it has become more powerful than even I foresaw."

Dash asked, "Why didn't we feel weak when Arthur used the sword to fight us?"

The Lady of the Lake answered, "In the hands of a mortal, even a deceased one, the sword's power is marginally used. It aids the wielder of the sword to win battles through enhancing their skills and offering protection. Also, the wielder can speak directly with Merlin, or the holder of the Mantel. While consumed with battle, the sword also offers the user an endless supply of physical energy and alertness. The power is an ocean to a man who cannot swim.

"Arthur's demise was a well-planned attack by Queen Mab. She discovered how to block the Mantel, and Arthur was left with only his own skills while in the heat of battle. He fought with such ferocity that many believed he still had the power of Excalibur aiding him." Her face turned sad at the memory. "Unfortunately, he did not."

The Lady of the Lake pushed the memory away and her face returned to passive. "This is not the case if the sword were to be in the hands of a Magic-Born, such as Lord Bonnevist. Excalibur becomes a direct connection to the power of the Mantel in the hands of the Magic-Born. The wizard or witch that wields the sword can take as much or all the power of the Mantel into their own and use it as they see fit. In essence, they can drain the Mantel and make themselves God-like in power. Having such leverage would also put the Mantel at his whim. He could control their actions by simply threatening to drain their lives without ever actually using his own power."

The sympathetic look that the boys had accepted as part of their training came back to the Lady of the Lake's face. "In Lord Bonnevist's hands, the plan would be simple. He would lock you both away in some dungeon and strap Excalibur to his side. He would have infinite power and you would not be able to fight back, because you would be weakened by both his attacks and your own."

"In the hands of the Mantel, as you just witnessed, Excalibur is only a sword. Using the sword is just to have access to your own power. It is your responsibility to find a person, specifically a mortal, who can wield the sword and the power of Camelot."

The Lady of the Lake crossed her arms, and a stern look crossed her face. "If no such person exists, it is your responsibility to hide the sword indefinitely and die as old and lonely men."

Cremont was a little stunned by that last line. "'Old and lonely men'? Why?"

Dash answered for the Lady of the Lake.

"Because the death of the Merlin bloodline means the death of the power of Excalibur."

Chapter 8

The guards that had been known to go down into the cells of the main castle would remark to their families and friends that the place had a scent. None of those same guards would ever agree on what the odor was or how to describe it, but they all agreed that it wasn't a good smell. They each blamed the usual source of smells; rats, mold, and rot were the most common causes that the guards chose.

None of them were correct.

Lord Bonnevist took a deep breath through his nostrils, taking in the scent deeply into his lungs. Only the Magic-Born knew the truth, and none more readily than Lord Bonnevist. The Magic-Born knew that it wasn't a smell at all that permeated the cells so much as it was an essence.

To those who were not born with the touch of magic, the cells smelled horrible. The cells smelled of death.

Lord Bonnevist wasn't immune to the other descriptions, such as the smell of rot from the wooden cell doors, the mold from the damp floors, and the rats that he almost enjoyed seeing scurry through the dark halls. Those were the actual smells that filled his mind, but they were blown away by the many souls that still resided in the cracks in the stone walls.

Bonnevist walked the halls slowly, enjoying the peace and quiet that the place afforded him. Ever since the fool Thordon's death, Bonnevist had been swamped in the day-to-day mundaneness of running this once legendary kingdom. On the one hand, this was exactly what Lord Bonnevist had always craved: to own and command all that Merlin had once held dear. Those dreams hadn't died, but they had been forced to the back of his mind with the revival of his other dream. The revival of his dream of commanding the Excalibur's power.

The realization that the Farthing twins were descended of the line of Merlin brought much hope and a smile to Bonnevist's heart. He had found little in his searchings for information in regard to the Lady of the Lake's realm and the resting place of Excalibur. Of what he did find, Bonnevist had learned that only those of the Lady's choosing could enter her home. Merlin's great-grandsons were evidently on that list.

If Bonnevist had known any of this before Jacob Cord had run to the authorities, he would have made certain to emphasize that they do not allow Evelyn Farthing to be killed. It would have been a much simpler task to convince the Farthing twins to aid him if he had shown some compassion at first. Undoubtedly, they blamed him for their grandmother's death, and Bonnevist was sure that the Lady of the Lake had told them the truth about him and his history as well.

No, while his hindsight saw perfection, Bonnevist was forced to work with the situation as it was.

His slow trek through the dungeon halls came to an end directly outside the cell that allowed him his audience with the long dead grand wizard of Camelot. The large, reinforced wooden door was still wide open and, per his request, Evelyn Farthing's body still rested on the stone slab in the middle of the dank cell.

The dark wizard entered the tight room slowly, dragging his hand over the slab and then Evelyn's blood-stained body. His fingers lightly played over her face before gliding down her neck, avoiding the hole in her chest, tracing down her navel, leaping over her thighs, brushing her legs, and lightly slapping her feet.

With that final touch, Lord Bonnevist spun away from Evelyn Farthing's corpse and pressed himself against the cold stone wall that Merlin's ghost had thrown him against previously.

"Where," Bonnevist whispered, "are you hiding?" He sniffed deeply, looking past the rats, rot, and mold for the souls that he had left in that room.

Hundreds of souls resided in that wall, and he could see all of them at once, just beyond his sight. It was the most crowded room in all of Camelot, and the crowd pressed forward. Some sought revenge for the wrongs that Bonnevist had conducted upon them while others only wanted to know why they had ever deserved such horrible treatment. All the souls pressed together, and

Bonnevist realized that they were working together to hide what it was that he sought.

The wizard pushed past each one of the spirits of the cell, looking into every crack in the walls, licking the stones, and wiggling his fingers into the seams of the ancient stonework.

All the while, he repeated his original questions, "Where are you hiding?" He chanted it, no longer choosing to whisper and made it a mantra as if the words themselves would be the spell that brought to him what he hoped to command.

He heard it then. It was a sigh of the breeze, heard and not felt. The dark wizard knew where to look.

With an agility unmatched in anyone his actual age, Lord Bonnevist spun again and leapt up onto the slab. He straddled the belly of Evelyn Farthing's body and leaned in closely. Pressing and squirming his fingers past her lips and into her mouth, Bonnevist pulled her mouth wide and shouted into it, "I found you!"

Sitting back up, Bonnevist slapped his hand onto her bare chest, directly over the hole that had killed her. Finding what he was looking for, Bonnevist pinched and then pulled, seemingly pulling at nothing, yet having a hard time doing it.

Finally satisfied with what he had done, he clenched his fist around the invisible beast that he had removed from the heart of Evelyn Farthing.

Lord Bonnevist brought his hands together in a sharp clap and shouted, allowing the roar of his voice to fill with the power of his will.

As if thrown there by Lord Bonnevist's bellow, Evelyn Farthing's faintly glowing spirit appeared standing at the head of her corpse.

Smiling at his handiwork, Lord Bonnevist allowed Evelyn's spirit a moment of squirming. Once she realized that she couldn't move, he spoke.

"Stop your struggling. You will not be capable of doing anything without my express permission." Bonnevist's smile shifted from one of triumph to one of malevolence. "I have bound your soul to my will."

Evelyn Farthing looked defiantly at the dark wizard. "You know who I am. It will not hold. He will not let it."

"I am willing to bet both of our lives that you're very wrong." He climbed down from her corpse and straightened his robes, tucking a hand inside the breast. "Merlin's intervention was a one-time thing. We both know that. I am certain that he will not come again."

Her defiant look wavered. "What do you want with me?"

"So very much," Lord Bonnevist answered. "Fear not: I do not want to consume your power. That honor is reserved for your grandsons. Unfortunately, I believe that I will need you if I am going to bring them to me." He shrugged. "They are young and stupid, and I will need you if I am going to have any hope of controlling them."

The defiant look returned at the mention of Cremont and Dash. "I will not help you."

Lord Bonnevist pulled something small from his robes. It was a very plain ad unremarkable yellow jewel attached to a long piece of silver chain.

"Fortunately for both of us," Bonnevist said as he held the amulet out to Evelyn, holding it by the chain, "you won't need to."

Evelyn Farthing gasped and light flashed all around her being. In another flash and a shudder through her spirit, Evelyn vanished into the yellow gem.

Bonnevist lifted the amulet and put its length of chain around his neck.

"But first, I need your help in collecting the Cord family."

Adrianna Cord sat beside her son, Martin, at their table in their quiet home. She was trying her best to keep Martin calm. Hold his hand tightly in both of her own, Adrianna prayed that Martin couldn't sense her own trepidation.

It had been an entire day since Jacob had gone into Camelot to make his statement to the authorities that would condemn their neighbor and friend, Evelyn Farthing, as a witch of the Magic-Born. He should have been back before dinner, but dinner came and went, and it was soon followed by the entire night. Adrianna and Martin hadn't slept at all, instead worrying about Jacob.

"We should go look for him." Martin said through his gritted teeth. It was the same argument that he had been making all morning, and it was everything Adrianna could do to stop Martin from storming off in search of his father.

"For the final time," her patience had worn thin, "Your father is safe and enjoying the gratitude of Lord Bonnevist himself."

Adrianna released his hand and folded her arms. "He will be home as soon as the Advisor is done with him."

Martin's face was tight with anger. "It shouldn't have taken this long, and you know that. He should have been home by now."

"Well, he isn't, and fretting over it will accomplish nothing." She needed to find her son a distraction. "Have you finished with your chores?"

By way of answering, Martin stood forcefully from his seat, rocking the chair back as he did. He stomped toward the door, hoping that the fields would shake the fears from his mind.

Before Adrianna could release her sigh of relief at her son's resignation, a shrill and ear-piercing scream tore through their home.

Martin fell to his knees and clutched madly at his ears. Adrianna slapped her own hands over her ears and cast her eyes about, searching for the source of their torture. She didn't need to look for long.

Standing over Martin at the door to the Cord home was Evelyn Farthing.

Whatever torture that Evelyn's screaming was bringing to Martin and Adrianna was nothing to the pain that Evelyn's face was showing. To their relief, the scream stopped as abruptly as it had started, leaving the silence to fill the gap.

Evelyn Farthing straightened, her eyes started their own search, darting back and forth across the home as she tried to decipher her location.

While it was obvious that it was indeed Evelyn Farthing standing in their home, it was also just as obvious that Evelyn Farthing was dead. Her body was transparent, and she was accompanied by a faint glow that encompassed her entire being.

Most awkwardly for the living in the room, Evelyn Farthing wasn't actually standing so much as she was floating about a hand's width from the floor.

Terrified, neither Martin nor Adrianna could do much more than stare at the apparition.

It finally dawned on Evelyn where she was, and she looked directly at Adrianna. "You must leave this place. Quickly." While her feet moved, Evelyn wasn't walking as she drifted toward Adrianna. "Lord Bonnevist is coming here, and he means to destroy you both."

Adrianna shook herself out of her stupor and stood to meet the ghost's eyes. "Lies. We have done nothing wrong. Lord Bonnevist would only come here to thank us." Adrianna's eyes grew wide with sudden fear. "Where is my husband? What have you done with Jacob?" She demanded.

Evelyn looked confused for only a split second before answering. "I have not seen your husband since..." she waved her hands at herself, indicating her current state. "He was alive the last that I saw him, but if you haven't heard from him, then it is likely that Bonnevist has had Jacob killed." She pointed at the door. "If I am here, then Lord Bonnevist cannot be far behind. You must leave before you share your husband's fate."

From behind Evelyn, Martin found his voice. "Are you dead?"

Evelyn turned, seemingly distraught, answered, "I was killed yesterday, by the Camelot Guard under orders from Lord Bonnevist."

"You were killed for practicing magic!" Adrianna spit. Rage filled her face.

Evelyn's eyes glowed brighter as she turned on Adrianna Cord. "I hurt no one!"

"You were a witch!" Adrianna returned. "That was illegal, and the punishment is—"

"Never mind!" Evelyn interrupted loudly. Her voice rattled the windows. "Lord Bonnevist is coming for you. You must leave now!"

Adrianna wasn't going to let Evelyn have any ground. "What could Lord Bonnevist possibly want with us?"

Evelyn's shoulders sagged. She could sense that they were quickly running out of time. "I am a Magic-Born, and so are my grandsons. They have escaped, and Lord Bonnevist needs your knowledge of them. He wishes to use what you know against them." She glanced over her shoulder, as if she heard a noise that wasn't there. Looking back to Adrianna, she continued. "His methods for getting such information are not pleasant. No matter the injustice that you might have brought upon my family, I do not wish to see the wrath of Lord Bonnevist brought down on Martin."

Adrianna smirked. "We will give him what he wants, freely. We have no allegiance to the Magic-Born."

A bright yellow streak crashed through the kitchen window and landed on the floor. The Cords examined it from where they stood and saw that it was a large yellow stone attached to a silver chain. It was plain, yet it was beautiful.

Evelyn was crying when the Cords looked back to her. "I hope that you are right, Adrianna, because you no longer have the luxury of choice."

The doors, both front and back, burst open as heavy boots kicked them in. Storming into their home were the Camelot Guard. Adrianna and Martin couldn't see past the first row of them to count how many had entered their small home, but they could see through the window enough to know that more waited outside.

The man in charge was someone that Adrianna didn't recognize, and she suddenly found herself wondering where Samuel Grand was. This new superior wasn't looking at Adrianna, but instead at the still present apparition of Evelyn Farthing.

"It's true." He whispered before drawing his sword. "Quickly men, grab the Necromancers!"

Adrianna understood all too late, and a heavy gloved hand had clasped over her mouth before she could shout in her defense. Martin Cord was just as subdued as his mother was and struggled only a little before understanding that he wasn't going to be able to get free. As the guards grabbed Adrianna and Martin, the yellow stone on the floor let out a scream that was not human. In response to that scream, Evelyn Farthing vanished from sight.

The crowd of guards parted as Adrianna continued to try to shout over the gloved hand and Lord Bonnevist stepped forward. His robes were tight on his muscled body, and his bald head still managed to gleam in the dark interior of the Cord home.

Lord Bonnevist looked to the guard in charge. "Was it as we expected, Clint?"

Clint nodded, seemingly afraid to speak.

"Necromancy." Bonnevist cursed. "The worst of the Magic-Born practice Necromancy." Lord Bonnevist walked over to the amulet on the floor and picked it up. "We're lucky to have brought the stone." He held it up, showing it to the guards present. "She could have taken all of our souls if we hadn't brought this."

The Camelot Guard let out a cheer for Lord Bonnevist.

Bonnevist stepped closer to Adrianna and looked past her to the guard holding her. "Keep your hand tight on her mouth. We don't want her unleashing any more spells." He turned his attention the Adrianna Cord. "Your husband came to us and told us of the horrible doings going on at the Farthing farm." Bonnevist frowned. "I was going to allow him to leave then, but he hesitated, obviously wishing to tell me more. His soul was obviously torn, so I asked him to tell me only if he wished to." He shrugged. "Jacob then told me, through sobs of betrayal, of how his wife was a practitioner of Necromancy, and how she had corrupted their son in the same arts. He loved his family but feared for their souls."

Lord Bonnevist spoke of Jacob in the past, and it caught Adrianna's attention. She yanked her head harder and managed to break free long enough to shout, "What have you done with my husband?"

As quickly as she had broken free, the guard grabbed her mouth again.

Lord Bonnevist leaned in close to Adrianna's face and said quietly. "Your husband was devoted to you, and it broke his heart to betray you." His eyes filled with sadness. It was obviously sad, and the false empathy made Adrianna sick. "Jacob Cord jumped from the castle in hopes that he could greet you in the afterlife."

Adrianna sobbed and screamed as much as she could through the hand that still was clasped over her mouth.

"Take them to the wagons. I will interrogate them in the cells."

Martin had a different reaction that Lord Bonnevist didn't miss. Martin's eyes were red, as if he wanted to cry, and they were filled with intense hate. The hate that radiated off Martin Cord was so strong that Lord Bonnevist could feel it in the air, warping the very magic of the home.

Bonnevist could almost see the anger in the air. He took a deep sniff and allowed it to fill him as the Cords were carried from their home.

Chapter 9

Cremont rolled just as a thin gout of flame arced over his back. He came to his feet with his staff, reinforced by his will, in front of him as a shield. The next blast of flame hit his staff squarely but instead of allowing the staff to take on the full power of the attack, Cremont redirected the energy, flicking his staff and sending the flames careening into a nearby tree. The bark blackened and the blast went out. Cremont smiled at his success.

The smile faded quickly, though, as Dash sent a wave of air at his brother. Cremont, still distracted by his accomplishment, took the full force of the blast and flailed backwards, slamming into another tree.

It had been a week since the boys had started training in combined weapons and magic. Arthur and the Lady of the Lake had not gone easy on them throughout the entire ordeal. Together the boys had grown more confident in both their fighting abilities and their powers, and it had not gone unnoticed by their tutors. As a reward, the boys were given a day of relaxation.

Firstly, they decided to change the scenery. It hadn't taken long for Dash and Cremont to realize that they could also change the look of their environment. They had toyed with mountains and deserts, but in the end they had settled for something they both loved: a beautiful pine forest.

Neither of the boys liked the idea of a day away from their studies. The trials of becoming wizards gave them distractions from both their upcoming responsibilities and their grief over their old life and their grandmother. Instead, Cremont and Dash had agreed to use the time to practice among themselves and focus on where each brother was weakest in their abilities.

In Cremont's case, that meant spells that focused on defense, stealth, and subtlety. Cremont had learned how to easily harness the "louder" powers, as Dash had labeled them. Cremont could summon any kind of attack, but his shields were weak, the shadows rebuked him, and silence was a foreign concept to him.

On the other hand, Dash was no better. He excelled at what Cremont could not easily grasp, but he could not shake the earth, his attacks were sloppy and meek, and instead of moving things with his mind as his brother could, he barely made them shake.

The boys knew why they were so well balanced, and it hadn't taken the Lady of the Lake to explain it to them.

It was the Mantel. Merlin's bloodline and power had been split between the boys, and they had become two sides of the same coin.

Except they were both beginning to learn that that wasn't the entire truth. In just the one day of practice, Dash and Cremont had already improved their skills by ten-fold in their weaker talents. It wasn't that neither boy had been born without the other ability, so much as they had developed weaker aptitudes for those spells. The muscles were there, they only needed to be worked to encourage their growth.

Dash was sweating through his tunic as he ran at Cremont. He pulled his bow from its place on his shoulder and summoned arrows of energy, as he had against the faux Lord Bonnevist. Instead of the faint green of the arrow-styled energy of before, the arrow grew to an orange color as bright as the sun. New sweat glistened upon his brow as he pulled back the string and let it go.

Cremont was still just standing as he became aware of the incoming arrow. He dropped to his knees and raised both of his hands in front of him, straining with all his will. Dirt and pine needles flew up from the ground to join in the wake of the power of his shield. The arrow met the shield at eye-level with Cremont. The shield wavered, flexing as Dash pressed his will against Cremont's.

To Cremont's relief, the shield held, but only barely. He could feel the shield and his strength collapsing, just as Dash's did. Both boys released their power at the same time, surrendering to the strength of the other.

Cremont laughed and stood slowly. "Is that," he panted, "the best that you can do?"

Dash was also panting and leaned against a tree for support. "I was going to ask you the same thing."

Cremont threw both of his hands forward. Flame erupted from

them and toward Dash. It was twice as thick as the gouts of flame that Dash had been launching at his brother, and twice as hot.

Dash threw up his hands only barely in time and caught the flame with a wall of wind that held it back from his face by only inches. Despite the power of the gust, Dash could still feel the heat of the attack on his face.

Cremont lowered his hands when he had thought Dash had had enough. The flame vanished as quickly as it had appeared and Cremont was shocked to see that Dash was nowhere to be seen.

Almost too late, Cremont spun around, raising his staff as he did so, and caught Dash's attack on the stick. Dash had blended with his environment and flanked his brother. Once he had maneuvered behind Cremont, Dash had used his bow as a club and swung it at his brother.

Having halted the attack with his staff, Cremont released the staff with his left hand and used that hand to summon his will and send a force of energy into Dash's chest. Dash, propelled by the sudden blow of power, flew from his feet and hit the same tree that his brother had hit previously.

Though stunned, Dash wasn't stupid. As soon as he hit the ground again, he began rolling. To prove his precautions correct, a bolt of lightning struck the tree directly where Dash had slammed into it. The attack only just missed Dash.

Dash summoned another shield, this one more of an invisible wall than a torrent of air. Cremont launched a volley of attacks, all hitting Dash's shield squarely before dying out. Dash walked the shield forward, closing the distance on his brother.

When only a few feet remained between the twins, Dash made his move.

Using the power in the shield, Dash spun on his heel as if he was swinging a large club or sword. As he spun, he dragged with him the wall of power that he'd been shielding himself with. Cremont had no time to react as the shield slammed into him and lifted him into the air.

The hit dazed Cremont and knocked the wind out of him. It took him a moment to realize exactly how hard he had been hit. His trajectory had lifted him high, and aside from the tower that the Lady of the Lake had summoned previously, he had never been higher in his life. He neared the tops of the pine trees that played audience to their practice. Fear gripped his insides and he grasped at ideas to save him from the crushing blow of impacting the ground.

As that very same ground came nearer, Cremont recalled that they controlled the shapes and contours of the realm. Sending his will out, the pine trees suddenly parted, giving way for a pond that sprung up in their wake.

Cremont barely had time for a quick breath before he hit the pond's surface.

He had insisted that the water be deep so that he didn't just bounce off the bottom of the pond. As soon as Cremont felt his momentum give, he began the climb back to the surface. Breaking through, he gasped and wiped his eyes looking around for Dash. He could hear his brother crashing loudly through the woods and began swimming to meet him at the shore.

Cremont beat Dash to the edge of the pond and immediately set about drying himself off. He pushed his will into a ball of flame and strained as he directed it to circle his wet body. The work was both fun and a personal test, as had most of the day been.

Cremont was mostly dry when he decided that the strength to hold the flame steady was getting to be too much. With a flick of his wrist, he cast it into the pond.

The flame went out, instantly sending up gouts of steam. Cremont smiled in spite of himself, but his smile faded as he noted something in the steam. He peered closer into it and watched as images flashed through the steam. They were moving pictures of people in Camelot, but it wasn't focusing on any one scene. First, he was looking at the market and then the image quickly changed to a fast horse, galloping over a bridge. The next scene was a cook, hard at work, in what looked like the Castle kitchens.

Cremont couldn't get the images to slow down and, as the steam vanished, he cast out his will to hold onto the vision, placing it on the surface of the water.

Dash was laughing as he came out of the trees toward his brother. "Great idea with the pond. I didn't think that I had hit you that hard."

Dash didn't expect a response as he saw what had captured Cremont's attention. He took the place to the left of his brother and leaned over the surface of the water.

"Wait." Dash said. "Let me try something." He reached out to the water's surface and closed his eyes as he touched it. The ripple from his hand touching the water rolled over the flickering images and they began to slow and come into focus. Both boys were amazed to see that they could also hear words and crowds milling about.

Cremont cast a frown at his brother. This was a subtler power that Dash had exercised. Cremont would need to work on it.

The scene was the market place within the walls of Camelot. The boys' elderly friend, Gregory Rogan, carried a somber look as he spoke to a woman and child that Cremont and Dash did not recognize.

The voices of their friend and his customers came to the boys as if they were standing right with them.

"I don't know what happened to the boys." Gregory was saying. "No one seems to know." He cast his eyes about, as if he was looking for the boys to jump out from behind the stall and surprise him.

The lady spoke next. "Is it true? That they were Magic-Born?"

Gregory shrugged. "Evelyn Farthing is almost my age, and she was able to take out an entire group of the Camelot Guard." The sadness in his eyes darkened. "It sounds like magic to me."

"She was living among us for years." Fear had crept into the customer's voice. "What spells could she have cast on us?"

Gregory seemed uncomfortable with talking about his friends in that manner and turned away from the customer and her son to tend his stall.

Sensing his discomfort, she pulled away from the previous question. "Are they hunting her grandsons?"

Gregory nodded, not looking at her. "It has only been a day since they disappeared near the lake. The Guard is good at what they do, they will probably have them soon."

Cremont grabbed Dash's shoulder. "Only a day?" His eyes were wide. "We have been training for almost two weeks."

Dash shrugged. "The Lady of the Lake said that our training had to begin immediately. Maybe she also meant that it must be quick."

The idea didn't sit easily with Cremont, and he shuddered. "I hope that our aging is still normal." Dash smiled at his brother. In the last week, or maybe it was the last day, the boys had been letting many things that they didn't understand fall under the label of "magic." This was just another spell they would need to learn.

While Cremont didn't know how to feel about the difference in times, he could see the tactical advantage in it and was already attempting to figure out how he'd work the spell himself.

The scene shifted as the boys became distracted and the new image managed to draw their attention back to surface of the water.

The scene that greeted them was the inside of a small home within the walls of Camelot. That meant that it was the home of a tradesmen or a member of the Guard. It wasn't a farming family.

Sitting at the table of the home was a woman in her middle years and a young girl around the age of five or six. Cremont held his breath, fearing he knew what he was looking at.

Across from the woman sat a member of the Camelot Guard. He must have been new because Cremont and Dash didn't recognize him. He was speaking to them, but it took a minute for the voices to reach the Farthing twins.

"...of course, be compensated for his years of service. I have been instructed to tell you that you may stay in this home until the end of the month. I am sorry. His friends are putting together a collection. It isn't much, but it should help you in finding a new home. We want to help you, Mrs. Grand."

Her eyes were filled with tears. "Then why are you pushing me and my child from our home?"

This was obviously not easy for the guard. "The housing is set aside for members of the Guard. While we respect and like you, we can't allow you to stay now that Samuel is..."

The little girl was sobbing, and her tears only fell harder as her mother cried.

Cremont was crying as well. Dash held his back, focusing on keeping the scene on the water steady.

Samuel's widow stood, her tears exploding to rage as her face brightened to red. "Get out!" She was shouting. The guard stood and walked silently to the door as she continued to bellow with anger.

As she took a breath, he said very quickly, "If you need anything, please don't hesitate to come to me. Samuel was a great man."

Defeated, she slumped back into her seat as he left.

The scene faded and was replaced by another.

Stables with sunlight streaming in. The light fell on a man in his early twenties with short blond hair. He was shoeing a horse.

A voice beckoned the man from outside the stables. "Daron! I need you out here. Now." The man lifted his chin, and his eyes were a sharp blue and his chin was sharp. The man had a noble look about him.

Dash looked at Cremont, confusing passing between them. "We don't know him," he said.

"Maybe we will." Cremont answered.

Again, the scene changed.

The twins were looking down into the water and into a very dark room. It took a minute of them cupping their eyes over the water for the scene to become clear.

A blond woman sat in the corner. Her clothing was dirty but more or less undamaged. She was crying and the boys could see her chest heaving with the sobs. Her face was swollen, and she had a black eye and blood drying under her nose. It took both of the boys a minute to recognize the beaten woman in the cell.

It was Adrianna Cord.

Her tears were leaking down her cheeks and catching on the gag that had been stuffed into her mouth. On top of the gag was a piece of rope that went between her lips and around her head, to stop her from spitting out the gag. As the sounds adjusted and came through to Cremont and Dash, they heard screams. The screams didn't come from the bound Adrianna, because it was obvious that she couldn't make a sound if she wanted to. Instead, the sounds came from the cell nearby, and suddenly Cremont and Dash both understood.

The mother's torture was to listen to the torturing of her son.

The pond magic shifted again, and more light came into the picture. The boys were looking down on another cell, yet this one had the door to it open with light streaming down into the room.

Martin Cord sat in the corner, in much the same manner as his mother in the previous cell, except his mouth hadn't been tied. His eyes were both swollen, but not from any sort of beating. His eyes were red with tears. Signs of beating were all over the rest of Martin, though. His cheeks were skinned, and his nose was still dripping blood.

Martin was kneeling, and over him stood Lord Bonnevist.

Cremont and Dash had fought him hundreds of times in the last week, but the reality was an imposing figure when compared to the illusion. He was dressed all in black and blended in to the cell perfectly. It looked as if his head and hands were only floating parts of him as he moved about. His bald head managed to shine in the dim light and his eyes were a penetrating gray that looked as if they alone were the cause of all of Martin's injuries.

"Where," Bonnevist demanded, "would the Farthing boys take you when you would...play?"

Martin opened his mouth to answer, it was obvious that he was willing to give anything that Lord Bonnevist asked of him. Martin wasn't given the chance to speak.

As Martin opened his mouth, Bonnevist punched him in it. A tooth flew from the boy's head and made a faint clatter as it hit the stone floor.

"Have the boys ever shown you that they were Magic-Born?" Lord Bonnevist backhanded Martin, again before he could answer. Martin fell back and hit the stone wall. Lord Bonnevist grabbed him by the collar of his blood-soaked shirt and righted him.

The scene faded back to the previous cell, and Adrianna was screaming through her gag, trying her hardest to show her son that she was there, that Martin wasn't alone.

The gag was too tight, and no noise escaped.

Martin was back in the ripples of the water. Bonnevist had stopped asking questions and made no pretense about beating Martin. It wasn't long before Martin was limp and unconscious.

Lord Bonnevist wiped his bloodied hand on his nearly invisible cloak and then reached down with both of his hands and grabbed Martin by the sides of his head.

Although he was still unconscious, Martin's eyes went wider than either of the Farthing twins had ever seen them go. His eyes rolled up and into his head and the whites were all that could be seen.

The pond itself shuddered and the image changed into pictures that Cremont and Dash both recognized.

Martin and Dash were swimming in the lake.

A young Cremont was pretending to battle with wooden swords with Martin and Dash.

Running through the corn, chasing close behind Cremont.

Dash asking Cremont about getting feed for Martin's horse.

They were memories. Memories of Cremont and Dash. Martin's life of knowing the boys. Lord Bonnevist was taking all of Martin's memories.

He was learning everything that he could about Cremont and Dash.

The Farthings were filled with rage and terror. The emotions were so mixed they didn't understand what they felt toward which parts. The confusion was part of the terror.

Dash was barely holding onto the image as he kept his tears back. Cremont wasn't capable of keep his emotions in check.

A tear fell from Cremont's cheek and landed in the water. The ripple of the tear hit the edge of the image and the image shuddered before switching back to the scene of Bonnevist holding Martin's head upright by Martin's hair.

Lord Bonnevist tossed Martin's head back, letting the boy fall from his grasp. He turned and looked directly through the pool and at Dash and Cremont.

"Boys," his voice was heavy with forced empathy. "I am truly sorry for what you have had to see. I'm very eager to meet you."

Cremont looked at Dash with fear in his eyes. "Can he see us?"

"Yes," Lord Bonnevist answered. "I can see you, and what a pleasure it is to finally meet you."

Dash tried to show strength, but his voice came out weak. "Let them go."

"I will. One way or another. Of that you have my word." He held up his hand. "But not one moment before you give me Excalibur."

Cremont answered before Dash did. "We won't do that. The sword is meant for only the right people. It is forbidden for the sword to be handled by the Magic-Born."

"You will bring me the sword." Bonnevist shrugged like they were discussing the weather. "Camelot means nothing to me other than the legacy it carries. If you don't bring me Excalibur, I will destroy first the people you love and then the rest of the kingdom. I will be slow about it, and I will make you feel every death."

Dash's face twisted with anger. "We won't do it. You can't have the sword."

Lord Bonnevist pulled a necklace out from under his cloak and held it out for the boys to see. He blew on it gently and suddenly the room was filled with light.

Standing next to Lord Bonnevist was Evelyn Farthing. The boys gasped in shock, their hearts leapt into their throats. Although they could see through her, it took them a moment to realize that she was a ghost. Once the realization dawned, the hope that she was still alive was shattered and tears poured from their already emotional eyes.

Then, they recognized that she could see them. Evelyn was looking at them with a smile on her lips but fear in her eyes. She was scared of the man that she stood next to and the promises that he made, and she had every right to be.

"I will do all of that," Bonnevist continued, "and I will make your grandmother watch. She will be there when I kill you and take the sword from your hands." He held his hands out as if to say that it was their decision now. "Or you can give me the sword and I will release the Cords and give you the amulet to do with as you please." He smiled and it was a predatory thing. "I will even give you a public pardon and we can tell the people that Martin is the bastard offspring of Thordon and the rightful heir to the throne. This could all work out very nicely if you just *give me Excalibur*."

His words echoed through the ripple and the boys could feel the command trying to root itself into their minds. It almost found purchase, but the boys had been practicing all day, and the power of Bonnevist's words glided around their brains for only another moment before giving up.

Cremont's rage bubbled up and he slapped the pond's surface. Dash released the image and fell back onto his heels.

"What do we do now?" Dash asked, his rage bubbling within him but nowhere near as visual as the stomping around of Cremont's rage.

"We find him, we free Camelot, and we kill Bonnevist!"

"Arthur!" Cremont was calling out to the former King. "I know you can hear me. Where are you?"

Dash wasn't calling, but he wasn't going to stop his brother from calling either. Instead, he called out with his mind.

Lady of the Lake, please come to us.

"Why aren't they answering us?" Cremont demanded to no one in particular.

Dash answered his brother anyway. "They aren't answering us because they know why we're calling them."

Cremont threw up his hands and, as one, the brothers stomped away from the pond.

A thud of invisible force hit them both in the chest and knocked them to the ground. Suddenly, they were looking up at King Arthur.

The deceased king glared at the twins. "You aren't ready to leave yet." He threw up his hands. "Hell, boys! You will never be ready. Bonnevist is goading you into a fight and you're taking his bait. He has the power of hundreds of wizards coursing through his body, and you think that you could ever be prepared to fight him?"

As the boys stood, Dash replied, "We have a plan. We are going to convince the people and then we will fight him. It won't be only us; we will have truth and right on our side."

Arthur huffed. "That and a sword and you'll have a sword." A lot of Arthur's fire died down then. "I love your spirits, boys, and if fights could be won on spirit alone you would have already taken back my throne." He shook his head at them. "If you leave now, then you'll be giving Bonnevist what he wants. You will be handing him Excalibur."

"He has Gran!" Cremon roared. His eyes were filled with emotion.

"Your Gran is dead!" Arthur countered just as loudly. "Fight for the living!"

Dash said, much quieter, "Bonnevist is holding all of Camelot hostage and will kill everyone if we don't go to him."

Arthur rubbed his temples. "Don't you boys get it? Camelot is more than the people; it is the idea. The people will come and go, but without the beacon of hope that is Camelot many more will suffer." Arthur was pleading with them. "The light of Camelot has almost gone out under Bonnevist's rule. If you give him the sword, the light will go out all together and many more people will die than are in Camelot."

"You can beg and bargain with us," Cremont said. "We know that you're right, but we cannot sit here and do nothing while he keeps his promises of death."

A voice from behind them, at the pond, startled Cremont and Dash, spinning them around. "Then you must go. Your hearts are true, and Arthur is proof that sometimes," the Lady of the Lake looked at Arthur with rebuke in her eyes, "all that you need is what is right and a sword."

Dash almost smiled, but the weight of what they were going to do still weighed heavily on his mind. "How do we leave?"

"The same way that you do anything in here." The Lady answered. "Will it and make it so."

Cremont raised an eyebrow to her. "Could we have left at any time?"

The Lady of the Lake nodded.

Arthur's face filled with resignation, and he stepped forward and jabbed Cremont in the chest. "You will need to hit him hard and fast, and do not let up." Arthur looked back and forth between Dash and Cremont. "If you are lucky, you can knock him off balance, maybe surprise him. If you can accomplish this, it could be possible for you to defeat him." A last-minute thought caught itself in Arthur's mind. "You must come at him like wizards. He's faced too many ill-taught Magic-Born over the years and his mind has grown accustomed to easy defeats. Plan ten steps ahead of him and then another five."

The Lady of the Lake's voice held no emotion, but the importance of her words resonated within the minds of the two boys. "In everything that you do, do not forget your purpose. Yours is to save Camelot and find the new King, the rightful heir to Excalibur. While they are separately defined, they might be jointly solved."

The boys said their goodbyes. They were eager to be on their way and made each farewell very brief, clasping arms with Arthur and giving a gentle hug to the Lady of the Lake.

Closing their eyes, the boys focused on not being in the realm of the Lady of the Lake and then faded from Arthur's sight.

"They'll die," Arthur said sadly. "We should have made them stay."

A wrinkled, old hand clasped Arthur's shoulder. "You could no more have made them stay than you could carry the moon." Merlin smiled through his beard at his old friend. "The Mantel has been idle too long and demands to be out of its scabbard."

The Lady of the Lake smiled to herself.

"They are far from ready, old man."

Arthur replied. "The Mantel will get them killed."

"They said the same thing about a king a few years back," countered the wizened wizard. "Look what he accomplished."

Arthur looked at his friend and frowned. "I hate it when you get all argumentative."

"No, you don't."

"Shut up."

Chapter 10

If it hadn't been for the Lady of the Lake's unusual manner of changing the environment on Cremont and Dash when they were battling, they would have drowned when they left her realm.

As they faded from her world and back into reality, they returned immersed in water. Assuming nothing, the twins had held their breath when they'd willed themselves out of the Lady's world and it had saved their lives.

It was completely dark, and they couldn't see anything. It was only by sheer luck and hope that they managed to swim to the surface instead of deeper. Once they broke the surface, they silently thanked the Lady that they were in a lake and not some never-ending expanse of ocean.

Dash emerged from the surface with a gasp for air. He wiped his eyes and tried to look around the lake. Any other night and he wouldn't have been able to see much of anything, but just over the tops of the trees sat the moon, giving him just barely enough light to see by. As it reflected over the lake, it took Dash only a minute to locate his brother. He swam toward Cremont.

"Where do you think we are?" Dash asked his brother as he reached him.

Cremont wiped his hand back and over his brow, pulling his hair out of his eyes. "I don't know. I think we're in the lake that swallowed us." He looked around. "Come on." He pointed to the shore. "We need to get out of the water."

Together they swam toward the moon and the nearest shore. Pulling themselves out, they rested their weapons and their cloaks out on the grass, off the beach. It was as Cremont was removing his cloak that he noticed the additional weight at his side.

"What is that?" Dash asked when his eyes fell on the dim image attached to Cremont.

Cremont unbuckled a belt that Dash hadn't realized Cremont was wearing and held the newfound item up to his face. "It's Excalibur. I didn't expect it to...attach itself to me."

"It's our purpose." Dash added. The sight of the sword in the moonlight finally made the reality of their situation click. They were alone. No more would they have the protection of the Lady of the Lake to watch over them. Arthur was incapable of reaching into this world and defending them. Now they held the sword, Excalibur, and they held its future. They had to find the future owner of the sword, the future of the Mantel, and the future king of Camelot.

That was so far down the road, though. They need to do so much to prepare the way for this would-be king.

Dash was overwhelmed with the thought of it all and almost collapsed to his knees until Cremont burst through his thoughts. "We need to get away from the lake. Maybe we should set up camp further into the woods."

Dash agreed and collected his gear as Cremont did the same. Dash noticed that as Cremont put the fabled sword back at his side that Dash's own eyes fought to notice it. That would make traveling with the sword much easier than either of the boys had expected it would be.

Out of habit, Cremont started from the lake in the same direction they'd traveled every time the Farthings had left the lake in the past. He was heading back home.

"Cremont, wait!" Dash's voice was an excited whisper. "Look at what you're doing. We can't go that way."

Cremont stopped and then looked at what he had been about to do. "Do you think they are still looking for us?"

"You know that they are, it has only been a day out here. Besides, home is the first place that they'll keep the Guard. We can't go back." He hesitated before adding. "Not yet."

"The other direction, then." Cremont agreed. "It will be quicker to get to Camelot from the other side of the lake anyway."

Dash agreed but added, "Arthur was right about one thing: this impulsive decision making will be the end of us. We're wizards now, or as close to it as this world has seen in many years. We are going to have to start acting like it."

Cremont hid a smile as he bowed elegantly and asked, "Then what do you suggest we do, great and powerful Wizard?"

"First, let's make camp. A small fire." Dash answered.

They trekked into the forest on the farther side of the lake, taking their time walking around the massive body of water. Staying away from the shore to avoid any eyes that might have been looking at the lake, they stomped through brush and pines, pushing their way as quietly as they could through the forest.

A mile from the lake, the brothers set up camp with a low fire. They kept their clothes close to the blaze and sat close behind it.

"Well," Cremont broke the silence, "I'm waiting, wise one. Regale me with your cleverness."

"We cannot give Bonnevist the sword." Dash stated, ignoring his brother's sarcasm.

Cremont protested despite the warning look. "He has Gran. If we can't give him the sword, how are we supposed to free her?"

Dash continued to defend his position. "If we give him the sword, then the people he kills will be on our heads." He folded his arms. "I'm not interested in giving the dead King of Camelot a chance to tell us that he told us so."

"I know that!" Cremont spat into the fire. "We're left with few other options. How do we keep the sword from Bonnevist without Bonnevist killing anyone?"

"As well as convince all of Camelot to see him for what he is?" Dash added. His face turned grim. "He will kill people. I don't know if anyone could stop that." His eyes lit up suddenly. "Or maybe we can."

Cremont looked curiously at his brother. "Are you going to tell me, or do I need to beat it out of you?"

"He doesn't know about the Mantel, only that the power of the sword exists." Dash smiled. "I think that I'm beginning to think like a wizard."

"Oh? Well, at least one of us is." Cremont said.

"We can win this, but you're not going to like how we do it."

Dash went about explaining his idea. Over the next hour and a half, Cremont and Dash put together their ideas and formulated what they hoped to be a proper battle plan. They weren't farm boys going into battle.

They were wizards.

Several hours had passed when Dash and Cremont dressed

again in their dried clothes and picked up their weapons.

Putting his hand over the dying fire, Dash looked at his brother and, with a wild grin, asked, "Are you ready?"

Cremont frowned. "I don't think that I could ever be ready for this, but I'll be damned if you think you're going ahead without me."

Dash nodded and pressed his will into the campfire.

Cremont raised his hands above his head and closed his eyes.

Dash's effort sent the campfire straight into the sky. When the fire was above the treetops it exploded, blossoming into an orb of bright light that lit up the entire forest.

Cremont's efforts were less visible in nature. The sounds of crickets and frogs vanished as the campsite boomed with the sound of thunder. The trees shook with the vibration of the ear shattering sound. Even with the protection that the boys had put around themselves, their ears ached from the noise.

Lowering their hands, the twins looked at each other and managed a feeble smile.

"I'll bet that woke up the Guard." Cremont said.

It was almost dawn before the Camelot Guard had located them.

"I don't remember that many men being in the Guard." Cremont whispered to his brother. "There must be a hundred and I don't see a single knight."

Dash nodded and then noticed something. "Look at their armor." He pointed through the branches of the tree that they had chosen to hide in. "They aren't all from Camelot."

Cremont looked at where Dash was pointing and saw the defining characteristic. About seventy-five of the hundred men had the emblem of the bear on their armor in dark blue.

"Lord Bonnevist has added his men from the North to the Camelot Guard." He snickered to himself. "How many of the Guard did Gran defeat?"

Dash flashed his own grin and shrugged at the idea, but the weight of what they were about to do came down on the smile as quickly as it had appeared. "What about the knights?" he asked.

"It's way too early for the knights to be awake. The Guard must have been on alert for word that we'd shown ourselves."

"When you're ready." Dash encouraged his brother, bringing the conversation to an end.

Cremont nodded and jumped down from the branches, landing directly in the middle of the nearest group of soldiers.

There were gasps of confusion as the startled guards leapt back from Cremont. Cremont smiled nervously at them and that seemed to bring them all back into themselves.

Swords cleared scabbards and in a fast moment Cremont was suddenly looking at dozens of angry blades. Cremont spread his hands in a movement of surrender, sweeping his staff out in his right hand as he did so. Gently, he allowed the stick to touch the ground, but he continued to grasp its end.

Someone behind the blades spoke up then. "In the name of Camelot and the acting ruler, Lord Bonnevist, you are under arrest for the crime of being a Magic-Born." Chains clanked as they were brought from wherever the Guard had been keeping them. "Bind him."

Upon the command, most of the swords relaxed to allow the guard with the chain to step forward. One sword stayed incredibly close to Cremont's neck as the guard came closer to him with the chains.

Cremont spoke quickly, before the guard could reach him. "The one with the sword. The rest are mine."

A lance of energy came down from the tree and sliced into the armor of the guard that held the blade so close to Cremont's neck. The guard lowered his sword and looked at the beam of energy that stuck out of his chest. It glowed, but it held the unmistakable shape of an arrow carved out of light. The magical arrow vanished, and the guard slumped to the ground.

Before the man had finished his descent, Cremont waved his staff in the direction of the guard with the chain. The chain suddenly jumped from the guard's hand and grew in length. The guard was instantly wrapped in it, and the chain didn't stop with him. It continued to grow and writhe as if it were some sort of incensed beast. As it flopped about it would grab onto anyone that it bumped, and soon three guards were disarmed and removed from the fight before the other nearby members of the Guard had caught on that they should avoid it.

Two more lances of energy came down from the tree and killed two more of the Guard before someone bellowed from the back, "Take down the tree!"

Cremont flashed bolts of his own energy at the guards coming at him and laughed with the excitement of the battle. Even with about a hundred of the Camelot Guard coming at him, it was nothing compared to King Arthur and the Lady of the Lake breaking him daily. Behind the enjoyment, he knew that he couldn't continue that kind of attack forever, and he began walking through the swath of bodies he sent to the ground.

As soon as the Guard had turned their blades on the tree, the arrows came down in a torrent like deadly rain from the branches. Four guards fell before the tree did. Once the tree fell, the Guard jumped upon it, hacking and slashing at the leaves and branches. After most of the tree was destroyed, one of the Guard called out, "There's no one in the tree!"

From amidst the rows of guards, Dash called out, "Because he's a wizard!"

The guards jumped away from the voice, turning at the same time and bringing their swords up. The blades all bent inward and away from Dash who was standing between them all. Dash propped up an invisible orb of energy around himself as several of the nearby archers of the Guard loosed their arrows.

His timing was perfect, the shield stopping the arrows and allowing them to drop just as they were about to reach their target.

Bringing his own bow from his shoulder, Dash started using it much as Cremont would use his staff, deflecting swords and slapping aside blows.

The Camelot Guard weren't Arthur, but they weren't children either, and they were learning to test Dash's attacks. He caught on quickly and began to adjust his attacks, changing his angles and adding a little bit of magic to each blow.

Catching one blade between the bow and the string, Dash twisted quickly allowing his magic to strengthen the bow string as he did so. With a quick tug, Dash was then holding a bow and sword in hand. With a twirl of his hand, Dash allowed the bow's length to cover his back while the string held the bow to his chest. He filled the weapons with his will, giving himself an almost indestructible blade and protection for his back.

Cremont stood about fifty yards from his brother, but he could hear the sudden clanging of swords as Dash entered into battle. Cremont batted aside blades and hit people with the added force of his magic behind his staff.

The brothers fought and knew that the fight wouldn't hold.

No matter how much they had learned, they were still only two men versus an entire army. Dash continued to vanish from sight before popping up behind an oblivious Guard while Cremont was pushing through the guardsmen with brute force. Cremont was hitting the men with his staff with such force that they would become projectiles themselves, slamming bodily into their companions.

Cremont was starting to get overwhelmed by more advanced fighters from the North than the traditional members of the Guard when he finally saw the signal. Dash was getting tired, and he knew that if he didn't begin the second part of their plan soon that he might not be able to. With a sharp pressing of his will, Dash lit up the morning sky with another arrow of magic loosed only from his palm instead of his hand. At its apogee the arrow divided into many littler arrows and fell down on the Guard.

With a wave of his staff, Cremont poured flames into men surrounding him, putting as much of his will into the flames as he could. The fire surrounded him and seemed to engulf him.

While Cremont scorched the earth, Dash pulled in all the shadows being cast by the dawn light. The darkness surrounding him was only matched by the sun that had become his brother. From inside the darkness the few of the Guard who had been caught inside began to scream as they became lost and bumped into themselves and other things that they couldn't see. They were terrified and their fear instilled their companions with trepidation. They stood as still as possible, not knowing if they should run away or run to the other guards' aid.

With a flash from Cremont's flames the orbs of fire and darkness, both having grown to the size of a horse cart, vanished. In both places where the boys had stood the ground was smoking even though the grass looked untouched.

The Farthings were gone.

Running through the woods, Cremont and Dash knew that it wouldn't be long before the Guard caught onto their little trick and gave chase.

"How many did you kill?" Cremont panted at his brother.

Dash frowned. "Too many," Dash was panting as well. "But not enough."

An arrow landed ahead of Dash in the path, and he suddenly was remembering running from their farm. It wasn't a happy memory, and Cremont could see the pain in his brother's face. He knew it well and shared it.

The next arrow that the boys saw passed through Dash's stomach and stuck in a branch ahead of him.

Dash fell, and Cremont dove to the ground with him.

The archer came upon them quickly. He had seen them dive into the woods and had given chase almost immediately. As he approached the Farthing twins, he drew his bow on them.

Cremont looked to the archer and began twisting his fingers in his direction as if he were trying to wind a string.

Grass and roots climbed from the ground with a flash of speed. The bow and the arrow were gone from the archer's hands quickly, and he squirmed and tried his best to wiggle from their grasp as they grabbed him next. His movements didn't help him at all and soon the guard was pulled into the earth, the only sign that he'd been near was his bow wrapped in roots on the ground.

"Sit still." Cremont told his brother as he placed his hands over the open wound.

Dash nodded and pressed his will into the wound as his brother did the same. The evidence of their work was slow to come, but soon the bleeding stopped and not long after that the wound closed itself.

Cremont almost collapsed with exhaustion. He hadn't expected that healing would take that much of his power, especially with Dash's help.

Looking at his brother, Cremont saw that Dash looked just as beat as he was, but Dash slowly stood nonetheless.

"We need to split up." He whispered to Cremont.

Cremont nodded. "The plan still holds."

Dash returned his brother's nod. "Stay safe. Camelot is to the south. You circle west, and I'll circle east. We can meet there."

Cremont slapped Dash on the back. "God help anyone who we run into."

Dash smiled, "Or us. I would be alright with a little bit of help coming our way instead."

Cremont laughed and took off at a quick pace toward the west while Dash moved toward the sun.

Chapter 11

Branches slapped against Cremont as he worked his way deeper into the thick brush. He ducked to avoid the periodic slaps to his face, but his attention was just too focused on his pursuers to avoid every branch.

Cremont jumped over a log and then under a low branch, moving with a stealth that surprised him considering his lack of knowledge in regard to this section of the forest. He was familiar with the area in a general sense but had never seen any reason to travel too far into this section of it. Cremont knew that if he continued this way, he would stay generally even with Camelot and able to turn to head in that direction at any time.

But not before he was able to lose those behind him.

Unlike Cremont, the section of Camelot Guard and Northmen that decided to take chase after him weren't trying to be quiet at all. If the scene hadn't been one of turmoil and chase, Cremont would have equated the sounds they were making the marketplace in Camelot. The guards thundered through the woods, hitting every branch that Cremont avoided and hacking their way through the smaller bushes with their swords.

From the noise alone, Cremont couldn't determine exactly how many chased him, but he had to assume that it was a large number. Even if it was exactly half of the Guard that had met Dash and Cremont at the campsite, that was still fifty well-armed and battle-ready men who chased the apprentice wizard.

If it were only half of that, it would still be a daunting task for the very tired Cremont.

Cremont wished that he could say the exhaustion he felt was from healing the wound that Dash had obtained, but that was far from the truth. The truth was that he and his brother were throwing magic as if they were still in the realm of the Lady of the Lake and magic was an easy thing to grasp. That wasn't the case in the world of Camelot and the Camelot Guard. Magic was something that you actually had to reach out and take, and it rarely came easily.

The best explanation that allowed Cremont to understand the magic and its use was that of the air. While Cremont was down and far from the sky, he could breathe very easily, and never really thought about the process. He never had to strain to get the air. By comparison, Dash and Cremont had spent many days practicing with their powers in different settings, and some of those included mountain tops. Cremont didn't understand why, but the air was always thinner at the tops of those mountains. Magic, to Cremont, was like that. When he had been in the Lady of the Lake's designable world, he had been on the ground and breathing the air, but once he and his brother had come back into the world that they knew it had equated to standing on a mountain peak and trying to take in gulps of air.

It wasn't impossible to use magic in the real world, just harder than he had expected.

That difficulty had worn on him both mentally and physically. He was breathing harder than he had during most of his trainings, and he wasn't exactly sure that he could escape the ones who chased him.

As Cremont pushed past another branch, an arrow slammed into it directly next to his hand. It was too late; the Guard had gotten too close to lose. He spun and dropped into a crouch, bringing up both of his hands and holding his staff out horizontally between them.

Although shields didn't come as easily to Cremont as they did to his brother, he had become better at bringing them about in the last few days and had faith in his ability to construct them.

A pressure upon his will, he put up a shield that taxed his energy and watched as three more arrows came at him and his shield. Two of those arrows stopped, inches from his body, and fell to the ground. The third arrow was low and passed through his shield as if nothing were there. He noticed this almost too late and jumped to the side. While his movements saved his abdomen from being pierced, it did nothing to save his leg. The arrow sliced through his muscle and tore through the other side. It stuck in his leg, held in tightly by the muscle.

Cremont fell with a gasp of pain, clutching at his leg. The damage to his leg burned with pain and he tried to keep off it as he fell to the ground.

Cremont's survival skills had been honed, if not perfectly, over the last week of training to push past the pain. Trying with all his might to ignore the arrow lodged in his leg, Cremont stood, putting most of his weight onto his left and undamaged leg.

Straining his will, Cremont snapped the tip from the arrow with a thought before grasping the feathers and pulling it out. He almost fell back to the ground as pain shot through the wound anew.

Blood oozed from the new hole in Cremont's leg, and he convinced himself to ignore it. There was nothing he could do about it now that wouldn't give the Guard time to put many more into him. Instead, he bent, slowly and with much pain, to the ground and scooped up sticks and rocks. He put as many as he could into his hands and rested his staff in the crook of his arm as he held them.

As he stood back up, he noticed out of the corner of his eye that Excalibur still rested on his belt. Idly, he wondered why he hadn't thought to draw the mythical blade during battle, or why no one had seen it.

The first question was fairly easy for Cremont to answer: The sword wasn't meant for him. His destiny was not to wield the legendary sword, but to find the one who would.

As for the second question, Cremont assumed that whatever magic the sword had to go unnoticed by even the Mantel, must work doubly hard on those not related to it.

The leaders of the charge broke through the brush ahead of Cremont then and blasted all thoughts of Excalibur from his mind. It was three Northmen that came through first, and one of them had his bow drawn while the other two brought about their swords. They were panting from the run but smiling in spite of themselves.

Cremont wasn't sure how he felt about his love of the battle. He hoped that this was some part of Merlin that he had inherited. The great wizard had been in untold numbers of battles over his lengthy lifespan and there had to be something to that. Dash didn't mind fighting, and was as good at it as his brother, but when it came to battle Dash preferred to out-think his opponents instead

of overpowering them. Cremont was clever, and on many occasions had shown to have a great ability to demonstrate just how
clever as he avoided the Camelot Guard as a child or only barely
defeated his twin in practice, but that wasn't what he enjoyed
doing. He loved the honor and the might, the sweat and the blood
of a fight.

Cremont felt certain that Merlin did as well.

Cremont flashed his own smile very quickly before tossing the
contents of his hands out and toward the Northmen.

The guards flinched as the twigs, sticks, and stones came at
them, and then stopped. All the debris hovered there as Cremont
held them tightly in his will. The guards could only stare as they
tried to figure out what it was that Cremont was planning.

With a release of his will, Cremont let go of the hovering debris
and pushed them forward. Hard.

Each small stone or stick became an arrow, only faster, penetrating the guards. The projectiles passed through the guards and
even managed to hit some of the other Northmen just breaking
through the foliage.

Cremont turned, forgetting about his leg, and made to run.
Instead, he fell as the pain of his leg reminded him that it was
there. He stood as quickly as his leg would allow and brought his
staff forward. He leaned on it, but he also held it ready for the fight.

The guards that hadn't been killed recovered from their shock
and stalked around the wounded wizard. Cremont watched as
more than twenty-five of the Camelot Guard, supplemented with
Northmen, came to surround him.

"For the last time," spoke the nearest member of the Guard,
"you are under arrest by the order of Lord Bonnevist. Stand down
so that we can take you in without harming you."

"That wouldn't be any fun, though." Cremont gave a half
smile. He looked at the guard and realized that he recognized
him. He didn't know his name, but he knew his face. The guard
had worked under Samuel Grand and had been one of his reg-
ulars. He was probably just like Samuel and had a family back
in Camelot. "I beg you, walk away. Just leave me here because if
you stay you might succeed and capture me, but many of you will
die." Cremont frowned. "I really don't want that. I want you all to
grow to be old men, holding your grandbabies and complaining
about the weather." He shook his head. "But if you press this, I will

defend myself. My purpose is greater than your orders. I will take many of you to your deaths. Please, consider this."

The guard obviously knew Cremont as well, and smiled, amused by the notion that the trouble-maker kid from Camelot could ever pose a threat to the Camelot Guard. He had somehow chosen to see Cremont for who he was, and not what he and his brother had just done to his guards. He was stupid, and Cremont knew his answer before he spoke it.

"Do you have anything else to say before we arrest you?" A Northman with manacles began to step forward.

"Yes," Cremont said, gripping his staff tighter. "I'm sorry for what I must now do."

All the Guard and Northmen were laughing, some nervously, but all in ignorance.

Cremont sadly lifted his staff and pointed it at them all. Focusing his will, he fell back on a trick that the Lady of the Lake had said had helped many wizards when focus was hard to find. He spoke his spell, and his spell was simple.

"Fire."

Spinning on his good leg, Cremont raised his staff and aimed it at the oncoming guards. Fire erupted from the end of his staff and cast itself over each of them. Trees caught fire and the earth was scorched. The guards hadn't expected the intense fire to come from the twin and were caught in the wave of heat and flame as it licked their flesh.

Cremont continued to spin and aim the staff at each of the guards surrounding him. The screams tried to penetrate his wall of concentration, but he just kept chanting "Fire. Fire. Fire," at the top of his lungs.

Suddenly, the exhaustion that Cremon had been feeling overtook him and he collapsed to the ground, oblivious to the pain in his right leg, and allowed the fire to recede.

On his hands and knees, Cremont looked around at what he had done. The Guard and Northmen that had found him were mostly dead. Those that hadn't died from the flames would be dead soon. In the back of his mind, Cremont knew that he should put them out of their misery, but he couldn't bring himself to do it. Instead, the new wizard lowered his head and wept, not caring for how loud he was.

When he raised his head, Cremont noticed that he was no

longer alone. Cremont stood slowly and watched as three very large Northmen walked among the smoking corpses.

As if it was part of their everyday lives, the men plunged their swords coldly into the men who hadn't died yet. Once they were done, they all turned to face Cremont.

No words came as they lunged for the exhausted Cremont with their swords raised.

In that moment, Cremont was no longer standing in the scorched forest. Instead, he and his staff were standing in a plain field, surrounded by tall grass. He turned and King Arthur faced him.

"Are you ready?" The dead King was smiling at him.

"Probably not, but since when did that matter?" Cremont answered.

Arthur answered with only a nod and lunged at Cremont much as the Northmen had just lunged at him.

Arthur was everywhere at once, attacking from several different angles, slashing and swinging with his sword. Cremont moved faster than he thought that he could, given his exhaustion and pain, and swung his staff to block every attack that Arthur sent. Arthur's managed to get inside Cremont's defenses once and sliced him along the chest.

Cremont jumped back and tried to shake off the pain. Shaking his head, he no longer saw Arthur, but instead two of the Northmen still coming at him in an attack. The blade of the nearest and biggest of the two was dripping with what Cremont assumed had to be his blood. Casting his eyes to the ground, Cremont saw that the third Northman was dead with his neck at an awkward angle.

As the Northmen raised their blades again, Cremont was back to fighting with Arthur. Arthur's sword swiped at Cremont's face, and Cremont went under it, bringing his staff up and adding to the momentum of the blade. Using his free hand, Cremont punched at Arthur's throat, passing through the ghost. Arthur smiled, but Cremont knew that he'd struck a great blow.

Suddenly, Arthur was behind him. Cremont spun and brought his staff around like a club. The staff went through the ghost King's legs. Cremont allowed his momentum to carry him around and he brought the staff up over his head and down onto Arthur's, dragging it down through his ghostly presence and slamming it into the ground with a heavy thud.

Arthur put his sword away and nodded to Cremont. "Get yourself some help. You'll bleed to death if you don't get help soon."

Cremont didn't get a chance to respond as Arthur and his field of tall grass vanished and was replaced by the scorched earth, the smell of smoldering corpses, and three newly dead Northmen.

Looking down at his chest, Cremont saw that the cut was deep. He tried his best to stop the bleeding with a little bit of dirt and then, using his staff, continued on his path back toward Camelot. He was confident that this had been all of the Guard that had followed him and hoped that his brother had fared equally as well.

The house of Gregory Rogan wasn't anything like his shop. An old and alone man, he had chosen to put his cleanliest efforts toward his wares. His home had become his place of storage and sleep. Along the walls and all over the tables were different vegetables, hanging meats, and shiny trinkets that the ladies of Camelot might find interesting, but then again, they might not.

He hadn't slept much that night and had been sitting at his table staring at the grain of the wood since long before sunrise. His entire life had been nothing spectacular, and that had been alright with him. He had never wanted for anything and no matter who ran the government they had never bothered him.

The rulers had all made changes to the world, and he could complain about them with the best of his customers, but those changes had never had any actual impact on Gregory Rogan and his long time in the land of the living.

Until the day before.

He hadn't had much of a family and friends were a dime a dozen, but no one had ever meant as much to him as the Farthing boys. Having grown up without their parents they had clung to the older man even during his grumpy times. They had become a part of his extended family, and it saddened him that they were now gone.

The business with them being Magic-Born or not meant nothing to the old man. He remembered Merlin, only barely, and hadn't ever thought him a monster. Over his years, he had seen so many of the Magic-Born arrested and put to death, and he had yet to actually see any of them do anything that actually suggested to him that they were evil.

A crash against the door snapped him from his reminiscences.

He stood slowly, hoping it wasn't thieves, as it had been several months ago. Digging through the junk on his table, Gregory pulled out a lengthy dagger and approached the door.

"Who is it?" He demanded, not really expecting any sort of answer.

"Not your mother," the familiar voice replied. "Open up before I bleed to death."

Gregory threw the latch aside and yanked the door open, just in time to catch Cremont Farthing as he collapsed.

Gregory dragged him in and placed him on a chair at the table, knocking the jewelry boxes that he had stacked precariously on it. Once Cremont was sitting comfortable, Gregory went back to the door to look out and shut it. Before the door was shut, Gregory noticed that his hands were covered in blood. He latched the door and ran over to Cremont.

"You're an idiot." Gregory said as he grabbed a towel and tied it around Cremont's arrow wound.

"And you're ugly." Cremont grunted through the pain. He grabbed a rag from the older shopkeep and carefully began wiping out his wound on his chest.

Gregory yanked the rag away from Cremont and started yanking the boy's shirt off. "Stop being stupid." He splashed a ladle of water on the wound, making Cremont flinch. "Where's your brother?"

"On the run." He grunted again. "He went east, I went west. We're to meet in Camelot."

Gregory didn't say anything more until all Cremont's wounds were dressed and the boy had begun to look more comfortable. Then he sat down across from Cremont.

"Is it true?" Gregory wasn't sure if he was afraid of the answer or not.

Cremont reached out and pointed at the candle at the center of the table. Instantly, flame lit the wick. "Which part? What do you know?" Cremont asked.

Gregory shrugged. "The Farthings are Magic-Born. Outlaws that killed Jacob Cord and have caused the drought."

"Jacob Cord is dead?" Cremont's heart sank.

Gregory nodded. "There are rumors going around as to how, but in the end they all say it was because of the Magic-Born."

Cremont shook his head. "This is news to me." He moved his

arms and regretted the action, new pain flashing across his face. "We are Magic-Born, Dash and I. That part is true, but we've only killed in defense of our lives, and not until after an archer killed Gran."

Gregory was quiet for a moment. "Where have you been?"

Cremont smiled. "You won't believe me."

"I'm old. I've seen magic. Try me."

"Dash and I are the great grandsons of Merlin. The Lady of the Lake saved us and took us into her world." Cremont snickered. It sounded so silly, and he didn't expect Gregory to believe it, but the man made no move and face against it, so Cremont continued. "Time is different there and the ghost of King Arthur himself taught us to sword fight while the Lady of the Lake taught us to use our power."

"How long were you in there?" Gregory asked, his face still an unreadable mask.

"A little over a week."

"Ha!" Gregory barked. "You trained for only a week? That's hardly enough time to learn much of anything."

Cremont nodded. This wasn't the first time that this had crossed his mind.

"Lord Bonnevist made a move, and we have to answer. He has Gran's spirit captive, as well as Adrianna and Martin Cord. He plans to begin execution if Dash and I don't go to him."

"Do you plan to fight him?" Gregory pressed.

Cremont nodded.

"Do you plan to win?"

Cremont hesitated before answering. "This is more than about winning. You know me and my family, Gregory. Are we bad people?"

Gregory shook his head. He wouldn't be caught with a bad word about Evelyn Farthing on his tongue.

"Magic-Born are just people. Some can be good, and some can be bad, but they are just people and if they are trained correctly, like Dash and I were, then they can become assets to any kingdom." Cremont's exhausted eyes frowned. "Lord Bonnevist is a bad one." He saw Gregory's eyes shoot wide. "He kills the Magic-Born so that he can absorb their power. He wants to be the only one."

"Bonnevist is a Magic-Born? How did King Thordon allow it?"

Gregory was genuinely surprised, as most of Camelot would be.

"King Thordon was no one but a puppet of Bonnevist, and he wasn't of Arthur's blood." Cremont shook his head. "The lies of the throne have corrupted Camelot once again." Cremont looked directly into Gregory's eyes. "That's why this isn't about winning. This isn't even about the Magic-Born, although that will come into play. This is about freeing Camelot from the hate that Lord Bonnevist has filled it with. We need to convince Camelot to see the Magic-Born for what they are, and then we need to remove Lord Bonnevist from power." He gave Gregory half of a grin. "Preferably by beheading."

Gregory gave a small smile. "You're asking people to change how they think and how they've thought for years. How do you plan to do that?"

Cremont's exhaustion vanished as he smiled even wider and, seemingly from the air, drew a sword. He set it on the table and enjoyed Gregory's shock as he said, "With this. With Excalibur."

Chapter 12

His abdomen was killing him.

Dash's wound had been healed through Cremont's and his joint efforts, but he couldn't help feeling that maybe they should have tried to put some more magic into it.

Of course, Dash was only slightly distracted by that. His main concerns were the legion of Camelot Guard and Northmen coming at him through the woods.

The section of forest that had been east of their campsite was known as Redder's Patch and had been used for logging by different groups sanctioned by the king for most of the last century. Unlike the rest of the forest, Redder's Patch actually had large swaths of clear ground where trees had been taken down. Normally, this was great for moving people, goods, and logs to and from Camelot. Unfortunately for Dash, this also meant that it was fairly easy to keep up with him.

Never had Dash felt so destined to be overrun in his entire life. Even in games of chase with Martin and Cremont he always felt as if he might be able to reach some point of escape, but as he ran away from the guards chasing him, he could only feel how desperately close they really were.

Hoping to gain some measure of distance between himself and his pursuers, Dash whispered through panting breaths, "Protect me," and forced his will out and into the forest.

In response to the image in his mind's eye, the trees he passed bent like flowers in the wind. They folded on themselves to square angles and together, creating a wall of trunks and branches. It wasn't going to be much, but the Guard would have to go around it and that would slow them down.

Dash continued his run, but he could feel the weight of the magic pulling at him and his energy.

He wasn't going to be able to stay ahead of them, but the trees had bought him some time and he might not have to stay ahead of them.

Running to the nearest tree, Dash spun and put his back to it. He pressed his will into it and then pulled from the tree what he needed. His flesh took on the hue of the bark and then the very texture of the wood itself. Where his cloak was visible it took on the texture and the color of moss.

Once the magic had finished climbing his body, Dash was invisible and in his place was a wider trunk covered on one side by moss.

The magical disguise was all completed just barely in time. Through his eyes of bark, Dash watched as the Guard and the Northmen ran past him. They were so loud that he could have called out to them, and they would never have seen him.

They numbered at around twenty men, and Dash silently hoped that Cremont had had to deal with fewer.

As the last of the Guard ran by, Dash released his hold on the tree and allowed his appearance to return to normal. He turned to head toward Camelot, to the south, and a fist slammed into his face.

Dash sprawled back and landed on the ground beside the tree. Looking up, he saw a member of the Guard and one of Bonnevist's Northmen. They had been lagging behind, probably hoping to catch the wizard in one of his tricks.

Dash cursed himself. He had been foolish and should have waited much longer before revealing himself to the world. He was tired and he was still feeling the ache of the arrow that had pierced him. Leaving his bow on his back, Dash cursed himself again as he remembered losing the sword he'd taken with him during the chase.

The guard turned toward the running crowd and opened his mouth to yell, but the Northman stopped him. "He's spent. We don't need their help. Let's play with him a bit first." The guard seemed unsure about this at first, but then the Northman raised his sword and brought with it the guard's confidence.

Together the guard and the Northman advanced on Dash. They moved slowly and spread away from each other, making it so that Dash could only keep an eye on one of them at a time. Dash quietly prayed that he'd be able to do this without his magic, but a quick glance at the size of the Northman dashed his hope.

The attack came during that quick glance. The guard, filled with excitement that Dash had looked away, took a swing at Dash's back. Dash had expected it and sidestepped it as quickly as he could. The blade bounced off his bow and glanced back toward the guard, as if he had struck metal. With Dash's will infused in the weapon, he might as well have.

The Northman wasted no time, and as soon as he saw Dash stepping away from the first attack, he swung in at Dash's front. He held the sword in both of his hands and swung it like a club at his waist.

It was a clever move and meant to give Dash the choice of taking the guard's attack or the Northman's attack. Against a normal person or soldier, it would have been deadly, but Dash was neither.

Still sensing his connection with the tree, Dash turned his flesh to that of the bark and caught the sword in his hand. Tearing the sword from the Northman's grip, Dash tossed the blade away. The guard at his back renewed his attack on Dash's back and came in fast. Dash spun and jammed his knotted fist into the guard's throat. The member of the Guard fell, clutching at his throat while he choked.

Continuing his spin unheeded, Dash came back to the Northman and batted the larger man's hands aside. He followed the attack up with a solid punch to the Northman's face.

Blood blossomed from the Northman's nose, and he fell over backward. At the same time, Dash found that he couldn't hold onto the power of the tree any longer and was forced to release it. His flesh reverted back to the flushed color of a man who had just been through battle.

Dash knew he shouldn't leave the men alive, but he didn't think that he had it in himself to kill more people. He wasn't averse to the killing; he was actually surprised with how easy it had become. Dash was averse to being used. Every time that Dash killed someone that Lord Bonnevist sent at him he was allowing Bonnevist to use him and chip away at who he was. He didn't like being Lord Bonnevist's tool.

He turned, hoping they wouldn't follow, and ran south and toward Camelot.

Dash only made it about thirty feet when he heard the guard calling after him.

"Stop!" He shouted.

Dash did as the man bade and turned back to face them. The Northman wasn't going to yell, he'd drawn a dagger and was preparing to throw it at Dash.

"Don't do it." Dash warned, but it was a useless waste of his breath.

The Northman threw the blade and Dash could see, long before it reached him, that the Northman's aim was true.

Of course, it would be, Dash thought. *Only the best serve his majesty, Lord Bonnevist.*

Dash lifted his hand in the direction of the blade, and it was suddenly gone from sight.

From the tree that Dash had hidden within, and that sat directly behind the guard and the Northman, the blade erupted. Bark blasted in all directions in the wake of the blade. The dagger passed through the guard's throat as if it were cloth. Its journey ended in the back of the Northman. He gurgled something unintelligible at Dash and then collapsed on the ground.

Dash almost collapsed with him. He had over-exerted himself in transporting that dagger into the tree. He'd relied on the connection that he had made with the tree, and it had been a connection almost too weak to use. His strength had been sapped and he didn't know how he was going to go on.

But he didn't have any choice.

Removing his bow from his back, Dash began using it as a walking stick, propelling himself along the path. He wasn't moving as fast as he would have preferred, but he was moving as fast as his body would allow.

It was around early to mid-morning when Dash finally found signs of civilization. Smoke from a recently doused campfire was filling his nose and he followed it until he found three men and a wagon loaded with sacks. Dash couldn't tell what was in the sacks, but the old-looking horse wasn't paying them or her owners any mind.

Dash could smell the remnants of whatever breakfast they had eaten, and the scent drove his stomach mad. He hadn't realized how long it had been since he or Cremont had eaten. The more that he thought on it, the worse that his stomach felt, so Dash instead chose to focus on the three men.

They were older and scrawny, much like their horse. Their

skin was as dry and tight as leather, and Dash was fairly certain that it wasn't because of the summer drought. Many droughts had brought on that tight skin, and probably the hard winds of travel. While Dash had no recollection of ever seeing these specific men before, he knew what they were.

They were traders, headed to Camelot to take advantage of its world-famous market. Gregory Rogan probably knew these three men as well as their mothers had.

Figuring that only the Camelot Guard and a few Northmen were hunting him, or even had any idea who he was, Dash decided to introduce himself.

Throwing his bow over his shoulder, Dash approached them with his hands up.

"Hail camp!" He shouted.

The men, who had been packing up their cart with their camp supplies, jumped grabbing for daggers and, in one case, a short sword.

"I come peacefully," Dash provided immediately. "I smelled your campfire and hoped that I could ask you for a ride."

The nearest to Dash leered at him and displayed a toothless maw as he asked, "Where are you headed?"

"Camelot," Dash provided. "I am supposed to be meeting my brother in the market." It wasn't a complete lie. He wasn't sure where he and Cremont were supposed to meet back up, but the market was as good a place as any.

"What will you pay us for the ride, boy?" Toothless asked.

His hands still in the air, Dash frowned. "I have no money."

The withered man directly behind Toothless, the man carrying the short sword, jabbed it forward and said, "Let's find out."

The three of them approached Dash and he suddenly found himself regretting his faith in humanity. If he and Cremont ever saved Camelot he would make certain that there would be a screening before anyone was allowed to sell in the fair.

"This really isn't necessary. I'll be on my way. I don't mind walking." Dash was trying to stop this from becoming more than it was.

The third man grunted. It had a cadence to it, as if the man couldn't talk but was trying to. Whatever the man was attempting to say, his companions understood it clearly and nodded in return. "Chop him up first, then we'll search him."

Dash lowered his hands and his frown seemed to take up his face. "That's not necessary at all!" Dash exclaimed, but the men ignored him.

Grabbing at his will, Dash lifted his hands and launched a volley of fireballs from his palms. The fire was dim and as it hit the first man's chest, it barely singed the cloth.

The man stopped in his tracks nonetheless and looked at Dash with wide eyes. "He's one of the escaped Magic-Born."

Dash was exhausted and doubted he could summon even another of his feeble fire blasts, but he chose against showing that to his attackers. "And that was only the warning shot. On your bellies, now!"

Dash's command might as well have been to leap up and down for all the good that it did. The men had seen his meager attack for what it was, and instead of their previous slow approach they took up a full-on charge then.

They were on Dash in seconds, and for all his training and power, he was tired to the point of barely lifting his arms. Fighting just wasn't in him.

They jabbed and punched at him, but they knew that any reward for the horrible Farthing twins was based on them being brought in alive, so they never used their blades.

In minutes they had Dash tied and his mouth gagged. They threw him on the cart with their sacks and equipment and were soon back on their way toward Camelot.

The entire ride was a bumpy and sore debacle that involved Dash being forced to listen to them laugh at him. Grunty was in the back with him, a knife pressed next to Dash's throat. Even if Dash could summon the energy to escape, he wasn't sure he could do so without Grunty plunging his knife into Dash's neck. Besides, Dash had gotten what he wanted.

Not exactly what he wanted, but he was headed toward Camelot and was grateful for small graces.

Bound and gagged as he was, his gratitude only soared when he saw the high walls of the city and began to recognize the sounds. No matter how long it had been for the people in this world, Dash had been away from his home for a week. He'd been without family, aside from Cremont, during that entire time.

He just hadn't realized how much he missed his old life, and the sight of the walls made his heart soar.

As quickly as it had risen, his heart fell when he remembered that his new merchant companions weren't headed toward the market anymore.

The Castle of Camelot was a sight to behold. It had been built by the people, with Merlin's blood and Arthur's spirit. The walls had blackened in the years since Arthur's death, and for the first time in his life Dash found himself wondering if that was related to souls of the residents of the castle.

The cart stopped, finally, directly in front of the castle, Dash was dragged from it and unceremoniously thrown to the ground. He started to stand, but Toothless and Grumpy held him to his knees.

Strong metal boots stomped up to him and Dash's head was almost pulled from his shoulders as a metal gauntlet grabbed his chin.

"Are you sure that this is one of them?" Asked Sir Parker Willingham, head of the Round Table of Camelot.

"Yes, sir!" Shouted Toothless. "I ain't sure which one, but he's got the magic in his blood. Tried to use it on us, but he's beat and weak." Toothless pointed at his shirt where it was still black from the fireball Dash had shot at him.

Sir Willingham pulled the gag from Dash's mouth and demanded, "Which one are you?"

Dash saw no reason to deny who he was. He had been caught, and no denials were going to convince his captors otherwise. "I'm Dash Farthing. Did you order the men to kill my Gran?"

Sir Willingham smiled. "I'm asking the questions. You're answering." He grabbed Dash's hair and pulled his head back. "Where is your brother Cremont?"

Dash ignored the pain in his scalp and held his defiant look. "I don't know. Did you order the Camelot Guard to kill my Gran?"

Sir Willingham slapped Dash with his gauntlet and let his head go. "Lord Bonnevist will loosen his tongue." He tossed a bag of coins to Toothless who turned and celebrated with his companions. "And for the record, it was a decision agreed upon by the Knights of the Round Table, but yes, I suggested it first and I gave the order directly to the Guard." He was smirking as he said it.

"Good," Dash said calmly.

"Good?" Sir Willingham asked as two of the Camelot Guard

grabbed Dash by the arms and began to walk him into the castle.

"Yes, good." Dash replied. "Now I know who must die before I kill Lord Bonnevist."

Chapter 13

The Cord family farm seemed the most likely place for a get together of any kind. Especially since the Cords hadn't been answering the door all day.

It had taken Gregory Rogan most of the morning and some of the afternoon to get the word out. It was difficult, as he wanted to get as many of Camelot's population as he could without inviting along the members of the Guard. He'd called upon his friends in the market and all the nearby farmers and when he'd finished, he had managed to convince a little under eighty people in the surrounding lands of Camelot to come to the Cord farm.

It had taken a white lie to get them all there. Gregory couldn't tell them that one of the recently persecuted Magic-Born was begging an audience with them to discuss overthrowing the government. Instead, he had told them that there was a huge announcement that everyone needed to hear about the recently passed King Thordon. While it wasn't entirely a lie, it almost wasn't enough to get the crowd that Gregory had managed to gather.

Gathering everyone at the Cord farm had been Cremont's idea. The Cord farm had one of the larger fields, and between the drought and the disappearance of the Cord family, that field was also the emptiest surrounding Camelot.

Keeping his hood up, Cremont walked among the gathering farmers and vendors. They all filled the energy of the place with a taste of anticipation and confusion. Mostly, the people and families were enjoying the break from their fields and conversing with their neighbors.

This was the first time that Cremont had been among a large group of people who weren't trying to kill him since he'd learned how to use his power. He was enjoying the feelings and thoughts that mingled thickly through the air as if they were part of the humidity. He could feel everything sticking to his skin.

His own feelings were an equal mix of pride and fear as he walked the crowd. Cremont had only seen a gathering as large as the one at the Cord farm when the people came to Camelot for the markets, and even then it wasn't all people of Camelot, but vendors and people from nearby lands. This gathering was entirely people of Camelot and the pride that welled up in him was so strong that he almost expected Merlin himself to appear.

The fear he felt was in knowing that this same group had been taught, as had he, to hate his kind. The Magic-Born were evil and corrupted all the way to their souls. Cremont and Dash were wanted men, and he had invited all his persecutors to meet him. Everything could go horribly wrong at any second and Cremont had no real plan other than to appeal to their sense of community: to appeal to that which made them part of Camelot.

Cremont was still trailing along the edges of the crowd when he found a face that he recognized. Samuel Grand's wife and daughter were in the crowd, and if it hadn't been for the vision from within the realm of the Lady of the Lake, Cremont would never have recognized her. He quickly moved away from her. His relationship with her husband was known and laughed about by many but most recently his grandmother had been the direct cause of Samuel Grand's death, and he could not bring himself to approach her with an apology yet. From the look of her face, she was in no mood for apologies.

Cremont saw another face as he turned away from Mrs. Grand. Gregory nodded to Cremont as he cut through the crowd. It was about to get started and Cremont needed to be ready, either to protect Gregory or to make a scene himself.

"If you could all quiet down just a bit, I'd like to get started." He said it twice and at the same volume both times, but the second time Cremont had added some of his own will to Gregory's voice and it carried out over the entire crowd. Silence wasn't what followed, but it was as good as Gregory or Cremont had expected to get.

Gregory had climbed up onto a wagon so that he could see and be seen and then went into his oration.

"I have asked you all to meet me here to beg you for your help."

The mumbling of the crowd began again, but Gregory just talked over it, and it died down on its own. "Not since the beginnings of

Camelot itself has this land been in such a heartache." He waved his hand over the dried husks that littered the field everyone was standing in. "Our fields have been dry for months, and the castle offers us no aid. No solutions, not even empty promises. Our farms feed the city, and the city is starving. Why would they ignore our pain? Why would they ignore their own pain?" He paused for breath, but it had an intense effect, punctuating his words with real silence. There wasn't a murmur among the crowd.

"The king, who has a son, has passed on," Gregory put his hands on his hips. "Yet his son, and no other man, has laid claim to the now empty throne. Rumor is that no one has even heard from Thordon's son since weeks before his death and now Lord Bonnevist, a man who has not hidden the fact that his only agenda is that of his people in the Northland, has claimed ownership over Camelot in King's wake." Gregory raised his eyebrows. "And what has he done for us? The Cord family is missing. Gone even through Jacob helped to uphold Lord Bonnevist's own laws. Has anyone heard from the Cords since they have vanished?"

Gregory's question was rhetorical, but Cremont looked at the faces that he walked past in hopes of some sort of answer. He knew, of course, what had happened to the Cords, but he wanted to know if anyone else might. Every scrap of information that Cremont could find on where the Cords were was helpful.

No response was given. The entire field of Camelot farmers and merchants was completely silent.

"Alright then," Gregory said. "How about I ask you a different question then?" He crossed his arms. "How have your market sales been?"

Silence again rang across the field.

"There is a reason for that, too!" Gregory boomed, answering the silence. "Lord Bonnevist has been keeping the roads filled with his Northmen and the Camelot Guard." The silence died to grumbling as the merchants realized that this was the truth. "They aren't actively stopping our commerce, but many of our customers and friends don't like the looks of a menacing guard. Yet, if you were to travel any of the roads that don't lead to Camelot, you would find them without Guard." Gregory sighed heavily, and many of the merchants sighed with him. "This isn't an accident. If the road to Camelot is inconvenient then our customers go elsewhere. Specifically, they go to Reddendale, and then they go to

Lundgate, and then the end up in the Northlands!" He let that sink in for a moment before explaining it. "All of the money meant for Camelot and her people is being *bled* to these other towns. *Bled* to Lord Bonnevist's Northland!" He was shouting then. "Bonnevist has done nothing to relieve our farms and he's choking off our market." His eyes fell on Samuel Grand's wife. "The only lucrative trade in Camelot is to join the Camelot Guard."

Someone near the far edge of the field shouted, "He protects us from the Magic-Born!"

Gregory looked out in the direction of the voice and just stared for a minute. Much to Cremont's surprise, and his hope, no one else added to the shout.

Finally breaking the silence, Gregory replied. "Yes, he does *protect* us from the Magic-Born. But what exactly has he protected us from?" Another cry went up, but it was drowned out as Gregory continued. "He protected us from the Hahn family. Alan and his daughters, yes, I see it in some of your eyes. You remember them. They had solved a problem in the market, only ten years after Merlin had disappeared. The Hahn's had gone to King Thordon and offered their power in service to him, much as Merlin had to Arthur all of those years ago." His mood darkened. "They knew the law, and they told the King anyway, hoping that he would allow them to better Camelot the only way that they knew how."

He crossed his arms. "The King reacted as he always did: He called upon Lord Bonnevist to come to Camelot and interrogate the Magic-Born." Gregory paused. "They were executed the morning after he arrived."

The crowd was groaning, but Gregory wouldn't let them. "Neville Strommer! Priest of our holy church! Some of the younger of you remember him. He never hurt a soul, and even tried to save a few. Neville took confessions and knelt with us in prayer. He married us and he blessed our babies. His prayers still reside over the buildings and farms of Camelot." Gregory grew quiet again. "Then one of us saw him using his gift to light candles. Bonnevist came, he interrogated our priest and friend, and then he executed Neville Strommer."

The crowd's emotional spectrum was all over the place, and Cremont was finding it very difficult to read what they were thinking and what was going on. He didn't need to be of the Magic-Born to sense the disquiet in the group as they grumbled and were getting louder as they argued among themselves.

"Evelyn Farthing!" Even though this speech had been rehearsed, Cremont's heart leapt as Gregory bellowed his grandmother's name. "What has she ever done? Or her children, Cremont or Dash? Jacob Cord was jealous of her crops that would grow when his wouldn't. He was jealous, so he went to the Camelot Guard and turned her family in. Her family had seen horrors like almost no one else in these lands. Evelyn had lost her daughter, but she had her grandsons, and they were her world. The Guard went to her house, and they killed her, but what had she ever done to any of us? She kept to herself, and she raised two boys when no one else could." Gregory smiled right at Cremont, but no one seemed to notice that his smile had a target. "And those boys? They were Hell, but all boys are Hell, and they never did anyone any harm."

There was a response to this, and until directly before Gregory spoke, Cremont hadn't expected it to come. "Evelyn Farthing killed my husband."

It was Samuel Grand's wife, and she had spoken up.

Gregory eyed her. "That wasn't her fault, and everyone here knows it," was his response and while it was barely over a whisper everyone was able to hear it.

Gregory continued. "Your husband took a job that threatened his life daily and how was he rewarded? After he died serving his masters with blind faith, his reward was that his family be removed from their home and thrown onto the streets to fend for themselves when he served no use to Camelot anymore." Tears ran down her cheeks, but Gregory didn't stop. "Your husband might have died at Evelyn Farthing's hand, but she was only the tool. Lord Bonnevist was the murderer."

The grumbling continued to grow until someone finally yelled out, "So what? What can be done?"

Gregory fought to bring his mind back to the here and now. He found that he had to do his best to avoid meeting gazes with Cremont as he said, "At this moment, Dash Farthing has been captured and is being interrogated by Lord Bonnevist. If history stands, it won't be long before Dash is standing beside his grandmother."

Cremont was shocked. This was news to Cremont, and Gregory hadn't brought it up during any of their preparation.

As if Gregory were explaining it only to him, he continued. "I heard of Dash's capture as you all arrived. He doesn't deserve to die. He has done nothing to harm anyone, and his only crime is that of his blood."

Cremont brought his wandering to a stop next to a woman about a year younger than himself and a man who's hand she held. The man was who caught Cremont's attention. He was the man from the vision of the stables. His name was Daron Cross. Cremont could see the love floating between them as thickly as any of the emotions of the crowd.

Daron nodded at Cremont and Cremont returned the nod.

"How can you expect us to fight off the Camelot Guard or the Northmen? How can we be expected to free the boy? What will become of us once it is done?" The voice came from about ten feet ahead of Cremont, but he couldn't see who was yelling it.

Gregory Rogan opened his mouth to answer but was interrupted by Daron Cross as he released his young lady's hand and ran through the crowd to join Gregory at the wagon.

"If we don't act now, together and as one, than it will only become harder for us to act later, and our families will continue to be stepped on. Our markets will continue to make no profit and our fields will continue to grow no crops!"

"Who the hell are you, boy?" Cremont shouted, deepening his voice as he did.

"Cross. I'm Daron Cross. I recently hired on at the stables. I've listened to the Round Table Knights, and I've heard the Camelot Guard. What Gregory says is the truth. They don't make the decisions for the betterment of us, the people of Camelot. They make their decisions based on orders handed down from Lord Bonnevist." He put his hands on his hips. "I've even heard Lord Bonnevist talk to King Thordon. There was no respect in his voice. He held only contempt for our King."

A teen near to Cremont shouted, "Who would lead us?"

As if the teen had summoned it, thunder roared across the sky and the ground began to shake. Suddenly the crowd parted between Cremont and the wagon. It was only a subtle force of his will, but for what came next, he needed showmanship.

Cremont kept his hood over his head and marched to where Gregory and Daron stood.

Before he pulled his hood back, Cremont grabbed Daron's arm and raised it above them. "Daron Cross shall lead us!" Cremont boomed.

Everyone gasped as they realized that this was a Magic-Born who stood before them. Cremont only confirmed their fears by throwing back his hood. "I am Cremont Farthing, and I am much more than a Magic-Born!" He drew Excalibur from its almost invisible sheath. No one there had ever seen the legendary sword before, but everyone knew what they were looking at. The gasps turned to murmurs at the sight of Excalibur.

Cremont was a little surprised. He didn't know if he could make the sword visible, but obviously, as an extension of his and his brother's wills, it was easier than he thought. "My brother and I are the last surviving children of the great wizard Merlin. He was our great grandfather and with that bloodline we have inherited the ability to name the owner of the sword." Cremont felt smaller than the words he sent to the crowd, and he still couldn't get a read on how they felt. "To hold the legendary sword, Excalibur, he should be true in heart, virtuous, and completely selfless." Cremont turned toward Daron. "Daron Cross, since the days of Merlin, no heart has rang as dedicated to the true spirit of Camelot and her people as yours. Take Excalibur and lead your people back into the light."

The silence was deafening. Daron's face was a mix of horror and surprise. Quietly, Daron said to Cremont. "I am no Arthur. I only work the stables."

Cremont smiled at Daron and while he didn't know where the information came from, he knew it was true. "Arthur worked the stables. This only seems more fitting." Louder, Cremont stated. "This choice isn't one made lightly. The sword chooses, I am only its voice." It was a white lie, but already Cremont could see the magic of his words as Daron's eyes lit slightly more. Not only Daron was growing to believe the myth, but so was the entire crowd, and Cremont could finally get a feeling for what the entire crowd felt. They felt pride.

Gregory broke the anticipation by grunting, "Take it, boy!" Daron gave a sideways glance to the old merchant and then lifted his hand toward the sword.

It was killing the crowd and Cremont that Daron hadn't taken the sword yet. As Daron hesitated one last time, Cremont pushed the sword's hilt into Daron's hand and made him take the legendary weapon.

The power of the Mantel surged through Daron, and Cremont

could feel the reverberation from it. Cremont could feel a connection between himself and Daron, and he hoped that Dash could feel it as well.

Cremont turned back toward the crowd as Daron held the sword and drank in its power. "As Merlin pledged himself to Camelot and to Arthur, I now pledge myself to Camelot and Daron." Cremont turned back to Daron and dropped to one knee. "My power is at your disposal."

Daron was still in shock and only managed to continue looking back and forth between Cremont and the sword and his young lady in the crowd.

Daron watched in fascination and horror as then Gregory Rogan dropped to his knees

Next went the crowd, and then Cremont's heart soared. He watched as one by one the people of Camelot pledged themselves once again to the wielder of the magical sword. The last to fall to their knees were Samuel Grand's wife and daughter. Their eyes were both stained with tears as they stared up at Cremont. Inside their emotions battled their senses and they didn't know what to do. Finally, in an effort that seemed to cost her all her energy, she quietly said, "For Camelot," and knelt to the ground. She pulled Samuel's daughter with her.

Cremont smiled.

Chapter 14

Consciousness came to Dash slowly. The first thing that came to his awareness was how sore his body was, especially his wrists. He recalled that when the Camelot Guard had dragged him into the palace, he had been beaten very thoroughly. This was partially Dash's own fault. He hadn't allowed them to take him easily and fought most of the way into the castle. The Guard was afraid that Dash would be using magic on them soon enough, so they started clubbing him before the idea found purchase in his own mind.

The blows rained down from every angle. Dash couldn't remember when he'd hit the floor, but before he knew it fists and boots were hitting him everywhere. A well placed one took him in the forehead. Between that moment and the sudden emergence of his consciousness, he had found nothing but darkness.

The second thing that came to Dash's attention was the smell. Horses living and dying in this place couldn't have smelled as horrible as the stench that filled his nostrils then. He could smell waste and age and death crawling through the walls, through the floor and filling his sweat. The smells also carried with them the magic of the place and that magic was filled with the same vile stench. It was despair and hate with anger and tears. He could feel the terrors of those who had been in there before as they climbed up and into his head, filling it with the voices of a thousand dying souls.

Dash opened his eyes in an effort to force the hate and death from his head. At first it worked. He was in a cell with little light. The cell wasn't much bigger than a stable stall and the cell door was a combination of wood and bars. What little light there was streamed in through that door. The floor had hay and dirt on it, but nothing else. It was an empty room.

The back of the cell is where Dash hanged by chains holding his wrists. Surprisingly, Dash's connection to the magical world, his heritage, hadn't been severed. Dash wasn't certain that he could be, even temporarily, cut off from his power, but if anyone or anytime was best suited for testing it out it was then when he was in the hands of Lord Bonnevist.

As a matter of fact, there were only two things keeping Dash from using his power. The first of which was his muddled head. At least half of the blows that he'd received had been directly to his head.

The second reason was that he had no want or need to escape yet. Dash and Cremont had planned on getting into the castle and freeing the Cords and Evelyn from Lord Bonnevist's grasp. They also needed to remove Lord Bonnevist from Camelot. Staying in the cell was the only way that he would get more information. It would put him halfway to his goal.

Unfortunately, the longer he was there, the less likely he would have any chance of fulfilling any of his or Cremont's goals. Lord Bonnevist was going to peel away the layers of Dash. He had him right where he wanted him, and it was very unlikely that Dash was going to survive through more than one or two of Lord Bonnevist's famous interrogations.

As if the very thought had summoned the images from the walls, Dash's mind was suddenly assailed by the past history of the cell.

Lord Bonnevist walked in, the door creaking open, and Dash was no longer himself. Instead, he was a little girl, hanging by the chains and her feet couldn't reach the ground. The chains were cutting into her wrists. Lord Bonnevist smiled the warmest smile at him, at her, and asked, "Are you comfortable?"

Lord Bonnevist walked in, the door creaking again as he opened it, and Dash was no longer the little girl. Instead, he was an older man, his brow had been cut and blood streamed into his eyes. The chains were loose, and he felt as if he could almost slip out of them. Lord Bonnevist smiled warmly at him and asked, "Are you comfortable?"

Lord Bonnevist walked in, the door's creaking echoing over and over again. A hundred times he entered that cell. A thousand times he gave a warm smile looking at whoever Dash was.

A young woman on the floor.

A little boy with tears streaming through the mud caked on his face.

A grandfather screaming so loudly that his throat bled.

A father praying silently, begging God to protect his family.

Each smile ended the same way.

"Are you comfortable?"

The assault washed over Dash, and he was as a man facing the ocean. It hit him hard, and he was drowning in it.

"I asked you if you were comfortable. It's rude not to answer. Didn't your grandmother teach you that?" One of the Lord Bonnevists wasn't smiling warmly at Dash. One was beginning to frown, and after his muddled mind had managed to sift through the magic fueled memories of his cell, Dash realized that one of the Lord Bonnevists was actually talking to him.

Dash doubted that he had a clever response in him and chose to stare at Lord Bonnevist as he dragged a chair into the cell and stood beside it.

Lord Bonnevist sat down in the wooden chair and leaned forward, looking up at Dash. "Allow me to explain a little about how this is going to go." He pressed his hand forward and held it just inches away from Dash's bare abdomen.

Dash howled as a white-hot pain sizzled underneath his skin. Immediately, Dash brought up his defenses, blocking the magical attack. In a swift swipe of Lord Bonnevist's other hand Dash's defenses crumbled, and the pain returned. Dash attempted to bring his defenses back up, but his mind was still too foggy from the attack to form any sort of force of will.

The fire burned along his abdomen and spread upward and into his chest, and Dash knew that when it touched his heart it had the potential to kill him.

Sudden relief washed over him as Lord Bonnevist pulled his hand away. Dash realized that he'd been crying and didn't even notice it until the pain was gone and his cheeks were soaked with his tears.

"If I ask you a question, you are going to answer. You will experience less pain by answering my questions truthfully." Lord Bonnevist smiled. "You will still experience pain, but not as much as you will if you remain quiet." He paused, locking eyes with Dash.

"Am I understood?"

Dash forced a smile and said nothing.

Lord Bonnevist didn't even lift his hand and Dash's every inch of skin was suddenly filled with pain. His body curled as much as it could in his hanging position. When the pain finally stopped, after what felt like hours but was certainly only minutes, Dash could feel fresh pain in his wrists where the shackles had been the only thing that had supported his weight during the attack.

"This is silly of me, and we both know it. We should be holding a civilized conversation." Lord Bonnevist's smile returned. "Let's start with something simple. The bond between twins is a magically powerful thing, and even more so in those that are Magic-Born." He poked Dash in the ribs causing a sharp yet mild jolt of pain. "Where is Cremont?"

Dash answered honestly when he said, "I don't know."

"Why don't I believe you?" Lord Bonnevist jabbed Dash in the ribs again.

Dash gasped before answering. "Because you don't understand the bond I have with my brother."

Lord Bonnevist let out a bark of a laugh. "You are correct. I don't understand your bond with your brother. Please enlighten me."

Dash saw no reason not to. "I know his heart. I know his feelings. I know that right now, wherever he is, he's both filled with fear and pride. Before you came in here, I felt a sharp pain of anger. He was told something, and that fear he felt changed from a fear of many and turned into a fear of one. Through it all, he still has that pride. Something, whatever he is doing right now, is filling him with pride." Dash was feeling strength flow into him as he thought more on Cremont. "Our bond is of the heart and that is all."

Lord Bonnevist nodded slowly and ran a hand over his bald scalp. "Dash, that is very helpful. It will be even more helpful when I've captured you both. It will save me a lot of time when I torture you both." He jabbed Dash in the ribs and along with the pain a lump of Dash's own meat fell away. "Now let me tell you what I know about your family bonds, Dash Farthing." Lord Bonnevist stood and then walked behind the wooden chair that he had brought into the cell. Leaning against its back, Lord Bonnevist spoke. "Through a poor attempt at consuming your grandmother's essence, I learned that you are Merlin's great grandson and through that I know that the Lady of the Lake has taken a particular interest in your brother and you." Bonnevist's smile was so wide that it looked almost painful. "That means that you have it within your power to give me what I want."

Dash, still bleeding from the recent hole in his side, knew what the evil wizard was implying. "You want Excalibur."

Lord Bonnevist snapped his fingers and two more holes opened up in Dash's torso. "Exactly. Now, how do I get it?"

"You don't." Dash answered. "Excalibur is too much power for you to have."

"No," Lord Bonnevist replied. "I don't get it from you. You don't have it, but Cremont does, and if you hadn't planned on giving me the sword you wouldn't have responded so quickly to my threat."

Dash opened his mouth to speak, but his tongue was suddenly missing.

Lord Bonnevist continued speaking while Dash panicked. "I'm sure that you both had some sort of ridiculous plan of defeating me and freeing the world from my evil grip, but you knew it wasn't a viable plan. The only way to win at all is to hand me the sword and hope that I see mercy and let you leave, maybe with the hope of taking me down when you're all grown up."

Dash's tongue miraculously reappeared and his panic subsided. "What would you know of mercy?"

Lord Bonnevist studied Dash for moment. "Good. Then you know that there is no chance of anything but failure on your part. You will not live, and I will get the sword, even if I must wait until you simple-minded children give it to me. I can wait forever. You cannot."

Lord Bonnevist pulled out a yellow stone attached to a chain around his neck. "And as long as you hold the sword, your grandmother's soul is mine." Dash felt as Lord Bonnevist pushed a small amount of his will into the amulet and suddenly the room was awash in a yellow light. It congealed and came into focus and Dash quickly recognized the sad look of his grandmother.

She said nothing, but stepped close to Dash, pressing her hands gently to his face. Evelyn Farthing's own eyes were filled with insubstantial tears. Her mouth was moving, but no words reached Dash's ears.

"As long as I have her, I own her. I own you." Lord Bonnevist said and instantly pain became etched in Evelyn's features. She writhed and more tears came and unlike her words, Dash could hear her screams.

It tore him apart.

As suddenly as the pain had etched her face, it was gone. Whatever magic Lord Bonnevist held over the amulet it was complete.

Evelyn reached for her grandson again, but before her hand could reach Dash, Lord Bonnevist called her back into the amulet. He slid it back under his collar and then returned to the chair in the center of the cell.

"Tell me everything that you know about Excalibur."

Dash bit his lip, not about to give up any information. As soon as he did so, he heard a voice in his head.

It was the Lady of the Lake.

Like a wizard... flowed into his mind and Dash suddenly had an idea.

Before he could act on it, he felt a surge of energy through him.

Dash could feel more than he ever had before. He knew emotions, pride and fear, his brother's emotions, but stronger and not only his.

Daron Cross.

The name came unbidden to Dash's mind, and he immediately understood the connection.

A smile crossed his face, despite the holes in his flesh.

Lord Bonnevist opened his mouth to demand to know what had made Dash smile when Dash interrupted him.

"I'll tell you about the sword," Dash said and turned his smile inward.

Chapter 15

Daron Cross and Cremont Farthing stood around a small table inside the Cord family home while Gregory Rogan gathered everything and anything that could be used as a weapon by the people of Camelot.

Once the crowd had finished their swearing of fealty to Daron Cross, Cremont had broken up the gathering to discuss their next plan of attack. The decision to attack and attack soon was simple enough to agree on, and Gregory had set about arming the troops almost immediately.

While Daron had been reluctant to take on the role of the bearer of the legendary sword, once he held the sword he took to the role quickly. The discussion in the old farm house had turned into an argument that was leading to raised voices.

Gregory slammed the door open and dropped hammers and blades down on the floor.

"What in the world is going on in here?" His eyes were wide with concern. Gregory jabbed a finger in Cremont's direction. "No sooner do you tell the whole countryside that this stable boy is going to lead us into battle, and then you two start shouting at each other." He swung his arm toward the door that he had just burst through. "They are barely going along with us as it is. If they hear you arguing they will back out. Hell," Gregory cursed, "I wouldn't doubt if one or two of them already ran to Lord Bonnevist screaming of wizards and stable boys."

Cremont waved his hand in Gregory's direction. "See? That is my point. If Lord Bonnevist doesn't already know that we are coming, then he will soon. If we don't move now then we will not succeed."

Daron slammed his hands down on the table top. "We can't go running into Camelot swinging pitchforks and hammers like madmen. They will be cut down before we make it a mile down the road. We need to take some time with them and train them."

Cremont didn't answer Daron and instead returned his attention to Gregory. "It has been like this since we came in here. Whichever option we choose, we risk so much."

Gregory looked from Cremont to Daron and then back. Disbelief was etched across his face. "Did you not listen to a single thing that I said out there?"

Cremont raised his eyebrow. "I heard it all. What did I miss?"

Daron was the first to catch on. "The Camelot Guard and the Northmen are patrolling the road to Camelot."

"And they are looking for you." Gregory added. "For now." He paused. "If Lord Bonnevist knows of our gathering than he will have recalled them."

"He might have sent some here as well." Cremont agreed. "Then now, more than ever we need to strike. Even if they were all in Camelot, the Guard alone is only a quarter of the men and women that we have at our disposal."

Daron was still not convinced. "They are untrained, and we are hardly against only the Guard. We also have Northmen and Knights to contend with."

"The Knights are old and slow. They haven't done anything even closely resembling battle in over ten years." Gregory said. "But you're right about the Northmen, we don't know what their numbers are."

Daron nodded. "I agree with you, wizard. We need to act now or cancel this plan entirely, but it will be leading many people to their deaths." He hesitated. "What good is it if we take Camelot and all her people are no more?"

Cremont was quiet, but he wasn't contemplating the plan. Daron had just referred to Cremont as a wizard. Being called a wizard hummed within Cremont and he felt a moment of pride almost overtake him, but then he remembered something else.

"We're thinking too much like men. Men fight battles with a frontal assault, they hack and slash until the problem is no more." He folded his arms. "That's too much work and too much bloodshed." Cremont closed his eyes for a moment. He opened them before he spoke again. "We also need more of the soldiers to leave the castle before we attack. The fewer men in there, the less likely they will wish to press any sort of attack against us."

Cremont unfolded his arms and leaned against the table, mimicking Daron's stance. "Once they are out, we will go in and shut the gate. Leaving us essentially alone with Lord Bonnevist and his Knights."

It was Gregory's turn to raise an eyebrow. "What will stop them from slamming the gate down before we get there?"

The gate that they were discussing was the main gate into the city of Camelot. Walled in, the city was well protected around its gates. Each gate faced a road and a direction. The gate that they were discussing using was the main or South Gate of the city. This plan would take them to Camelot's front door.

"I will." Cremont answered.

"They will expect us through the South Gate." Daron said.

Cremont nodded. "And it will be quite the surprise when they can't stop us." Cremont smiled. "When they can't stop me."

"Once Lord Bonnevist sees our numbers and his missing soldiers," Daron returned Cremont's smile, "and you just walking through his locked gate, he'll surrender Camelot to us."

Cremont's smile vanished and the Farthing boy knew that it was time to tell Daron the rest of what they would be up against.

"I highly doubt it." Cremont replied.

Daron's smile faded and his look turned confused. "Why? He would be defenseless before us."

Gregory answered for Cremont. "He's a wizard, boy."

"What?" Daron's shock was written across his face. "He's not a wizard. He can't be, he's been killing wizards and witches for years."

Cremont touched Daron's shoulder gently. "It's part of the lie that he's convinced all of Camelot of. Somehow, he gets more power from the Magic-Born that he kills." Cremont's face was one of understanding. He also had a hard time believing that the man who had protected their people for so many years was really the thing that he was protecting them against. "Camelot, and its past relationship to Merlin somehow attracts the Magic-Born, that's probably why Bonnevist chose us."

"How would he..." Daron didn't finish the sentence. "Now that you say it, it all makes sense. How else could a normal man have killed so many Magic-Born?"

Cremont nodded. "At least one of them should have been able to break away, but that was never the case. Bonnevist always kills those he interrogates." Cremont suddenly realized what he said and lowered his head.

"Not this time, though." Gregory closed the gap and placed his hand on Cremont's shoulder. "We'll get him out."

Cremont nodded. "We're getting ahead of ourselves. Camelot must be empty first. We will need a distraction."

Daron agreed. "What will we do?"

Cremont smiled. "You will take our new army to Camelot; I'll meet you there. Stick to the forests and away from the roads. By the time you get there Camelot will be as empty as its going to get."

Daron frowned. "Somehow I've come around to attacking with untrained soldiers. You wizards are clever."

"Let's hope that Lord Bonnevist isn't as clever as we are." Gregory replied.

The entirety of the gathering at the Cord farm only required one good speech from Daron Cross before they were marching off toward Camelot through the forest. There were still many who were afraid of going into the fight, but Cremont had Daron explain to them that with the great grandson of Merlin by their side they would not have to worry about too much combat.

Cremont hoped that he had been right.

His feelings told him that he was. All of the Camelot Guard were family men born and raised in Camelot. They had lived and loved in the walls and the Camelot Guard had become a career choice for them. Their loyalty was to Camelot, and if they were to see their family members demanding aid from a nonexistent government their resistance would wane.

The real problem would be the Northmen. They would be loyal only to Lord Bonnevist and would probably turn on their Camelot Guard allies as soon as they sided with Camelot. The only way that Cremont could stop the fighting would be to end Lord Bonnevist quickly, and if Cremont was going to have any hope of that he would need Dash. Lord Bonnevist would be too much for Cremont alone to take. He could get in, but he'd need his brother to stop Lord Bonnevist and bring the peace back to Camelot.

That was the plan for once they got into Camelot. Getting them in is why he had lagged behind.

Once the last of the farmers and merchants were out of sight, Cremont ducked into the nearby woods. He didn't need magic or the light of the now-visible moon to see where he was going because his was a path that he knew very well. He ran through the woods only barely letting his feet touch the ground and moved as quietly as he could.

It was very likely that there would still be Guard stationed at the Farthing farm, and Cremont did not want to alert them any sooner than he had to. As he neared the farm, he wished for Dash to be beside him, because Dash would be capable of moving between the Guard without any risk of being seen. For Cremont, that would be slightly harder.

He halted before he broke from the woods and looked out among the still tall crops. From where he hid, he could see the last place that Evelyn had been alive before the Guard had claimed her life. Cremont could feel the love and the bonds that the family had shared on the farm. He could almost see every event of their lives played out on the field before him. Cremont could almost smell his grandfather again.

He also realized that while it wasn't the first time that he had felt the mass of emotions connecting him and Dash to that place, it was the first time that he had been capable of recognizing it for what it was. It was the magic of his home.

But it was also his and Dash's past, and he could only hope that Dash and Evelyn would understand what he was about to do and that they would forgive him.

Casting out his senses, Cremont quickly located the nearest member of the Guard. He stood only about thirty feet to Cremont's right, directly on the edge of the forest line. Cremont continued to expand his senses out and could feel more of the Guard surrounding the farm.

In total, he could sense six members of the Camelot Guard. It wasn't many, and Cremont wasn't certain if that counted in his favor or not.

Reaching out to the guard who stood the farthest from his current position, Cremont strained his magic and lifted the man before launching him into the forest that he stood in front of.

In reaction to his spell, Cremont was awarded with a piercing scream and smiled to himself. The scream was answered by every member of the Guard near the farm. Cremont felt the snap of attentions as the other five members of the Guard unsheathed their swords from their scabbards and ran toward their downed companion.

Cremont didn't hesitate.

As the guard nearest him ran past, Cremont walked out of the forest and directly toward the house, knowing that no eyes would be on him.

As he approached, Cremont poured his rage and hate for all that Lord Bonnevist had brought to his home, to his family, to his lineage, and now to his brother into a ball of energy. He stopped only feet from the door and released it into the house that had been his home for the last seventeen years.

The orb of energy blasted the wooden door to splinters and then stopped directly in the center of the home where Cremont held the power in check just long enough to add a little more power to it. Then he released it.

The orb didn't explode or expand in any way, it simply flowed out of its shape and filled the expanse of the home. It had become a liquid fire and poured itself over memories, emotions, mementos, and other scars of lives well lived.

Before the Guard could recover from the search for their tossed companion, Cremont swiftly returned to the woods and then sprinted to catch up with the marching force he'd helped create.

Chapter 16

Sir Parker Willingham stood beside the guard left behind to tend the wall. From the wall he could see the blaze in the distance licking at the already blackened night sky. He knew what farm that was, and he didn't know what to think of what he was seeing.

At first Sir Willingham had thought the people of Camelot had decided to raze the Farthing farm in a show of unity against the Magic-Born. That kind of united front brought forth a strong sense of pride in his people that he hadn't felt in years. He was fully aware of Camelot's slow death, but he wasn't the man who would do anything about it. Instead, he had decided to ride it out until it inevitably consumed him. He long ago decided that he would rather sit on top of a crumbling castle than be the one it collapsed on top of.

This possible display of Camelot's people standing up for what they believed in, no matter how backward he knew it to be, awakened something of the knight that he used to be. Back when he had been much younger and had yet to be disillusioned by the legends of mythical Camelot.

Then a ride had come in, and Willingham still couldn't make out what it meant. One of the Guard had been assaulted by a Farthing boy directly before the fire began.

Why would he burn down his home? Why would the boy go to the farm at all? The boy had seemed intelligent in all the previous meetings between himself and the Guard. This was a move that seemed very much in the direction of imbecile.

The report of the fire was also something he hadn't expected. Previous reports from Lord Bonnevist had stated that whatever power the boys had inherited, it was uneducated. The boys were untrained, yet the previous battle with the Guard in the forest and then the reports of this fire being unstoppable was showing that not to be the case. Lord Bonnevist was either wrong or lying to the Guard.

Lord Bonnevist was rarely wrong.

Yet, Sir Willingham wouldn't hold it against the Lord to lie to the Round Table Knights and the Camelot Guard. If Lord Bonnevist had told them that they would be fighting a fully trained wizard it was very unlikely that any of the Guard would have gone into battle at all.

A sudden thought struck the Knight.

Willingham turned to the nearest guard on the wall. "Take two men with you and don't let anyone near the Farthing boy in the cell. Only myself and Lord Bonnevist." The guard nodded and quickly moved to fulfill his orders.

Willingham winced inwardly as he realized that now he would have three fewer Guard patrolling the walls. He had already recalled the Guard and Northmen from the roads, but they had yet to return. Camelot was facing a frontal assault from a wizard; it was minimally defended, and Lord Almighty knew that the Knights were in little to no condition to fight. Thordon had turned their role into something honorary more than necessary. Sir Parker Willingham had the most recent battle experience and that was over six years ago.

Then there were Bonnevist's people, the Northmen. Willingham didn't know what to think of them. They could fight, and in a battle Willingham was certain that one of Bonnevist's Northmen was worth six or seven of the Camelot Guard, but they lacked something.

Willingham knew what it was, but it made him shiver to think about it. They lacked spirit. They lacked that special something to fight for. The only reason they fought was for that beautiful moment when a life ended. They lived for the spray of blood and the taste of sweat on their tongue. While one Northmen could best six of the Guard in a fight, one guard could outlast ten Northmen in endurance. The Guard were homegrown soldiers of Camelot and proud of their families and lineage. What did the Northmen have? Willingham didn't rightly know, but with the lust for blood that filled their eyes he had to assume that it wasn't a family or children that waited for them back in the Northlands.

Willingham shook the distracting thoughts from his head. He didn't need to be frightening himself with thoughts of Northmen when wizards would be knocking on his door any day now.

As if on cue, a holler went up the along the wall. Sir Parker Willingham felt his hair stand up on end and a chill ran down his spine. This was it, and he had a horrible feeling that there would be nothing he could do about it.

While he didn't understand the words being shouted, he did understand the message they conveyed. Willingham sprinted along the wall toward the South Gate.

"Drop the gate!" He shouted as he ran. "Drop the gate now!"

Before he'd repeated himself he already heard the loud slamming as the iron gate dropped into place along the southern gate of Camelot. He was panting and out of breath when he got to the gate itself and joined the Guard standing watch. There were only six men on the south wall, but Willingham had assumed it to be more than enough to drop a gate and call for reinforcements.

Looking at what greeted him outside the gate, Willingham was forced to reconsider his previous assumptions.

Looking angrily up at the Guard from the ground outside of the walls of Camelot were a little more than sixty farmers and merchants that Willingham mostly recognized. They each carried farming tools and boards of wood and looked ready to throw themselves at the walls of Camelot.

Of course, sixty of Camelot's men were not nearly enough to break through the walls of Camelot.

Then Willingham's eyes moved closer to the gate and saw the man, who looked eerily familiar, standing with his head high and holding a sword directly up into the night sky.

It was the stable boy from the castle.

Beside him stood a cloaked figure that Sir Willingham didn't need to guess at. Pulling back his hood, Cremont Farthing looked up at Sir Willingham and smiled.

"Sir Knight! I have two questions to ask of you." Cremont called out, his arms folded.

"Ready your bows!" Shouted Willingham.

"First, would you mind fetching Lord Bonnevist for me? I would like to speak with him in the castle drawing room." Cremont looked up at the sky. "In about ten or so minutes would be fine."

Only two of the Guard on the wall had bows that they could ready, and they must have recognized some of the men down in the crowd below, because they hesitated to draw.

"The second question that I have for you is would you mind taking a look at the sword currently being held by the man to my left?"

That drew complete silence from everyone on the wall, and Willingham finally gave the stable boy and the sword he held a good look, and it didn't take long before all that Sir Willingham, or anyone on the wall for that matter, could only see the sword. The name echoed among their lips as they each recognized the sword that none of them had ever seen.

"Excalibur," the whisper spread across the wall.

Sir Willingham was the first to break the mesmerizing spell that the sword had over each of the men on the wall. "How did you get that sword, boy?"

Daron didn't get a chance to answer as Cremont shouted a reply, rage dripping off his word. "Watch your tongue, blasphemer to the cause! He is the rightful King of Camelot as decreed by the laws of Camelot and the wielding of Excalibur!"

Sir Willingham didn't know what else to say, so he said the first thing that came to his mind. "Lies! Only the wizard Merlin can choose the next King and he's been dead for years!"

Cremont unfolded his arms and aimed them at the wall. "Only the bloodline of Merlin can deliver the sword to the next king of Camelot." The gate let out a loud creak of noise as if the metal itself was under an intense strain. "I am Cremont Farthing. Now if you'll go and get Lord Bonnevist, I'll show myself in, thank you."

The entire wall shuddered with such force that it almost tossed the Guard and Willingham from its top. Willingham no longer wished to be the man in front of this boy-wizard, and he wished not to lose any men. "I'm going for Lord Bonnevist," he said to the nearest Guard. "Keep the gate down. If they get in, do not stand in their way." He left the wall as quickly as he could and ran to find Lord Bonnevist.

Cremont continued to press his will into the gate. He didn't want to destroy it so much as just lift it. They would need to replace it if they intended to keep the Guard and Northmen out of Camelot long enough to accomplish their goals.

There was another groan from the gate before it shuddered enough to cause dust to fall from the old stone walls. The gate lifted. Only a few feet at first and then, after a long hesitation, the gate rose the rest of the way.

Cremont let his arms drop and allowed his shoulders sag. He was already starting to feel the toll of the last few days. He hoped that Dash hadn't been using his abilities and would have the energy to hold up his end of the battle to come. Otherwise, it was going to be a short and sad confrontation with Lord Bonnevist.

Daron Cross took up the charge and shouted. "Forward, into Camelot, and do not attack unless they attack. We are here to negotiate the release of our city! The release of our lives from the fist of Lord Bonnevist!" His shout echoed across the courtyard as they entered through the gate. Cremont found power in Daron's words and wondered exactly how much of that was his own power coming back to him through the sword and how much of it was just Daron's own strong personality bolstering Cremont's will.

The courtyard of Camelot was mostly reserved for markets and the socializing of the people of Camelot. There were several permanent shops and a place for alcohol, but with the threat of a Magic-Born on the loose they were both closed up tight for the night. The courtyard itself, it being the evening, was empty of the market and stands stood unmanned and naked. The courtyard seemed so much larger to Cremont than it ever had when it was filled.

The few people they did come across belonged to the Camelot Guard and they didn't seem as eager to fight as Cremont has suspected. They backed away from the incoming entourage, but they kept their hands on their hilts.

Once the entire group of Daron and Cremont's followers had made it through, Cremont returned his attention to the gate. The chains were slack. Instead of cranking the gate open, Cremont had only lifted it and had been holding it open by his sheer force of will. Now that they were all in, Cremont slowly released his grip on the gate and brought it down to the ground, allowing the chain to return to taut.

Then Cremont turned his attention to the rightful King of Camelot. "Daron, could you cut the chains please?"

Daron looked at the newly trained wizard with complete and total confusion in his eyes. "Cut the chains? You're the wizard, how am I supposed to cut chains?"

Cremont smiled at Daron. "You are the rightful King of Camelot and are holding the legendary sword Excalibur. How do you think you are going to cut the chains?"

Daron looked at the sword and then back to Cremont, disbelief filling his eyes. He returned his gaze to the sword. As he stared at it, he seemed to be reading something along the blade. It looked to Cremont as if knowledge itself had chosen that moment to enter Daron's mind, and the stable boy was unsure what to do with it.

After a minute of that Daron looked at Cremont again and smiled. He seemed to know what needed to be done. He might have known something more than that.

Daron ran at the chains, which were stretched tightly only a few feet from where they stood. As he approached he let out a roar as he swung the legendary sword. Daron's first cut went through the steel chain as if it wasn't even there. It was only another moment before the second and final chain was dispatched in the same manner.

Now they had stopped anyone from letting the Northmen and the rest of the Guard in. Now Cremont had to make sure that they didn't try to let themselves in.

Cremont bent low and touched the ground at his feet. The ground rumbled and it heaved before a final course of energy rippled the ground and a wave of dirt lifted and buried the bottom three feet of the gate.

"That won't keep them out permanently," Cremont said, turning his sweat covered face to Daron, "but it will keep them out long enough to do what must be done."

Worms burrowed through Dash's flesh. Tearing and ripping at his flesh, Dash couldn't tell if he was alive or dead. He could feel each pop and break of his skin as the tiny creatures burst out of and into his meat. He only knew that the pain he felt must be what Hell is.

Then he remembered the fact that had kept him tethered to the reality of his situation.

Lord Bonnevist was getting very frustrated.

It wasn't from failing to cause Dash any pain, because Dash was a writhing testimony to that truth. Lord Bonnevist was frustrated because he couldn't make Dash do whatever he wanted him to do. It took Dash a while to understand where the frustration was coming from until he finally allowed himself to be open to his magic. That was when he had found Lord Bonnevist's pain.

When he made a command, Lord Bonnevist would attach his will power to that command. Dash had to admit that on several occasions he had felt the subtle pull of the commands, but he had assumed it was just a weak attempt by Bonnevist to control him. It wasn't until he had felt the strength of the power Bonnevist put into the commands that the Dash realized the dark wizard was upset that it wasn't working on Dash.

Meaning that, until Dash, Lord Bonnevist could even control other wizards and witches with his power. Yet, something about Dash made this more difficult, if not impossible.

This little fact gave Dash more hope than anything so far. Bonnevist hadn't shown off Dash's grandmother since the initial attempt to torture him, but he hadn't needed to. Every time that he gave Dash a break long enough for Dash's mind to return to the reality of the cell, Dash couldn't help but fixate on the amulet just out of sight underneath Bonnevist's cloak.

Dash wasn't certain how, but he needed to get that necklace away from Lord Bonnevist and something deep within his soul told him that his chance was going to come soon.

As if the thought itself had summoned an action from somewhere in the castle, Dash could hear the quick stomping of boots down the hall toward his cell. The door to his cell had been left open during his torture. Lord Bonnevist had shown himself to have quite the deep understanding of how to torture someone and closing the door hadn't become necessary.

Dash wouldn't be going anywhere as long as Lord Bonnevist was in the room.

Rounding from the hall and into the room, a Guard came crashing in and almost ran directly over Lord Bonnevist.

"Lord, sir!" The Guard was panting. "Cremont Farthing is in the walls. He has brought a large number of Camelot's people with him, and they are demanding to have an audience with you."

Lord Bonnevist smiled and looked over his shoulder toward Dash. "Tell them to come back later. I only have time for audience with one Farthing."

"Sir..." The guard seemed hesitant to follow the order. There was something that he hadn't told Lord Bonnevist yet. Dash and Bonnevist both had an idea of what it was. "There is a man with him and he carries the sword."

The fury radiated from Lord Bonnevist's eyes and he turned them on Dash as he demanded, "What sword?"

"The sword, my lord." The guard must have been a local, or

maybe he was just smart, because he straightened with respect as he answered, "The man carries the sword Excalibur, sir."

"Leave me." Bonnevist whispered to the guard. Without hesitation the order was followed, and Dash was once again alone with the dark wizard.

"It seems that your captivity has encouraged the brash actions of your brother." Lord Bonnevist smiled. "Whether he believes it or not, he's come to give me Excalibur." The wizard turned to the door. "I'll greet your brother with less hospitality than I have shown you. I hope that your last words to him were heartfelt."

Dash couldn't even remember the last words he had shared with his brother. It had been less than a day ago, but it felt like another time altogether.

Lord Bonnevist turned back to Dash. "I just threatened your brother. Do you have nothing to say?"

"No." Was all that Dash could bring himself to speak. It wasn't from lack of hatred, it was from lack of distraction.

Focusing his will, Dash sent a sharp stab of his mental powers directly into the chain around Lord Bonnevist's neck. The chain snapped and fell through his robes as he stepped forward. Before it could hit the ground, Dash caught it with his will and left it to float to the corner of the cell.

Bonnevist reached him in two steps and grabbed his chin roughly. He was seemingly oblivious to having lost the amulet.

"I am currently deciding if he would be more fun to torture. What do you think? You hardly scream loud enough anymore."

Dash had his mind back inside his head and the words came to him then. "You should bring him and give him a cell near mine. I think the sound of his screams would only further strengthen my resolve to kill you."

Bonnevist let go of Dash and smiled. "That's the spirit I was looking for." He straightened his robe and stepped to the door. "I will give him your best and show him my worst."

He left Dash alone with a heavy slam of the cell door.

Alone with the Amulet.

Dash waited only a moment or two. It was long enough for Lord Bonnevist to fall from earshot and therefore, Dash hoped, allow Dash to move without being heard.

Dash didn't even try to focus his will, instead aiming a blast of poorly honed concentration at the manacles holding his wrists.

With a loud clank of noise Dash's sore wrists were finally released from their captors.

Doing his best to ignore the pain, Dash ran to where the amulet had come to rest and picked it up with all the care that one would show a newborn baby. Looking into it he wondered how something so small could hold someone so grand as his grandmother.

Dash slipped the amulet around his own neck after mending the chain with a little of his will.

The magic was coming so much easier to him now that he'd been out of the magical realm of the Lady of the Lake for almost two days now. That as well as his not using magic at all in the presence of Lord Bonnevist had helped him to shore up his reserves.

With another pump of his energy, the cell door creaked open, and Dash ran out into the hall in nothing but his pants and a rather simple-looking amber amulet.

Chapter 17

Lord Bonnevist was almost glowing with excitement as he stalked the halls of the castle. The member of the Guard who had come to inform him of Cremont's demands had waited just outside of the prison. He had informed Lord Bonnevist of the added fact that they would be hosting the outlaw wizard in the dining hall of the castle. Lord Bonnevist barely heard the guard's explanation over the sound of his own thoughts.

Cremont Farthing had done as he asked and brought him the sword.

Excalibur, which had eluded Lord Bonnevist throughout his entire unnaturally long lifespan was finally within his reach and all that he had to do was snuff out a man who thought himself powerful enough to command the sword and a boy who allowed his heritage to go to his head.

It was almost too perfect.

Lord Bonnevist slammed open the large doors, standing at least twelve feet and very heavy, and entered the dining hall. The room was elegantly designed with golden trim on just about everything. From what Lord Bonnevist had heard, the gold was not the original look. Arthur had preferred the colors of red and purple throughout most of the palace. If that was the case, then that only meant Thordon must have updated the color scheme and Lord Bonnevist had no doubts that gold was all that was on Thordon's mind. When he had first chosen Thordon to be the illegitimate heir to the throne of the famous king, he had chosen him simply because of how much the boy's mind was filled with greed.

From then it was a very simple thing to manipulate and control the new king of Camelot.

Standing on the far end of the long oak table (also trimmed in gold) stood the dirt-covered visage of a cloaked boy and the simple clothes of another boy.

Boys, not even men. Lord Bonnevist had to restrain himself from laughing out loud at the pair of them.

The boy in the peasant's clothes raised the sword, Bonnevist's sword, and pointed it at the dark wizard.

"Where," the boy asked, "are the Cords?"

Lord Bonnevist smiled and nodded, acknowledging the query. "They are in their cells in the prison."

"All of them?" Cremont asked. He was definitely Cremont. He looked very much like his brother and, of course, he held a staff.

*Delusions of grandeur...*the thought came to Lord Bonnevist suddenly.

"Well," Bonnevist answered casually, "you are unfortunate to have missed Jacob Cord. The poor man went to pieces early yesterday." Lord Bonnevist admired the attempt by Cremont to keep his expression neutral. It was an utter failure, but the attempt deserved its due respect.

The boy holding Excalibur hadn't anywhere near the reserve that Cremont did and began to stomp forward. Cremont stepped in front of him quickly and gently placed the staff across the boy's chest, stopping him from advancing. The boy's rage only intensified with the restraint.

"What did you do to him?" He shouted, but Lord Bonnevist could sense how much the boy didn't want to know the answer.

So he told him anyway.

"I imposed my will on him, and through the use of my voice I commanded him to eat himself." The boy stared at Bonnevist in disbelief, so the dark wizard continued. "Jacob Cord ate most of both of his arms before death finally consumed..." he gave a short laugh at that, "him. I could have revived him and returned his arms to him." Lord Bonnevist looked directly into Cremont's eyes at that point. "Yes, I am that powerful." He returned his eyes to the boy holding Excalibur. "I chose not to. I wanted him to die because he served no purpose in this world after he led me to the Farthing woman."

Making a conscious effort not to take the bait that Lord Bonnevist had laid before him, Cremont asked a different question. "Where's Dash? Where are you keeping my brother?"

Lord Bonnevist was only becoming more impressed with the

amount of self-control that this boy, this son of Merlin, continued to show in his presence. The wielder of Excalibur was raging in place and only not attacking because he held faith in the orders of the youth wizard. Maybe that, too, showed a little bit of wisdom in the boy. Lord Bonnevist was unsure.

He had no reason to lie, so Bonnevist told him. "Your brother is in a cell in the prison as well." Lord Bonnevist tried another tactic and added, "He will be dead by tomorrow."

There it was, the little bit of emotion that showed where the real weakness was in this Farthing boy. His brow rosed before he could get it back under control and Bonnevist could feel the rage break through like a blast of sunlight through a cloudy day. Just as quickly as he saw it, the unrestrained emotion was gone.

Lord Bonnevist had found the button, though, and he still had one more card to play.

"Where's my grandmother?" The boy wizard demanded.

"She is in a very safe place." Lord Bonnevist answered.

"Yes, some necklace prison that you hold her in. Where is it?" Cremont demanded.

Lord Bonnevist felt for the chain around his neck was surprised to find it missing. The rage he had seen in his challengers' faces began to fill his own emotions. Bonnevist didn't allow the betrayal of his control over the situation to become evident on his face. It was obvious where the amulet had to be, and he was certain that Cremont's brother was having a tear-filled reunion with his grandmother.

When Lord Bonnevist got back to Dash's cell he would kill the boy then, no longer would he wait until morning.

"I left her with your brother." He forced a smile. "I am not some monster. I did not wish for him to be left alone on his last night alive."

This sent evident confusion over Cremont's face, and even the boy with the sword seemed to calm a little bit. Lord Bonnevist hated himself for having allowed them some sort of comfort. He decided not to allow them the chance to enjoy it for long.

"Now give me Excalibur and you can all be reunited." Bonnevist didn't make any false promises about allowed Dash to live. Adding a lie like that would be detected.

"You must also release Dash. I don't wish for him to die here." The Farthing boy had taken the bait and Lord Bonnevist relished the return of his control over the situation.

"That," Lord Bonnevist said slowly, "was not part of the promise that we have made to each other." He folded his arms. "The barter was the lives of those that I had for the sword. I did not have your brother at the time of the deal and therefore the outlaw child will be executed per the law."

Cremont didn't attempt, or maybe found it too difficult, to hide his rage from his face or from Bonnevist's senses. Warm and heavy, Cremont's rage filled the giant dining hall and Lord Bonnevist loved the taste of it.

He felt the clumsy attack before Cremont could deliver it. To Cremont's credit, Lord Bonnevist couldn't figure out where the attack was coming from until it was already upon him.

The high vaulted ceiling of the dining hall had been covered in decorative chandeliers hanging from thick metal chains. The lighting was more than likely an original from the time of the famous King Arthur as they lacked the over stylized gold coverings of the rest of the dining hall. These large chandeliers weren't gold at all and were instead heavy steel with equally heavy steel chains.

Cremont must have been building up his power the entire time they had been talking, or he must have been more powerful than Lord Bonnevist had expected. The chains snapped with a sharp crack that echoed around the hall and kept the source well hidden from Lord Bonnevist. It wasn't until the nearest chandelier was almost upon him that Bonnevist noticed it.

A quick curse leapt from the dark wizard's lips, and he dove to the side. In the same instance that he dove, Lord Bonnevist sent his own will up and out, filling the rogue chandelier with an earth-melting amount of heat that liquefied the steel.

Molten steel began to rain down, but Bonnevist caught it in his mind and threw it at the young wizard.

He didn't get a chance to see what happened to Cremont. Through the wave of molten metal, a sword slashed, carving a way for the boy to leap through and swing at the head of the dark wizard.

Hardening his cloak to almost the density of stone, Lord Bonnevist raised his arm to deflect the attack. It wasn't until he heard the crack of his rock-hard cloth that he remembered this was no ordinary sword. Excalibur could cleave the fates.

Lord Bonnevist felt the blade bite down into his forearm and allowed the pain, surprise, and rage to flow out of him. The wave of magic that hit the boy with the sword sent him tumbling back the way that he had come.

Bonnevist had missed what the great grandson of Merlin had done to avoid the molten metal, but whatever Cremont had done it had kept him from harm. He came at Bonnevist then, and he flung bolt after bolt of lightning at the dark wizard. They were not powerful attacks, but they came in fast. Cremont would fire a lightning blast from his left hand and then immediately follow it up with a blast from his right hand and he advanced as he continued that rotation.

Those attacks weren't meant to hurt Lord Bonnevist. They were meant to distract him.

Bonnevist collected two of Cremont's lightning blasts and sent them into the would-be king of Camelot. The combined attack blasted the oncoming boy in the chest and sent him across the length of the large dining hall. The effect was instant as Cremont used the emotions he gained from the damage to the boy to fuel his next attacks. Lord Bonnevist deflected the next lightning bolts, but they actually caused his hands pain as he slapped them aside.

Cremont didn't let up and began to roar as Lord Bonnevist's blackened hands deflected fewer and fewer of the blasts of lightning. Cremont was still marching toward the dark wizard, who still stood near where he had entered through the large doors of the dining hall.

Lord Bonnevist remembered the doors then and with a quick wave of his hand he tore one from the wall and dropped it neatly in front of him on its edge. The door was wood, but more than sturdy enough to take the full force of the lightning attacks coming from Cremont.

Lord Bonnevist gathered his breath during the respite. The Farthing boy was much more powerful than he had anticipated. The blood of Merlin was strong within his offspring.

That thought brought him to a newer and slightly more upsetting idea. If one brother was more powerful than Cremont had anticipated, then the other one might be as well.

The thought had only just climbed into his brain when the other door tore from its hinges and swung down to bat Lord Bonnevist into the wall that his will held to protect him from Cremont.

Slamming into that one, the dark wizard almost lost his

concentration. In reaction to the attack from behind, he sent his mind out in an explosion. Gathering all the power at his command he allowed the explosion to ripple out and over the entire dining hall.

The gold encrusted doors squeezing Bonnevist exploded outward first. As his energy touched the wood it lost all ability to keep itself together and fell in splinters around the older man. The wave of energy then hit the table and its companion chairs. The power had the same effect on them that it had previously had on the doors. They fell to the ground in splinters, only faded memories of what they were.

The wave hit Cremont and knocked him into the air. Invisible blades crashed into his flesh and tore at his mind. He rode an invisible wave of pain very similar to the smaller tortures that Bonnevist had used on his brother.

As the pain flayed his skin from his body and tossed him into the air, Cremont kept hurling lightning. The blasts struck Bonnevist in his chest and in his face, and they arced burns over his body and set his robe on fire. His power already released, Bonnevist jerked with the power of the lightning racking his entire body and fell to the floor.

The table continue to explode as Bonnevist's wave rolled outward, yet it managed to miss the area directly behind Lord Bonnevist as Dash came running into the room.

A blind man could see the power in the room, and Dash was far from blind. His eyes fell first on his still airborne brother as his bloodied body fired more and more power in Dash's general direction. Dash followed the course of the attacks and allowed his eyes to take in the jerking, yet evidently still strong, body of Lord Bonnevist. Bonnevist was slapping some of the bolts away as his robe burned, but Dash could send the power of the still expanding wave of power and knew that it came from the spasming wizard. Dash ran forward, about to tackle the dark wizard when another figure came into his view.

Dash didn't know his name, but he knew who he was. He was the man who Cremont had chosen to wield the Mantle of Excalibur in the charge for Camelot's freedom.

Dash didn't need to approach the fallen man to know that he was dead, and that Excalibur was doing no one any good in his quickly cooling hands.

Reaching out with his power, Dash tore the sword from the dead hero and ran at Bonnevist. Lord Bonnevist saw Dash coming and managed to sidestep the clumsy swing of the legendary sword. The dark wizard grabbed at the hilt in an effort to take it from the Farthing boy, but the blade shocks him with a bolt as powerful as any that Cremont had thrown at him previously.

Lord Bonnevist pulled his hand away gingerly and together he and Dash stared at the sword.

"You cannot take it, it must be given." Dash said quietly, but he had no doubt that Lord Bonnevist could hear his words.

Instead of a reply from the dark wizard, Dash was surprised that the next sound was a crash from the far side of the dining hall.

The wave of uncontrolled power had collapsed, and the bloodied body of his brother had crashed against the wall of the dining hall and fell to the floor.

Dash forgot all about Lord Bonnevist and sprinted to his brother, closing the great distance of the hall as quickly as he could.

He came to a stop sliding on his knees up to his brother's gasping body.

"Cremont!" Dash shouted.

Cremont was a skinless heap of blood and meat. The power had done to his skin what it had done to the wood of the place and had shredded upon touching the dark lord's power.

"Don't move," Dash was whispering in panic. "I will heal you."

He raised his free hand over his brother's bloody chest and began to focus his will.

"Don't," Cremont barely gasped out. "This is all...part of the plan..." Each word was an enormous effort for Cremont to get out. "Come here."

Bonnevist is watching the entire spectacle and doing his best not to laugh out loud. The dark wizard's hands were burnt, and his body was bloodied from the battle, but the sight of the dying Farthing boy was bringing ecstasy to his body. He couldn't hear what the dying one was saying, but he knew that it was only a matter of minutes before he would be finally holding Excalibur.

Dash leaned away from his brother and nodded. Cremont reached up and touched the amber amulet hanging from his neck.

Dash nodded. "I've got her, and I'll get the Cords, too. Camelot will be free."

Cremont nodded, forced a smile, and died.

Dash hung his head and cried. While it was only for a few seconds, they were the tears of true grief and his entire body heaved with the burden.

Finally, broken and defeated, Dash stood and slowly turned to Lord Bonnevist. He walked then, dragging the sword with him, its magical tip cutting a deep furrow in the tiled flooring of the dining hall.

After what seemed to Lord Bonnevist like hours, Dash stopped before the dark overseer of Camelot and knelt. He raised the sword above his head as an offering to Lord Bonnevist.

"Take Excalibur. It is yours." Dash didn't look up at Lord Bonnevist.

With only a small hesitation, Lord Bonnevist demanded, "What trick is this?"

"No trick. You can have the sword." Dash looked up at Lord Bonnevist and allowed their eyes to meet. "This time, I choose to lay down the sword and not fight you as a man, but instead I choose to fight you as a wizard."

Lord Bonnevist snatched up the sword and held it in his hands. No bolt of power surged from the weapon as it had previously. This time the sword was his.

He held it high over his head and closed his eyes.

Lord Bonnevist felt no different at all.

He had expected the power of the Lady of the Lake to wash over him and fill him with its vast fathoms of power. The dark wizard had expected god-like power and was instead feeling nothing different at all.

"What have you done?" He demanded of Dash.

Dash shrugged. "It is not what I have done, but what you have done. You've destroyed Excalibur."

Lord Bonnevist was confused, and the confusion was frustrating him. He kicked out at the still prone Dash Farthing and sent him sprawling onto his back. "What? I did not destroy Excalibur! What is wrong with the sword?"

Dash sat up slowly and began a slow journey to his feet.

"The sword is not, as you and so many assumed, powered by the Lady of the Lake."

Lord Bonnevist looked down at the weapon and some of his rage bled away to confusion. "What do you mean? Of course, it is connected to the Lady of the Lake." He paused as realization dawned. "You lied to me."

Dash shook his head. "Do you really think that she would put her powers in the hand of a mortal? What would the world gain from that? She is wise beyond anything we can comprehend. She would not put that kind of power into the hands of some stupid wizard."

The sharp words and their implication brought Lord Bonnevist's anger back in full force. Whether it had power or not did not affect the ability of Excalibur's blade to cut. Bonnevist brought the sword up and held the tip of it against Dash's throat.

"I am not stupid." The dark wizard resisted the urge to plunge the blade into Dash's throat. "Explain to me why the sword isn't working."

Dash smiled. "The Mantle is broken."

"I am tired of asking questions that you know that you should answer." He put more pressure behind the blade and drip of blood mixed with the dirt and sweat that covered Dash's throat. "What is the Mantle?"

"The Mantle is where Excalibur does get its power." Dash had no problem with giving Lord Bonnevist the truth now. The truth of the Mantle could not hurt anyone now. "When Merlin went to the Lady of the Lake and begged for her to create a symbol for the King of Camelot to use in a time of crisis, she did as he asked, but she only did it with the knowledge that anything done with that sword would be the responsibility of Merlin. She put a spell on the sword tying it to Merlin and his power. That spell is the Mantle of the Merlin bloodline. In order for the sword to have power, bloodline of Merlin must be alive and strong for it to draw its power."

Bonnevist's face contorted with confusion. "But you are of Merlin's bloodline. The power should still be there."

Dash shook his head. "It is a rare thing, but I don't believe that it was an accident." He waved his hand in the direction of his brother. "Cremont and I were twins, and we inherited the full command of Merlin's power, but it was split between us. Together we are as powerful as our ancestor, but apart we are not as strong as we could be. The Mantle was tied to both of us. By killing Cremont you destroyed the Mantle."

"No!" Lord Bonnevist hissed. "No, I will not believe this!" He pulled the sword away from Dash's throat and swung it around in the air attempting to channel the power that he knew the sword should have been capable of bestowing upon him. "No!" He shouted and the echo filled the dining hall.

As suddenly as he had gone into tantrum, Lord Bonnevist calmed. His back was turned to Dash, but Dash could sense the danger preparing to lunge at him.

"If the Mantle is broken, then I have no need for half of a Merlin." He spun, bringing the blade toward Dash in an arc that would cleave the boy in half.

Dash brought up his shield of energy. Normally, Excalibur and its power would cut through it as if it were a soap bubble, but the sword was powerless now and stopped in midair between himself and Bonnevist.

"Wait!" Dash shouted. "Can't you revive him? Fix the Mantle and lock my brother and me away!"

Lord Bonnevist paused, still holding the sword high in the air. He almost kicked himself because that plan would work. He could mend the boy wizard with the flesh of the downed king, and he could then put one of his stolen lives into the boy. Preferably, he would have liked to have had a guard or prisoner to steal the life from but fixing the sword would repair any damage that giving life to the Farthing boy would cost.

"Why would you suggest such a plan? You would be prisoner and powerless, left to die...and to breed...in my prisons." Bonnevist was genuinely curious.

Dash shrugged. "I would rather live in captivity with my brother than die without him."

There it was. Just as it had been in the other Farthing boy. The weakness that had allowed Bonnevist to manipulate the feelings of the attacker. Now he would do it again and get what he wanted.

"Very well. Drag the corpse of the peasant to your brother. Touch their hands together."

Dash was stunned at first. He hadn't been sure if Lord Bonnevist would accept his proposal. Once the shock had worn off he ran to do as he was bid.

The boy had a handsome face and looked younger even than Cremont and Dash. Dash couldn't help but feel a lump of heartache in his chest at the sight of the failed would-be king. This was Daron Cross, the man who was true of spirit that was whispered to him by his connection with the sword.

This was the fate that would become of the men he and his brother chose for the sword. It was a heavy burden and saddened Dash.

Once Dash was done dragging the body of the Camelot boy to the body of his brother he placed the boy's hand directly on top of Cremont's. The body of his brother was even harder to look at than the boy he didn't know so Dash averted his eyes and did his best not to look at Cremont's skinless corpse.

Lord Bonnevist came over once he saw that Dash had aligned the bodies and knelt over their heads. He didn't have the mud he had mixed when he had performed the spell on Evelyn Farthing, but with the bodies touching he shouldn't need it.

Dash didn't understand any of the words that flowed from Lord Bonnevist's mouth as he held both of his hands over the foreheads of Cremont and Daron. A bright green light flitted between the dark wizard's hands and their faces, and it took Dash a moment to see what the wizard was doing.

Where their hands touched, the flesh was spreading. Like water running downstream it flowed up and over Cremont's arm and then under his burnt and torn cloak. It climbed up his neck and over his shredded scalp. Dash was caught somewhere between shock and horror as the flesh left the corpse of Daron Cross, leaving him exactly as bloodied and destroyed as Cremont had been, and filling in the gaps in Cremont's own flesh.

When the healing had been done, Bonnevist took Excalibur, which had been tucked under his arm during the spell-casting and placed it at his feet. Leaning forward he placed his hands directly onto Cremont's chest and pressed down. His chanting grew louder, and his eyes closed. With a burst of energy that Dash felt but did not see, Lord Bonnevist sat back on his heels and smiled broadly.

"Rise, Cremont Farthing. You are to serve me now."

Cremont's eyes fluttered and then his memory caught up with his body. He slid away from Lord Bonnevist as quickly as he could and jumped to his feet.

He was in perfect health. Dash was impressed.

Looking past the still prone Lord Bonnevist, Cremont asked, "Do you have him?"

"I think so, yes." Dash said from behind Bonnevist. The dark wizard reached for the sword at his side and realized that it wasn't there as he felt it poke into his back.

"Clever move boys. Was what you said about the Mantle even true?"

Cremont answered. "Yes, he told you the truth. The Mantle of the Merlin bloodline powers the sword, and my death broke that Mantle."

Lord Bonnevist spun, floating to his feet as he did so and shot a quick wave of energy at the boys. It wasn't enough to harm them, but it pushed them both back enough to give him room to prepare for battle.

He turned on Dash first and lashed out with a whip of energy.

Dash reacted reflexively and brought the sword up to defend against the magical blast. The power caught on the sword and suddenly Dash felt something surge through him.

It was familiar and new all at the same time. He felt stronger and more powerful than he ever had yet at the same time he knew the sensation he felt. It was the least foreign thing that he had ever known in his life.

It was Cremont.

Dash looked down at the sword, and Cremont's eyes followed his. Together they could feel it: Dash was accessing the Mantle.

Their surprise stemmed from what the Lady of the Lake had told them. They couldn't access the power of the Mantle because they were the Mantle.

Their surprise gave way to fast realization as the power surged through Dash. At no time previously had two born of the Mantle existed at the same time. A single child of the Merlin bloodline couldn't use the power of the Mantle because they would only be taking from their own power, but twins could access each other's strength through the sword. They could touch the half of the Mantle that the other represented.

Cremont had shown over and over again that he was the more combat proficient of the two.

That was the half of the Mantle that Cremont represented. That was the half of the Mantle that Dash now had control over.

A flick of the sword sent the whip of power splashing to the ground and then Dash threw his palm out toward the corrupt dark wizard. Lord Bonnevist's spells bounced off the wave of power that came at him. It caught him and threw him far against the wall. Dash ran forward, still pressing Bonnevist against the wall and off the ground. He filled the sword and himself with all the power that he could gather, and he could see as his efforts made his brother collapse to the ground.

Guilt flooded into Dash, but he could not let that stop him. If he weakened his resolve than Lord Bonnevist would be able to stop his next move.

Stopping his run, he put the momentum into a throw that hurled Excalibur at the dark wizard. All the magic of both boys filled the sword as it arced through the air toward its target.

Lord Bonnevist bellowed as he sent waves of energy and power at the sword. Lightning, fire, and the sheer force of his will pushed outward and crashed into the sword, attempting to alter its course.

None of them even touched the sword.

The power of the Mantle, Merlin's full power, carried the sword through the air and slid it through Lord Bonnevist's chest stopping only after it had pierced the stone.

The hilt of the legendary sword was pressed tightly against the dark wizard's chest.

He squirmed for only a moment more before sagging as the life left his body.

Epilogue

In the twenty-four hours that passed after the death of Lord Bonnevist, the Farthing brothers were very busy.

Camelot was made up of a lot more than just the seventy-five farmers and folks from the market, and the rest of the town still had to be informed that the presiding ruler of Camelot had been overthrown and that the Magic-Born were not to be feared.

The first difficulty was explaining to all the Northmen rubbing their heads outside of the gates of Camelot that they had been compelled by Lord Bonnevist, a Magic-Born himself, to faithfully follow his every order. While they might not have believed it or understood, they soon surrendered to their confusion and started the long trek back toward their land, the Northlands.

Taking on the actual people of Camelot had been next in their to-do list. It was a lot to ask of people to change the ways they had known their entire lives, but Gregory Rogan had an idea, and the Farthing twins had decided that no idea had ever sounded so clever.

Dash's half of the plan was one of face-to-face meetings with each and every owner of crops in all of Camelot. He went from farm to farm and poured a healthy dose of his magic into the crops. He didn't do much, and he couldn't without killing himself in the process, but he was able to get the majority of the plants toward healthier shades of green and the farmers that he helped were very grateful for his efforts.

The other part of Gregory's plan was carried out by Cremont. Cremont nervously walked the distance to the lake and knelt beside it.

"M'lady, on behalf of all of Camelot, I beg an audience," he whispered into the water.

At first nothing happened and Cremont wondered if she knew

why he was there before casting the idea aside. Of course, she knew why he was there, she was the Lady of the Lake.

No sooner had he experienced the thought that she burst from the water. Not a splash or drop of water came with her, but he noticed that the lady in the shimmering blue robe was standing gently on its surface.

"You have destroyed the dark wizard." It wasn't a question, yet Cremont chose to answer it anyway.

He nodded. "Lord Bonnevist is dead, but Camelot is far from healed."

She returned his nod with a barely perceptible one of her own. "Wise you are to have recognized that. Camelot has an entire future ahead of it and the people must be taught again how to trust. This world is in constant need of nurture." Her gaze drifted toward the forest that surrounded her lake and then came back to Cremont. "Thus, why you are here."

He nodded again. "Yes, that is why I am here."

She nodded. "I will do it and you must take credit for it. Let the world know that Camelot is once again home to the feared and all too powerful Merlin." The Lady of the Lake's eyes seemed to bore into Cremont. "Let the world know that it is protected."

Cremont nodded and thanked her but didn't stand again until she had receded into the lake.

He returned to Camelot and met with his exhausted brother in Camelot's marketplace as the people bustled about.

Dash was looking at everyone as they went from stall to stall. "They don't even know things have changed."

"They know." Cremont replied. "They are Camelot and the darkness at her heart has been destroyed. The Guard is reforming, and Gregory is spreading the word among the marketers. They know and they are appreciating Camelot in the only way that they know how."

Dash looked to the sky and smiled. "If they don't know, they will know soon."

The sky had darkened and filled with clouds, yet no one moved their wares or covered their carts.

"We must make a show of this." Cremont whispered to his brother.

Dash laughed to himself and nodded. "Very well. I'll shout, you can wave your hands."

Dash raised his hands into the air and looked at the sky while his brother mimicked his movements. Then Dash shouted from the top of his lungs. "In the name of Camelot, I call forth the rain!" Cremont didn't miss his cue and shot a ball of fire directly into the sky above them. The shot of flame disappeared into the distance.

The boys waited and hoped that their timing had been perfect. Everyone just stared at them as they stood there with their hands over their heads.

Breaking the silence, a rush of rain came down as the city succumbed to the heaviest rain storm they had seen in years.

Normally, the rain would make everyone pack up and run for cover, but everyone just stood in it, frozen.

After a moment of that they began to cheer and scream their excitement. The boys received slaps on their backs and hugs as the entire city of Camelot rejoiced at having wizards in the castle.

After most of the cheers of rain had died down, Dash and Cremont returned to the castle. They ordered the Camelot Guard to arrest the Knights of the Round Table and, surprisingly, the orders were followed without hesitation. It seemed the members of the Guard were more Camelot than Guard and more than ready to follow the orders of the new protectors of the city.

The old knights didn't fight much either and the grumbling among them made it sound as if they hoped for leniency.

It was growing later in the evening when Dash went in search of his brother. Dash found Cremont in the dining hall. They had taken Daron Cross' body to his family and, as it turned out, his fiancée, but the blood from the stable boy's corpse had yet to be cleaned. Cremont was kneeling over the sticky dry stain.

"Who will be king of Camelot now?" Cremont asked when he heard his brother approaching.

Dash had been wondering much of the same thing but had decided to revel in the rain-lust of the town. "We will have to locate another one who can wield the sword."

Cremont spun on his brother. "If that man is in Camelot, then the answer is simple, but I highly doubt that it will be that easy." He waved his hand at the broken doors of the dining hall, indicating the city outside. "We just announced to them that they could trust us and that they are protected. We cannot just leave now to go find them a new king."

Dash smiled. "That is why we are both very lucky that there are two of us."

Cremont raised his eyebrow in response to his brother.

As an answer, Dash pulled the legendary sword, once again invisible at his side, from its sheath and offered it to his brother. "We know that the sword will work for us, and we are not both needed to find the new king. I will hunt for the new king, and you can keep the sword and protect Camelot until I come back. If the need arises, you will have the full power of Merlin at your disposal."

Cremont took the sword and didn't know what to say. He didn't want his brother to leave but the plan was sound. "But..." he grabbed at the only thing that might slow this plan down, "what about gran?" He nodded toward the amber amulet still on the golden chain around Dash's neck.

Dash shrugged. "I've tried releasing her, and she came to me and told me that only Bonnevist could have released her, but she is no longer in torment now that he's dead. I don't believe her; I think that I will be able to find someone who can give her the freedom that her soul deserves." He shrugged. "I will search for that while I look for the new king."

Cremont wasn't happy with the idea of his brother going any-where without him, but Dash grabbed Cremont by the shoulders and looked into his eyes. "I will be alright, and this is the best way to succeed at our goals. Camelot will have a good and decent king. Until then, they have you."

Cremont returned his brother's look and after a moment smiled. "Alright. Together we will give Camelot what it needs. We will do what is right by our lineage."

Still smiling and with minds set on a path that they both agreed on, the twins of the Merlin bloodline walked back out of the castle and into the rain.

About the Authors

Matthew Davenport hails from Des Moines, Iowa where he lives with his wife, Ren, and daughter, Willow. When his scattered author brain isn't earning weird looks from the ladies of his life, he enjoys reading sci-fi and horror, tinkering with electronics, and doing escape rooms.

Matt is the author of the Andrew Doran series, the Broken Nights series (along with his brother, Michael), *The Trials of Obed Marsh*, and *Satan's Salesman* among other titles.

He's also a self-styled student of the Cthulhu Mythos and exercises that influence in his stories and as part-time editor at the blog Shoggoth.net.

You can keep track of Matthew through his Twitter account: @spazenport
and his blog: authormatthewdavenport.wordpress.com.

Robert Reynolds lives in Cedar Rapids, Iowa with his wife Liz. He is a lifelong artist of multiple mediums, including photography, paint, and clay. His writings include large collections of poetry with *The Sons of Merlin* being his first novel. His other passions include collecting Science Fiction and Fantasy books as well as leisurely playing video games.

Curious about other Crossroad Press books?
Stop by our site:
http://store.crossroadpress.com
We offer quality writing
in digital, audio, and print formats.